Chasing Hunter

Chasing Hunter

ISBN: 1-4196-7743-8
ISBN-13: 978-1419677434
Library of Congress Control Number: 9781419677434

Chasing Hunter

Cort Malone

2007

This book is dedicated to the memory of my grandfather,
Bernard Schuss.
I think he would have been proud.

PROLOGUE

15 years earlier

In a sparsely furnished Italian restaurant named *Mama's* on the upper west side of Manhattan, two men sat at a table adorned with a red and white checkered tablecloth. The table was in the far corner of the restaurant next to the kitchen, and both men sat with their backs to the wall, facing the front door.

Carmine and Anthony Valenti were brothers, both in their sixties, and they represented the last vestiges of a formerly widespread and well-connected crime family that had controlled much of the Bronx and northern Manhattan for the better part of the twentieth century.

"Hey, Carmine, pass the parmesan cheese."

Anthony Valenti was shorter, heavier, meaner, and two years older than Carmine. He enjoyed his role as the family's enforcer and still spent many days strolling the local neighborhoods with a couple of beefy lieutenants, collecting "protection" money from the various shopkeepers and other business owners.

"Here's the cheese. Try to keep it on your plate for a change."

Carmine Valenti, unlike his sloppy brother, wore an expensive, tailored suit, and his hair was neatly combed and parted, in stark contrast to Anthony's unruly curls. Carmine was smarter than his brother, having graduated from law school before fully immersing himself in the family business. But he was no less vicious when the situation required it. Carmine handled the family's business concerns and, even when conducting entirely legitimate negotiations, his opponents often caved to his demands when subjected to the intensity of the stare from his coal-black eyes.

Both brothers looked up as the small bell attached to the front door chimed softly and a tall, well-dressed man walked into *Mama's*.

The Honorable Arthur J. Diamond had recently risen to the position of Chief Judge of the Criminal Courts of New York. He assumed that his presence had been requested by the Valenti brothers because many of their "employees" would be active participants in the criminal justice system during his tenure.

The Judge had no trouble spotting Carmine and Anthony at the back of the small restaurant, with their bodyguard standing a few feet away. The only other patrons in *Mama's* were a young couple talking quietly at a table to the left of the entrance, and three men, who looked like they had just come from playing basketball, sitting to the right by the front windows, which were covered by dark red shades. Judge Diamond strode to the rear of the restaurant and sat down in the one open seat across from the Valentis.

"Hello, Judge. Congratulations on your promotion," Carmine greeted him with a smirk.

"Thank you. Now, do you want to tell me what this meeting is all about?"

"Hey, you want something to eat, Your Honor?" Anthony asked, spraying marinara sauce across the table as he spoke. "This place makes the best chicken parmigiana in the city."

"No, thank you. Actually, I can't stay very long, so is there something you gentlemen want to discuss with me?"

Anthony simply continued eating his pasta, but Carmine cocked his head slightly to the side and seemed to be studying the Judge for a moment before speaking.

"Well, if the Judge wants to get down to business, we'll get down to business. Your Honor, you are the fourth Chief Criminal Judge to meet with us over the years, and we'd like to maintain the same good relationship with you that we had with your predecessors. The last three Chief Judges that walked through that door came in expecting to receive bribes—money and other services they believed my brother and I could provide in exchange for certain favorable treatment should any of our associates ever find themselves before the criminal courts."

Carmine again paused for effect and stared at Judge Diamond, who had been leaning toward Carmine as he spoke, but now sat back in his chair in response to Carmine's harsh glare.

"Unfortunately," Carmine continued, "those three Judges were a bit presumptuous. You see, my brother and I do not offer bribes to cops, politicians, or anyone else, especially judges. We have no need to do so, as we do not consort with persons of a criminal element."

Judge Diamond began to shift in his chair and appeared visibly uncomfortable as he attempted to interject.

"Mr. Valenti, I don't think you understand. You invited me he—"

"Shut up!" Anthony interrupted, practically growling at the judge despite a mouth full of food. "My brother's not finished talking to you."

The Judge, now gravely quiet and shaken, listened as Carmine continued speaking in a much more relaxed tone.

"Artie—do you mind if I call you Artie? Ah, doesn't matter. Your predecessors were presumptuous to expect a bribe offer, but you are the worst of all. Not only did you expect us to offer you a bribe, you were so sure that's what we would do that you wore a wire to this meeting and have cops waiting outside to arrest us for trying to bribe you."

The Judge looked stunned, as if he'd been slapped in the face.

"How did you know?"

It was Anthony who responded, "It's his job to know. My kid brother—the freakin' genius!"

"Anyway, Artie," Carmine continued, "sorry to disappoint you, but it looks like it's time for you to leave now. I hope you've learned your lesson. And I hope the lesson gets passed on to the next Chief Criminal Judge after your term ends, whenever that might be."

Judge Diamond rose slowly from the table, pushed in his chair, took a couple of steps backwards, and then turned around to leave the restaurant. As he turned, a drop of sweat fell from his forehead and landed on his hand. The Judge felt the sweat hit his palm, and then felt a searing pain in his back as the first bullet hit him right between the shoulder blades. The next three riddled his lower back and exploded through his stomach. As the Judge collapsed forward, the other customers began screaming and diving to the floor. When the cops burst into *Mama's* moments later, the scene as a whole was utter chaos. Yet Anthony and Carmine were seated at their table, eating quietly as if nothing had happened and there wasn't a dead body lying on the floor ten feet away from them.

The gun used to kill Judge Diamond was found in the restaurant's kitchen, but it had been wiped clean of fingerprints. Of all the people at *Mama's* when the shooting took place, only one was still alive when the Valenti brothers were tried for murder the following year.

When that lone eyewitness finished testifying, Anthony Valenti jumped out of his seat and over the defense table in an attempt to attack the person who fingered him as the shooter, but he was quickly restrained by the bailiffs. Anthony's face grew beet red as he screamed while the witness was led out of the courtroom.

"You're dead! I'm going to kill you with my bare hands! You hear me? You're dead!"

PART ONE

THE CHASE

CHAPTER I

Present-day, Friday, 3:47a.m.

Sitting behind a large desk in a cavernous and oddly decorated office, an attorney, who appeared to be slightly drunk, was drafting an e-mail on the computer directly in front of him. He paused to re-read the e-mail and then chuckled to himself as he clicked the *Send* button.

Despite the late hour, the attorney was hardly surprised when one of the three phones on his desk began to ring. After all, he had clients all over the world, and even his domestic clients knew that they were likely to reach him in his office no matter what time it happened to be.

But when the attorney checked his Caller ID and saw that it read *Restricted Number*, his heart rate quickened. He'd been receiving several unwanted calls over the past few weeks, always from an unavailable or restricted number, and he feared that the same caller would be on the other end of this call as well.

As the attorney lifted the phone from the receiver, eschewing his normal use of a hands-free headset, his fears were confirmed. A distorted, mechanical voice came across the line.

"You know you're eventually going to tell me what I want to know, don't you?"

"I don't know what you're talking about," the attorney responded.

"I'm talking about your biggest client. The one behind all of that business you bring in."

"Is this some kind of joke?" the lawyer asked. "Are you with the cops or something?"

Laughter cackled through the phone, and the mechanized voice answered, "No, I'm not with the cops, and this definitely isn't a joke. I'm tired of playing games with you. Either you tell me your client's name and where I can find him, and you'll never hear from me again—"

"Or what?" the attorney cut in, speaking with a false sense of bravado.

"Or I'll spread the word that you're planning on turning your client in, and you'll be dead before you even have time to get scared enough to soil yourself."

The lawyer slammed the phone down and immediately buried his head in his hands, massaging his temples with his index fingers. The reason these calls were so troubling was that the attorney had never told anyone about the true source who provided the majority of his business. In fact, this client was so careful about maintaining his privacy that he'd spent millions of dollars in legal fees merely to set up front companies and dummy corporations to serve as the law firm's actual clients. But if the caller knew about the existence of the reclusive client, it would only be a matter of time before the client knew that someone was asking questions about him. And if the client believed that his attorney was sharing information about him with anyone—the cops, his enemies, even his friends—he would be extremely displeased, to put it mildly.

The disturbing conversation sobered up the lawyer, and he thought back to another phone call he'd received earlier that day from the lackey of his biggest client—the same client that the mysterious caller was seeking information about. The client's Russian bodyguard, who always purposely mispronounced the attorney's name, had called with an unusual request.

"The boss wants to meet with you tonight in your office, after you are finished with your dinner party and everyone else is gone. You know how much he values his privacy. I trust you will be available, even at the late hour."

At the time, the lawyer had agreed to wait in his office for his client to arrive, even though he found the demand for a face-to-face meeting strange in that this client had never come to his office before. But he hadn't made the connection between the threatening phone calls and his client's odd behavior until now. If the client had any doubts about his attorney's loyalty, the result of the meeting could be much worse than simply losing a lucrative source of business. Realizing that he could be in grave danger, the lawyer decided that there was only one person he could trust. Whether he ended up in jail, on the run, or even dead, he at least hoped to get certain information into the right hands, which would prove to be a powerful bargaining chip in exchange for his safety or, at worst, provide a bit of revenge should the unthinkable occur. And if everything went smoothly with the meeting, he could easily retrieve the information that he would pass along before it was discovered.

The attorney suddenly turned and looked down at the bottom drawer on the left side of his desk. He reached into his pants pocket and pulled out a set of keys. With his hand trembling slightly, the lawyer unlocked the bottom drawer with one of the keys and removed a thin briefcase, placing it on the desk in front of him. After manipulating several numeric dials on the briefcase, the attorney popped it open and took out a laptop computer. He moved the briefcase onto the floor and opened the laptop on the desk in front of him, directly in front of the large flat-screen monitor attached to the computer on which he'd been drafting an e-mail just a few minutes earlier. The lawyer entered his password to access the files on the laptop, which emitted several beeping sounds as it churned to life.

While typing feverishly on the laptop keyboard, the attorney pulled open another drawer to his right and removed a small, metallic object about two inches long and half an inch wide. The small object was a USB flash drive, which functioned as a second hard drive, providing a simple way of storing and transferring information between computers without requiring the use of a floppy disk or a CD. As the lawyer inserted the flash drive into the side of his laptop, he stopped typing just long enough to scribble a quick note on a plain sheet of paper.

"Come on, come on," he urged the computer to complete its task.

Finally, the dialog box in the center of the laptop screen indicated that it had finished downloading the contents of the computer onto the flash drive. The attorney quickly disconnected the flash drive, but immediately shoved a small floppy disk into the laptop's disk drive and typed a few keystrokes. He then grabbed an empty rectangular yellow envelope from the corner of his desk and swiveled around in his chair. He stuffed the note he'd just written and the flash drive into the envelope, got up, and walked over to the side of the office nearest to the door.

In front of him on the office wall were several ducts that made up part of the office air conditioning system and a narrow opening into which he hastily shoved the envelope. The narrow opening was actually a mail slot built specifically at the high-powered lawyer's request, and his personal mail dropped from the chute into a bin located in the mail room several floors below. The attorney felt this was necessary because his mail was far too important to wait for the standard pickup from his firm's normal mail service, which only came by once every hour between nine thirty a.m. and six thirty p.m.

Due to the size of the law firm and the volume of mail and copying projects it generated, there were at least two employees on staff in the mail/copy room twenty-four hours a day. One of these employees would immediately deliver any mail that dropped in from the lawyer's specially built mail slot. Although this occasionally forced the mailroom workers to temporarily abandon their other projects, the attorney knew that anything he dropped down that chute would be in the inbox of any other lawyer in the firm within minutes. And that's the way he liked it.

Just as the whooshing sound of the envelope going down the chute faded, the sound of a familiar voice with a heavy Russian accent caused the attorney to jump back and stare with his mouth open at two large men entering his office wearing heavy black overcoats and leather gloves, despite the mid-August temperatures.

"Sergei wants to know who you've been talking to, Mee-shell," one of the large men sneered at the attorney, who had hastily moved back beside his desk.

At first, the lawyer did not respond. He was not surprised at his visitors' attire, but his worst fears were confirmed when he saw that one of the men was holding a long, jagged dagger. The attorney also thought that he recognized a sadistic look of anticipation on the Russian's face. As he eyed the two men nervously, the lawyer slowly pulled open the top right-hand drawer of his desk and groped around inside without taking his eyes off the other men. Finally finding what he was searching for, the attorney's mouth curled into a smile as he spoke.

"That's the last time I'm going to have to listen to you mispronounce my name, you big Russian gorilla."

Despite his brave front, the lawyer was afraid. As he removed his hand from the drawer, now holding the gun that he'd purchased only one week earlier, he stepped around the front of the desk just a few paces away from the men he intended to kill. Although confident in his shooting accuracy, these were shots the attorney could not afford to miss.

Distracted by his thoughts of aiming the gun properly, the lawyer suddenly realized that the two Russians did not look even slightly concerned. In fact, they seemed somewhat amused. The larger of the two men actually began to laugh.

"What's so funny, Boris?" asked the attorney. But even before he heard the answer, his heart began to sink. Boris answered him in a mocking voice.

"I know something you don't know. While you were down there at your little summertime lawyer party, Ivan come up here and take bullets out of your gun."

In a last desperate moment of hope, the lawyer pulled the trigger. The empty gun clicked. In one swift motion, Boris stepped forward, grabbed the attorney's outstretched arm, twisted it around behind his back, and drove the knife he was holding up into the lawyer's chest. The wounded man fell flat on his back on the floor in front of his desk, and a small pool of blood began oozing around the knife and staining the carpet beneath him.

Boris quickly picked up and pocketed the attorney's useless gun. He then walked around to the other side of the desk and ejected the disk from the laptop computer. He inserted another disk that he pulled from his inside jacket pocket and typed a few strokes on the keyboard. Almost instantly, a virus began downloading onto the attorney's laptop that would wipe out everything on the computer and hard drive. Once he was sure that the virus was working, Boris ejected the disk and returned it to his jacket along with the other disk that he had just taken from the computer.

The lawyer was alive but was in tremendous pain from the knife, which still protruded from his torso. He could hardly move at all and felt like he was losing consciousness and going into shock from the agony. Just before he passed out, the attorney heard Boris's voice, mocking him one last time.

"Good-bye, Meeshell. You were right about one thing—that's the last time you'll ever hear me mispronounce your name."

CHAPTER 2

Jake Hunter, Friday, 7:15a.m.

When he was younger, Jake Hunter always said that he would never be a lawyer, and he would never live in New York City. But after graduating from Brown University, where he'd played football and majored in biology, Jake had taken the LSAT and enrolled at Fordham Law School in the heart of the Big Apple. Now twenty-four years old, Jake was living in a neat, one-bedroom apartment on West Sixty-third Street in mid-August after his second year of law school.

Jake's eyes flickered open and he quietly reached out for his watch on the dresser next to his bed. It was seven twenty in the morning. That was good. There would be plenty of time to get ready for his last day of work as a summer associate at the prestigious New York law firm of Davidson Palmer & Wilcox. The reason for the stealthy effort to check the time was lying in the bed beside him still asleep. Her name was Anna, and Jake knew little else about her except that she was a very sweet girl who had moved to New York from North Carolina two weeks earlier, and that she looked incredible when she was naked. The previous night was the end-of-the-summer dinner event for the summer associates at DPW, and several of the junior attorneys had kept the summer class out drinking until the wee hours of the morning. Jake had called Anna on his way home from the bar and she'd agreed to meet him at his apartment.

Jake eased slowly out of bed, reached down to the floor to pick up and put on his boxers, and walked out into the living room, closing the bedroom door behind him. He went over to the window with the unimpressive view of three brick walls and the narrow courtyard below. His apartment was located in a building that was actually attached to seven other buildings, with four located on West Sixty-third Street placed back-to-back with an identical four buildings on West Sixty-fourth Street. Jake opened the window and climbed out onto his fire escape.

One of the reasons that Jake was on the fire escape this morning was a beautiful, fiery Italian girl named Jen. They had dated for over a year, but had recently broken up. In fact, Jake realized that they hadn't so much broken up as she had broken him down. He'd somehow gone from a near-hopeless romantic when they met, to a near-complete cynic afraid to trust a woman entering his life in any way farther than his bedroom. But Jake knew that time would heal the wounds, and that the romantic in him would return eventually. Right now, though, he couldn't help but think of Jen.

Jake didn't consider himself a "real" smoker, just an occasional social smoker when he was out drinking with friends. As disgusting as he recognized it to be, he also enjoyed a cigarette after having sex. Jake and Jen had fought surprisingly long and fiercely about this habit, but in hindsight it seemed that they fought surprisingly long and fiercely about a lot of silly things. The argument ended back in February with Jen telling Jake that he could smoke if he wanted to, but he would have to do it outside on the fire escape. To prove to her how happy he was with that solution, Jake had maturely climbed outside in twenty degree weather in his boxers and patiently lit his cigarette with shaking hands and visible plumes of frozen breath coming out of his mouth. Best cigarette he'd ever smoked.

Jake glanced around at the neighboring windows, but no one else was awake in those apartments. He turned to face the wall on the east side of the fire escape and removed the third brick up from the railing. The brick appeared to be perfectly in place, and Jake had only discovered that it could be removed while he was tracing and tugging at the wall during one of his first smoking breaks six months earlier. He'd been pleasantly surprised to discover the small, hollowed-out hole in the wall behind the brick. It wasn't just a convenient place to stash his cigarettes, but also held a separate plastic bag containing one thousand dollars in cash and a folded, wrinkled piece of paper with a phone number on it. Jake knew the number by heart, but he kept the piece of paper because it had great sentimental value. The phone number had been given to Jake years earlier, but it was made clear to him that it was only to be used in a dire emergency. Jake had never had a reason to dial the number, although sometimes he wished that he had.

Half an hour later, Jake had shaved, showered, and dressed in a white button-down shirt and tan slacks. Even beneath the common business-casual work attire, his broad shoulders and sinewy frame were apparent. Anna was awake, but still looked sleepy as she sat on the small couch in Jake's living room wearing only one of his t-shirts, but huddled beneath a blanket as she watched him making coffee. She'd asked him to come back to bed with her, and the offer was certainly tempting, but Jake wanted to arrive on time for his last day of work.

Jake pulled open a cabinet above the coffee maker and grabbed three generic coffee cups and lids. Anna was curious about Jake's supply of paper goods and asked in her soft, southern accent, "Hey, where'd you get that stack of coffee cups from?"

Jake turned around to face Anna and smiled mischievously at her as he answered.

"You have to promise not to tell anyone, but I stole them from work."

"Well I didn't promise you anything. So I think I'm going to hold that information against you, and if you ever do me wrong, I'm gonna tell them that you're a thief and you'll get your license to practice law revoked."

Despite her threat, Anna smiled broadly at Jake as she spoke, and his only concern seemed to be not spilling her coffee as he walked across the room.

"Well, darlin'," Jake responded, teasing Anna by imitating her with his own southern drawl, "it's going to be hard for anyone to revoke my license to practice law anytime soon since I don't even take the Bar Exam for another year. And if you're going to be holding something against me, there's a few things I'd prefer a lot more than that not-so-scandalous information."

Jake took the seat next to Anna on the couch, leaned toward her, and kissed her as he placed her coffee on the table in front of them. They'd met only ten days earlier, but they both had very easygoing personalities and clicked physically right away. Still, Jake was hoping that they would get to talk a bit more over the upcoming weekend so that he could figure out if his initial instinct about Anna was right and she might be the type of woman that could make him start to believe that he could trust his heart again.

As Jake got up from the couch, he asked, "Can I see you again tonight?"

"If you're lucky," she responded playfully. "Is it okay if I let myself out after I shower?"

"Of course. Just be careful you don't leave anything important in here when you go because the door locks automatically behind you."

"Okay. And, hey, I'm looking forward to seeing you later."

As Jake backed out the door of his apartment with Anna's melodious accent still ringing in his ears, he smiled at her, showing off his dimples, as he realized that he too was already looking forward to seeing her later.

Jake checked his watch as he exited the apartment and saw that it was precisely five minutes after eight o'clock. He heard the familiar dinging sound of the elevator reaching his floor. Realizing that someone had just stepped through the doors, Jake yelled down the hall, "Hold the elevator!"

Jake lived on the sixth floor of his building in apartment 6-F, which, coming from the elevator, was all the way at the end of a long hallway and around a short corner to the right. When Jake exited his apartment door, there was a stairwell immediately to his right that went up to the top floor of the building and also down six flights to the ground floor. At almost all other times, Jake took the stairs down when leaving his apartment, but on the way to work, he sometimes shared the elevator with his neighbor from across the hall in apartment 6-G.

After exiting his apartment, Jake took three strides forward and then made a left around a corner and walked down the long hallway toward the elevator, passing the doors to the other five apartments on his floor along the way. As Jake stepped into the elevator, a beautiful, dark-skinned Indian woman in her early twenties took her finger off the *Door Open* button.

"Good morning, Jake."

"Good morning, Neha. You look ravishing today, as usual."

"You're such a flirt, Jake. But I'm on to you. I just heard you talking to a girl in your apartment. Was it that cute little blond that I saw you with the other night?"

"So, spying on me again, eh? Why won't you just admit that you have a crush on me?"

"Because I don't. I have a boyfriend you know."

"That's not what you were saying a month ago."

"We were on a break, and it was just one kiss because you're cute. It meant nothing to me."

"It's tragic to see such a nice young woman living in denial."

"The only woman in denial is that little blond if she thinks she's ever going to hear from you again."

"Hey. That's not fair. In fact, I'm seeing her again tonight."

"Whatever. Hey, why do you have two cups of coffee with you? Do you really need that much caffeine in the morning?"

"No. They're not both for me. One is for a friend."

The elevator reached the ground floor and creaked to a halt. Jake let Neha exit first, which served the dual purpose of allowing him to demonstrate proper manners while at the same time enjoying the view as she walked in front of him.

"Hey, Neha, I'll see you later."

"Bye, Jake."

Jake sauntered out of the elevator, letting Neha leave the building before him. He made a left out the front door and headed toward Amsterdam Avenue. The rent in the apartments where Jake and Neha lived was cheap, in part because they were surrounded by several city housing projects reserved for low-income families. Between Jake's building and the low-income apartments, on Jake's left as he walked toward Amsterdam, was a small park and playground with two basketball courts, several benches, swings, and a jungle gym. Jake entered the park and approached a bench on which a tall, thin, black man with a graying beard appeared to be sleeping. The homeless man wore a heavy woolen overcoat, mismatched sneakers, and a green ski cap. Jake roused the man by gently shaking his shoulder.

"Morning, Ollie."

The older man's eyes opened and blinked several times. He sat up, and then his face broke out into a wide smile.

"Hey there. What's up Jake?"

"Same old. Just heading in for my last day of work."

"Are they firing you?" Ollie grew angry at the thought of Jake losing his job.

"No. In fact, they should be hiring me, hopefully. I've got one more year of law school to finish first, and then I have to take the Bar Exam." As Jake was speaking, he handed Ollie one of the two cups of coffee he was holding.

"Why do you bring me a cup of coffee every morning, Jake? Most of the lawyers I've known were real selfish people. Are you trying to make up for some kind of past sin or something by being nice to me?"

Jake was somewhat disheartened that Ollie did not remember the impetus for their friendship, but he'd grown used to the homeless man's haphazard memory lapses over the course of the summer. During his first week of work, Jake had been hurrying to the office to meet his boss at the crack of dawn one day and hadn't noticed that his watch had slipped off his wrist as he passed the park next to his apartment building. While waiting for the Sixty-third Street traffic light to change so that he could cross Amsterdam Avenue, Jake hadn't been all that shocked to be approached by the disheveled black man who he presumed was about to ask him for some spare change.

Much to Jake's surprise, however, the man had simply held out Jake's watch and said, "You dropped this back there. Wouldn't want you to lose track of time during your first week at work."

Flabbergasted, Jake thanked Ollie as he strapped the watch onto his wrist. But then it dawned on him that there was something very unusual about the interaction and he asked, "How did you know it was my first week at work? And why didn't you keep the watch?"

Jake could tell immediately that Ollie was offended by the question, and his response was in a less than friendly tone.

"I didn't keep your watch because I ain't no thief. I figure it's better to return someone's property to them and hope they see fit to maybe pay me back with a few dollars to get something to eat or a cup of coffee. And I know it's your first week at work because it's my job to watch over people. Used to do it in the war until..."

Ollie's voice trailed off, and he became lost somewhere in his memories, although Jake had no idea whether the memory was real or imagined. Still, he was thankful that Ollie had returned his watch and pulled his wallet out of his back pocket and grabbed a twenty dollar bill out of it.

"Hey, what's your name?" Jake asked, holding out the twenty and startling Ollie out of his reverie.

"You can just call me Ollie," the man responded as he reached out and took the money that Jake offered him.

The following morning, Jake brought Ollie a cup of coffee in what would become a daily routine. Over the next few months, Jake learned that Ollie had in fact served in the Gulf War in the early nineties, where he'd been part of an advance scout team whose job was to travel a short distance in front of the rest of the unit in order to scope out the upcoming terrain and ensure that passage would be safe and free from ambushes or hidden explosive devices. At times, Ollie spoke proudly about his military service, but on other occasions he grew dark and would not discuss the events that led him from the war to his present situation of living on the streets of New York City.

One thing that Jake eventually learned was that Ollie often got upset when confronted with his failing memory. So when he asked why Jake brought him coffee every morning, rather than remind Ollie of the first day they met, Jake simply responded, "I'm not making up for any sins, Ollie. But bringing you coffee every morning is selfish. See, the way I figure it, it's cheaper for me to brew the coffee myself and bring it to you than to give you a dollar every day to go buy it."

Ollie laughed at Jake's facetious logic and then said, "Man, Jake, maybe you is just like the rest of them other lawyers—too damn smart for your own good!"

Ollie laughed again, and Jake patted him on the shoulder as he got up to leave.

"Take care of yourself today, Ollie. Be safe."

"You too, Jake. And thanks."

Jake checked his watch again and saw that it was a quarter after eight. He wasn't really worried about being late to work, especially not today. At eight-fifteen on a Friday morning in mid-August after a late night out, not many attorneys would be in the office yet at all. In fact, some wouldn't show up until the afternoon, and some wouldn't show up until Monday. But there was one attorney that Jake knew would be in the office—Michael Kelban.

Kelban was forty years old, but looked ten years younger. He was a baby-faced genius and the most ambitious person that Jake had ever met. Kelban graduated college from NYU in three years at age twenty and immediately applied to NYU Law School. When he was not accepted at NYU Law, Kelban ended up going to George Washington instead. Every year since he became a partner at Davidson Palmer, Kelban hosted an impressive, thousand dollar a plate charity gala to raise money to support the scholarship program at George Washington's Law School. Kelban's stature in the upper tier of New York legal circles, and his natural charisma as a party host, made his event one of the most successful and talked-about celebrations in New York every year. Just to be sure that NYU Law School got the message that they had made a mistake in not admitting him, Kelban always had special gold-embossed invitations sent to all of the administrators and faculty at NYU. Of course, if they wanted to attend Kelban's charity function, any alum or administrator from NYU was required to pay two thousand dollars a plate—double the normal rate.

On Jake's first day of work as a summer associate three months earlier, the recruiting coordinator had taken him and the other six members of the summer associate class on a tour of the firm. They'd stopped at several offices to meet some of the partners and associates with whom they would be working. Kelban always met with the summer class for two reasons. First, he liked to appear intimidating and impressive, and the summer associates were an easy group to awe with his tales of hundred million dollar jury verdicts and billion dollar mergers. Second, he liked to test the mettle of the class to see if anyone stood out. After Jake and the other summer associates entered his office on their first day, Kelban spoke to them about what it meant to be a lawyer.

"The saddest thing about the legal profession is that it takes most lawyers twenty years of practicing before they figure out the key to being a great lawyer."

As Kelban began speaking, it was hard not to focus directly on him, but Jake's eyes had wandered a bit around the vast, eclectic office. Kelban sat behind a tremendous wooden desk, covered in stacks of papers, and with two computers—one in the center of the desk and the other off to the left. Hanging from the ceiling directly behind the desk was a large painting signed by an artist named Kandinsky. The windows were open and a soft, early summer breeze blew in, and the painting rotated around and around. The Kandinsky was painted on both sides, and Jake immediately presumed its main purpose was to distract any adversary, or perhaps even any client, who found himself seated across the massive desk from Kelban.

"Well," Kelban continued, "I'm about to give the seven of you a twenty-year head start on the rest of your classmates. The question is, what are you going to do with that head start?"

As Jake scanned the rest of the room, he realized that the Kandinsky painting was far from the most distracting prop in Kelban's office. The rear wall of the office was lined with bookshelves containing an impressive collection of legal treatises on every subject from torts to trusts, but the distraction was what was placed in front of the rear wall facing directly toward Kelban's desk.

"The key to being a great lawyer is the ability to create business." Kelban's speech took this odd turn, and the quizzical looks on the faces of the summer associates caused him to sigh and begin shaking his head in disgust.

"What you kids don't understand is the importance of the fact that we live in the most litigious country in the entire world. Some people consider that to be a problem, but for us, and for all of our fellow attorneys, not only is it a solution, but it's also a salvation. You see, there are far more lawyers in this country already than could ever be necessary to work on all of the legitimate legal scenarios out there, whether they are litigations, corporate matters, bankruptcies, or anything and everything else. But the key word in that sentence is legitimate. If people only hired lawyers when they had legitimate legal causes, half the lawyers in this country would be unemployed tomorrow."

As Kelban droned on, Jake turned back toward the rear wall of the office where there were three large chairs lined up next to one another from the window to the wall. The chairs were occupied, but not by people—at least not living people. Rather, seated comfortably in the back of Kelban's office were wax-like figurines, which could have come straight out of Madame Tussaud's famous museum on Forty-second Street in Times Square. The first seat was occupied by a silver-haired man with a creased forehead and a stern, serious look upon his face. He was dressed in the traditional flowing black robe of a judge, and this is precisely what Jake presumed this gentleman to be. However, the face was not of any judge that Jake was familiar with, and instead seemed to be more of a representation of the typical incisive judge, sitting on the bench and presiding over his courtroom.

"The point of course," Kelban drew Jake's attention again with reference to a supposedly forthcoming meaning to his tale, "is that our business depends on the very illegitimate legal actions pursued by our clients that, in all honesty, we know from the outset are more than likely to lose. But there's the catch. If a case is more than likely to lose, there's still a possibility that it might win. And while we cling to the possibility that our client's case could win, we advise him that it probably will not, and we continue to collect our fees until each and every final appeal is exhausted."

The second chair contained a smaller, younger man. He had dark hair and green eyes, but was otherwise bereft of unique physical characteristics. He was of medium height, medium build, and medium complexion. His clothes were ordinary and his expression was placid yet mildly interested. The man was paying attention, but you wouldn't be surprised if he missed something. Jake had almost chuckled out loud when he read the nametag affixed above the man's left breast. It read: *Juror #1.*

Kelban was gathering steam and growing excited as he spoke, but the excitement showed only in his eyes. It reminded Jake of someone, but he could not place who. At any rate, Jake got the impression that none of the others had picked up on the charge that Kelban was getting out of his own speech because he was superb at keeping his true emotions beneath the surface.

"Now I'm sure that some of you will want to go running back to your ethics or professional responsibility professors and tell them that the awful partner told you to take on clients and cases that you knew would lose and milk them for all they were worth. Well, if that's what you're thinking, then you weren't paying attention. One of the great things about the law is that it's never perfectly clear how it will be interpreted. Give the same set of facts to different judges and different attorneys and you will get an unbelievably broad range of results. So, like I said, the client who wants you to take his supposedly illegitimate case all the way to the Supreme Court of the United States, if it can get there, has just as much of a right to our legal expertise and efforts as the client with the open-and-shut, slam-dunk, can't-lose case—as long as he's willing to keep paying the bills."

The third chair was more disturbing than the other two, but Jake assumed that a weapon made of wax couldn't really hurt anyone. The tall, broad figure sitting in the third chair cast an imposing shadow over the room, and was cloaked in a long, dark, hooded robe that completely covered his face. All that was visible was one thick, hairy arm, extending out of the sleeve of the robe and holding a two-sided, medieval axe. Jake soaked in the physical appearance of the three characters—judge, jury, and executioner—but he would not understand their purpose until months later.

"The problem with all young attorneys is that they are far too idealistic about their place in the world, and far too scared to push the boundaries and risk making a name for themselves."

Jake could tell that Kelban's speech was winding down because his voice calmed ever so slightly and he walked around the front of his desk, perching himself upon the corner closest to his mostly rapt, yet confused, audience.

"I graduated college when I was twenty, law school at twenty-three, and began working here immediately. I busted my ass and put in my time, but I was always, always pushing harder to make connections, meet clients, sell them on who else they should be suing, or merging with, or protecting through a trust, and on and on. I didn't bully people and I wasn't pushy. I just presented them with legal options and opportunities that they hadn't previously considered. And that is how you can be a great lawyer—by learning early on how to generate business. But to be an excellent lawyer, you've got to learn how to generate business with extremely wealthy clients. That's what I did, and that's how I became a multi-millionaire and a partner at this firm by my thirtieth birthday. Any questions?"

"Yeah, what took you so long?"

Jake had asked the question mostly because he was annoyed at Kelban's smug attitude and couldn't help himself from trying to knock the partner down a peg by throwing him off after his self-important and cynical little speech. But there was another reason as well. Jake had sensed that Kelban wasn't just telling the story to inflate his ego—he could do that in front of a crowd of people far more important than a group of summer associates. Instead, Jake felt that Kelban was challenging them as a group, to see if anyone had the nerve to respond to his well-rehearsed spiel.

There was a palpable silence in the room for at least fifteen seconds after Jake spoke, and then Kelban finally responded, "What's your name, kid?"

"Jake Hunter." Jake presumed that Kelban obviously needed to know his name in order to have him fired.

"Well, Jake Hunter, you think you could reach partner here faster than I did?"

"Perhaps. But only if I learned from the best, sir." Jake had decided to cut his losses and make a passing attempt at flattery in order to save his job on his first day at work.

"Interesting idea, Hunter, I've never had an apprentice before. Perhaps it's time I took one on. Enjoy the rest of your first day today, and report to my office at six a.m. tomorrow. We'll get to work on making you a partner bright and early."

For the next three months, Jake hadn't worked for any attorney at Davidson Palmer other than Kelban. He logged twice as many hours as any other summer associate, but he gained a hundred times more knowledge and experience than any of them. Jake also got to know Kelban better than most people and, at one point, actually felt sympathy for Kelban, who he learned was an only child whose parents had both passed away. It was clear that Kelban focused all of his energies toward working—the firm was his life—and it was just a matter of time until Jake found himself caught up in Kelban's ambitious and exuberant pursuit of clients, money, and excellence in practicing law. As the summer progressed, Kelban had trusted Jake with more and more responsibilities.

On his last day of work as a summer associate, after his usual fifteen minute walk from his apartment, Jake was about to enter the building at 1251 Avenue of the Americas, where his firm's offices were located on the forty-second and forty-third floors, when he heard a familiar voice call out from behind him.

"Hey, Jake! Hold on a sec buddy."

Jake turned and caught the amusing sight of his fellow summer associate, Greg Hansen, sprinting toward the doors, drops of sweat running down both sides of his forehead. Hansen was about five feet, five inches tall, with a round midsection, and a mass of tangled dirty-blond hair. He'd graduated from the University of Wisconsin, and some people said that he resembled that school's mascot—the badger. Hansen also attended Fordham Law School with Jake, and was his closest friend in the summer class at Davidson Palmer & Wilcox.

"What's the rush, Hansen?" Jake asked, smiling at his out-of-shape friend. "You could have caught up to me inside, you know."

"Actually," Hansen gasped, pausing to catch his breath, "I couldn't. I think someone stole my i-disc last night, and you know they won't let anybody into the building without it unless you're with someone else who has one."

"Well, at least you got your exercise for the day by running that last twenty yards."

"Exactly. Now let's get upstairs before I have a heart attack down here."

As they rode up in the elevator, Jake and Hansen discussed the previous night's party and their hope to receive full-time offers from the firm. Hansen got off the elevator on the forty-second floor, where his office was located, and Jake exited on the next floor up. Once upstairs, Jake entered his office, put his cup of coffee down on his desk, and logged on to his computer. When Jake double-clicked on the *Microsoft Outlook* application, he was blown away by the e-mail message waiting for him from Kelban. It read:

Jake—urgent! You screwed up on the hotel merger. Your mistake is going to cause a $500 million merger to fall through, and the firm is going to lose one of its biggest clients, not to mention millions of dollars in fees. I will try to cover for you and take some of the blame, but they'll find out from my files that you were running the deal. See me as soon as you get in this morning—we have to discuss this immediately! MK

Jake felt an involuntary shudder run through his body as he got up from his desk and began walking toward Kelban's office wondering what he could possibly have done wrong on the merger. He was so distracted by the e-mail message that he didn't even notice the bright yellow envelope sitting in his inbox.

CHAPTER 3

Charlene Stanton, Friday, 7:30a.m.

While Jake stood on his fire escape, smoking a cigarette and thinking about the women in his life, a woman who he did not yet know, Agent Charlene Stanton of the New York office of the Federal Bureau of Investigation, stood in front of her bathroom sink in a white tank top and light blue boxer shorts surveying her appearance in the mirror. Her dark eyes had matching dark circles beneath them that never seemed to go away, perhaps because Stanton rarely slept well. She was olive-skinned and had jet black hair cut short above her shoulders. Her nose was slightly pointed and she had a short chin and a long neck, giving her a somewhat birdlike appearance. Stanton had never been accused of being beautiful, but she was not unattractive and often received backhanded compliments along the lines of, "You could look really nice if you'd just take better care of yourself."

As far as Stanton was concerned, she'd been taking care of herself just fine her entire life, because no one else had ever done it for her. Stanton was a foster child and had never known her biological parents. She'd been shuttled between various foster families and group homes, but never found a place that she considered a real home. After graduating from Martin Luther King Jr. High School in New York City, Stanton earned a scholarship to John Jay College of Criminal Justice. She graduated college with honors, joined the Crime Scene Investigation Unit of the New York Police Department, and four years later was accepted into the FBI's trainee program. After another four years of treading water as a junior agent, Stanton requested and received a transfer to the FBI's International Organized Crime Unit, a relatively new division where Stanton hoped she'd have an opportunity to make a name for herself.

Stanton knew that the major mission of the IOCU was to prevent the infiltration of foreign organized crime into the United States. But the IOCU was not created until after many of these organizations were already operating in this country. The group that took the most advantage of the delayed reaction to foreign organized crime in the United States was the Russian mafia. Stanton had studied their history and found that beginning in the late 1980s, Russian gangsters were losing power and facing apprehension in their homeland as a result of their country's embracing of ideals such as glasnost and capitalism. Fleeing to America, and New York City in particular, these former Russian gangsters found that there existed untapped potential for numerous criminal ventures. By the early 1990s, the criminals who had emigrated from Russia to New York were involved in an extraordinary number of illegal activities, encompassing everything from traditional Italian mafia-controlled operations involving the construction and waste collection industries to high-tech computer crimes, stock market swindles, and online gambling. Perhaps the most dangerous aspect of the Russian mafia was its ability to maintain a near-invisible profile by ruthlessly eliminating anyone who stood in the way of, or threatened to reveal, its various illicit schemes.

Stanton learned that because of the secretive nature and low profile of the Russian crime families, confidential informants and undercover operatives were critical to the IOCU's attempts to bring down the existing gangsters and prevent the influx of new organized crime cells. Stressing her background as a New

York City resident who had worked her way through college as a bartender, Stanton persuaded her superiors that she was the perfect candidate to fill an undercover assignment working at the Russian Vodka Room, a bar and nightclub on West Fifty-second Street known to be frequented by members of Russian organized crime. As part of her cover, the IOCU paid for Stanton to rent a studio apartment located a few blocks away from where they hoped that Charlene "Smith" would soon be working.

The Russian Vodka Room had a dark, foreboding décor, and was divided into several discrete sections. There were private rooms, roped-off booths, and two small side bars in the far corners of the dimly lit establishment. The main bar ran along the front of the club and served as a barrier between the clientele that came to the Russian Vodka Room to be seen—like the B-list celebrities, hockey players, and a certain attractive young female tennis player—and those patrons for whom privacy was a priority. The Russian gang members always congregated in the back of the club, but very rarely spoke to the bartenders working behind the two side bars.

After talking her way into a bartending job at the beginning of the summer, Stanton had been largely ignored by the men she served drinks to in the back of the club. But on the Tuesday after a long Fourth of July weekend, everything changed when a customer who had recently seemed to take an interest in Stanton approached her and ordered a scotch "neat." As Stanton poured the brown liquid into a glass, she could feel the customer's eyes staring at her, and as she served the drink they struck up a conversation.

"I've been watching you, you know. You're new around here. What's a woman like you want to work in a place like this for, surrounded by all these tough guys?"

Stanton wanted to keep her chatty new friend talking, and decided to try an open-ended, ambivalent response.

"These guys talk tough, but it seems like it's all talk."

Looking discreetly in both directions to make sure there was no one nearby, the customer answered quietly, "I happen to know that some of it is not just talk."

Deciding to make her move and push to see just what, if anything, this stranger knew, Stanton asked, "Oh yeah, now you're gonna tell me that you're involved in this gangster stuff."

The customer paused briefly before responding, "No, actually, I'm not involved myself. But I know the people who are and I know what they are capable of."

Stanton tried to not seem overly interested or eager, but didn't want to lose contact with this potential source. She flipped her hair to the side, trying to look sexy, and said, "Sounds kind of scary to me, but also kind of exciting."

"Well, if you'll give me your phone number, maybe we could get together and I could tell you some stories that you might find exciting...and scary."

Stanton did her best to remain passive and control her excitement. After all, this customer might be doing nothing more than hitting on her by pretending to be a big shot. Stanton acted as if she had cooled slightly at the thought of giving out her phone number to a customer.

"Maybe it would be better if you gave me your number and I could call you instead."

The customer seemed to consider this for a moment and then reached into a pocket and pulled out a business card, handing it to Stanton. The card had nothing on it except for a small ten digit phone number in bold type at the center of the card. The customer handed the card to Stanton and started to walk away.

"Wait," Stanton said. "This card doesn't even have your name on it."

"Well then I guess you'll have to call me if you want to find out what my name is."

And with that, the stranger had turned and left the bar, leaving Stanton staring at a phone number and a half-empty glass of scotch.

After waiting two days in an attempt to not seem desperate, Stanton had finally called the number on the card. She'd agreed to meet the mysterious customer for a drink that night, hoping to cultivate a source of useful information on the Russian mafia. Much to Stanton's surprise, she thoroughly enjoyed the night out, though she tried to remain focused on the fact that she was working a potential informant. The evening ended with the two of them talking and sharing several bottles of wine before falling asleep together on the beat-up old sofa in Stanton's living room. After their second date, Stanton was beginning to get some details about her source's involvement with the Russian mob, and she also realized that there was a strong mutual attraction between them. The morning after the second date, they had woken up in Stanton's bedroom, rather than on the living room couch.

Since Stanton had made that first phone call, just over a month had passed, but her life had been such a whirlwind during that period that it felt to Stanton like barely any time had gone by at all. In the interim, both her career and her personal life had reached heights she'd never dreamed possible as a shy, awkward orphan growing up on the hard streets of New York City. And Stanton knew that she owed her newfound success and esteem to the mysterious stranger, who had also proven to be a valuable source in her work for the IOCU.

Just two weeks earlier, Stanton's source had provided her with detailed inside information about a high-powered Russian weapons dealer, which led directly to the gangster's arrest, and to Stanton being pulled from her undercover assignment and promoted to a full-time field agent. Though she was thrilled about the promotion, the only thing Stanton found more exciting than her career taking off was the fact that, for the first time in her life, she'd fallen in love with someone who truly loved her back.

As Stanton finished getting ready to leave her apartment and meet up with her new partner, she thought about how the past month had been one of the happiest times of her life. But despite everything going so well lately, there were still a couple of things that were eating away at her. First, Stanton was concerned that her secret relationship with her source would get her in trouble at work. Her much greater fear, however, was rooted in the many stories she'd heard, at least some of which she believed to be true, about the cruelty of the Russian mafia. The worst of these tales were always about the torture of informants who had turned on the mob. Stanton had seen the crime scene photos from the murder of one man who was known to have provided information about the Russians, and the images had made her stomach turn. Stanton knew, without a doubt, that if anyone ever found out her source's identity, it wouldn't be just their relationship that would come to an end.

CHAPTER 4

Sergei Ilanov, Friday, 8:30a.m.

In a relatively modest one-bedroom apartment on West Forty-ninth Street between Ninth and Tenth Avenues, one of the wealthiest men in New York sat at a computer desk that had been purchased at an Ikea furniture store several years earlier. Dressed in a simple light-blue button-down shirt and gray slacks while tapping away on his computer keyboard, the man could have passed for a mild-mannered website designer or a computer programmer. But this man was far more dangerous than he appeared.

Although it would seem unlikely based on his appearance, Sergei Ilanov was actually in the process of manipulating bank accounts in several Caribbean Islands by transferring millions of dollars between them. The money he was moving around included proceeds from numerous illegal activities, but after the funds were transferred from several of the Caribbean accounts to banks in the United States, it would appear to have come from perfectly legitimate sources. The price paid for the laundering of these funds included certain taxes and an occasional payment to foreign banking officials to help speed the transfer process, but these costs were a pittance compared to the resources that being a wealthy man in America could bring. And so Sergei acted the part of a wealthy, reclusive foreigner, and people rarely had the opportunity to question where his money came from.

There was a time when Sergei had made a fortune in his home country of Russia by using skills other than exploiting lenient Caribbean banking regulations. But he'd lost everything when the regime changed hands, culture and society were turned upside down, and the authorities that Sergei once controlled were suddenly after him.

What had made Sergei rich in Russia was, to put it simply, stealing and killing. Sergei was very intelligent, but using his intellect legitimately in Russia would have led him to either working for the government or at a boring banking job. Instead, Sergei found that he could acquire much more money from a bank by devising a clever way to take other people's money out of it. Though he possessed great skill as a thief, his reputation for violence and brutality while robbing banks and shopkeepers soon led him to a new career specializing in torture and contract-killing for some of the Russian gangs. Sergei rose in power and ultimately took command of one of the largest Soviet gangs after murdering the gang's previous leader by bludgeoning him to death with a shovel.

After a decade of prosperity in the 1980s, the gangs were being prosecuted and driven apart, and a manhunt was on for Sergei throughout Moscow. Sergei was hiding out with his family in a secret apartment he kept for emergencies, when one of his lookouts knocked on the door and hurriedly informed Sergei that the authorities had discovered his location and would be there shortly. Sergei turned to his wife, who was clearly upset at the thought of running from the police. Speaking in his native tongue, he ordered her to prepare to depart immediately.

"Get ready to leave for the boat. We have to go now."

Sergei's wife began to cry and folded her arms in front of her chest, refusing to move as she spoke.

"Sergei, my family is in Russia, my home is in Russia. I am afraid of the dangers of traveling, of running from the authorities."

Sergei stopped packing his things for a moment, stared harshly at his wife and said, "Pack your things. We leave now!"

"No. I won't go with you."

In a flash, Sergei's hand reared back and swung forward, connecting with the side of his wife's head. The force of the blow sent her flying into the wall. Two young girls went running toward their mother to protect her, but Sergei threw them off her and onto the sofa nearby.

"Stay!" he shouted, and the girls sat trembling, frozen with fear and terrified of what would happen next.

"Are you ready to come now?" Sergei asked his wife.

Sobbing heavily, she shook her head from side to side. Sergei looked disgustedly at her, and then turned to stare briefly at his two daughters before speaking again to his wife.

"You could never even provide me with a son to follow after his father. You have always been useless. I shall be burdened by you no more."

Sergei reached out, grabbed his wife's shoulders with both hands, and pushed her violently backwards away from him. She'd been standing a short distance in front of one of the apartment walls, and the force of the blow caused her head to crash into the wall behind her with a harsh thud. Her body immediately went limp and dropped to the floor, while her eyes rolled back in her head and her mouth sagged awkwardly open. Moments later a slow trickle of blood began to leak from one nostril, and Sergei's daughters ran from the couch to their mother and attempted in vain to wake her.

Sergei surveyed what might have been a heart-wrenching scene to another person, but despite the fact that he was husband and father to the women on the floor in front of him, he felt nothing for them. Before he walked out the door, Sergei looked into the eyes of his children one last time. His youngest daughter stared up at him in fear, a look that Sergei saw often in the eyes of the people who came in contact with him. But his other daughter, three years older than her sister, was looking at him with a less familiar expression—although he'd certainly seen it in others as well. Her eyes burned with pure hatred. With a thin smile on his face as he considered his daughter's insolence, Sergei turned and left the apartment, never once looking back.

It had been fifteen years since that day and Sergei had never looked back. It did not take long for him to rebuild his gang, as many members of the Russian mafia had sought refuge in the boroughs of New York City. Because Sergei knew that he'd been betrayed by several members of his gang in Russia, he became extremely protective of his identity as he built his new empire in America. He operated almost entirely through intermediaries, and only a handful of people knew his real name. Sergei enjoyed the deception involved in using various cover stories when he did venture out in public, and worked hard to perfect different accents and craft suitable backgrounds for the characters he would inhabit. No matter what role Sergei assumed, his alter ego always possessed great wealth. But it didn't require any acting for Sergei to demonstrate his vast financial resources, as he was soon making more money in America than he had during the height of his reign in Russia.

Sergei was quite adept when it came to managing and manipulating the income produced as a result of the numerous illicit activities in which he was involved, and he had no need for an accountant or banker when he relocated to the United States. However, the extensive and complex legal requirements involved in acquiring businesses, completing real estate deals, and merging corporations in New York made it necessary for Sergei to find an attorney that he could trust to handle such matters.

Shortly after Sergei had come to New York, he crossed paths with a cocky young attorney who often came into one of the underground high-stakes gambling houses that Sergei ran throughout the city. The attorney was logging major hours at a large law firm, earning six figures in salary plus bonuses, yet he would spend several nights a week playing poker in the dank, smoky club. One night, one of the other regular players, an old enforcer in Sergei's gang back in Russia who had retired to run a deli in midtown Manhattan, asked the young lawyer, "Hey, Junior, why do you spend so much of the little free time that you get working at that fancy law firm down here playing poker with a bunch of old men like us of—how should I put it—questionable moral fiber?"

Sergei had been watching the game and the attorney's response caught his attention.

"Most of the other junior associates at my firm are trust fund babies, country club raised rich kids who've been handed everything in life and are just following in their daddies' footsteps. I may be able to work twice as hard as they do, but I'll never be able to make the big-time connections they already have when it comes to bringing business into the firm, which is the only thing that matters when it comes to making partner. So, I figure the best chance I've got to bring in some major clients is to cater to a crowd with just as much business to offer to me and my firm, but perhaps of a bit more—what did you call it—questionable moral fiber. That's why I come here, and it's also why I don't take even more of your money every time I'm here, because then you'll never let me represent you."

Most of the patrons had laughed appreciatively in response, some because they found it funny, and others because they'd simply been surprised, as this speech contained almost as many words as they usually heard the kid speak during an entire night of card playing. But Sergei hadn't laughed at the attorney's comments, for he found them much more intriguing than amusing. Shortly after the lawyer left the club that night, Sergei began making several phone calls to have a complete check of his background prepared.

Over the next few months, Sergei had arranged for the lawyer to represent several of his associates in legal matters varying from criminal cases to corporate transactions and real estate deals. In each case, Sergei made sure to test the attorney's willingness to bend, and even break, the law if it would mean a successful result for his client and more business for his firm. Without fail, the lawyer had agreed to the underhanded tactics, and between his devious behavior and brilliant legal mind, the attorney consistently achieved outstanding results and was bringing in more and more business.

As he was leaving the poker room one night, the lawyer was invited to meet with Sergei in his office, where the Russian had explained that he knew what it was like to try to reach the heights of a profession when you had to start from the bottom and fight for everything you got. The attorney kept quiet, listening to Sergei's offer of a partnership in which they would both have a great deal to gain. Sergei painted a general picture of his legal needs and the opportunity he was offering, being careful to refrain from referencing any illegal activities, but allowing the young lawyer to read between the lines of his proposal. When Sergei finished speaking, the attorney had asked only one simple question.

"So, what's the catch?"

"The catch," Sergei responded, "is that once you agree to work for me, it is a lifelong commitment. And if I ever have reason to doubt your loyalty to me, you will undoubtedly be terminated."

The lawyer swallowed hard under the glare of Sergei's dark stare and his sinister implication, but then stood up from his chair and extended his hand as he said, "You'll never have a reason to doubt my loyalty, sir."

As they shook hands on their agreement, Sergei thought to himself, *For your sake, I'd better not.* Over the years, as the lawyer's career had taken off, due in large part to a tremendous amount of business brought in through his particularly reclusive client, Sergei had always made sure to keep very close tabs on his attorney. After all, he was the first, and only, outsider that Sergei had ever allowed access to him and his empire, and Sergei would spare no expense to protect what he had built.

Although the gang under Sergei's control was one of the most diverse and successful, it was not the only Russian gang to re-form in New York. Throughout his fifteen years in America, a turf war had existed between Sergei's gang and that of his friend and former lieutenant, Yevgeny Pulachin. The respect between the two leaders was enough to keep full-scale war from breaking out between the gangs, but there were often competing interests that led to fighting and, occasionally, bloodshed.

Pulachin had been caught two weeks earlier by the FBI and the ATF in a raid of one of his warehouses that was storing thousands of illegal weapons, and it certainly didn't hurt Sergei's business to have one of his main competitors in jail for the next twelve to twenty years. But Sergei often relied on having the best sources of information reporting back to him about both his friends and his enemies, and he was concerned that he hadn't heard anything beforehand about the raid. The only intelligence he was able to obtain was that a female FBI agent had an informant who had tipped her off about the warehouse and, more importantly, when Pulachin could be caught there in the act of brokering the sale of illegal weapons. Sergei's lack of knowledge regarding this informant made him very uncomfortable. After all, if his rival could be brought down by a traitor in his ranks, could Sergei be vulnerable as well?

Following Pulachin's arrest, Sergei immediately set up surveillance and phone taps on several of the people closest to him to make sure that he was not being betrayed the way his former lieutenant had been. And after listening to tapes of several unusual phone calls, Sergei had given the order for his attorney to be killed.

CHAPTER 5

Jake Hunter, Friday, 8:38a.m.

As Jake walked the long, foreboding hallway that led to Kelban's office, he glanced around at the portraits that hung on the walls of the firm that had been founded over a century ago. Even the old men in the pictures seemed to be staring at him accusingly, and Jake could feel the heat of his body rising through his neck and the backs of his ears. It was about twenty minutes before nine o'clock—the latest Jake had come in to the office all summer, but Kelban himself had told Jake that it would be all right to sleep in a bit before his last day of work. While talking to Jake at the party the night before, Kelban had pointed to an attractive blond cocktail waitress carrying around a tray of champagne flutes.

"Have you noticed that she's offered you about twenty more glasses than anyone else at this party? Hell, I haven't been able to get a drink all night. Every time I come close, she's already heading back in your direction. Seriously though, Jake, have some fun tonight. You've earned it."

Shortly thereafter, Kelban had snuck out of the party and back upstairs to his office.

Now, less than eight hours later, Jake found himself staring at the door to Kelban's office, replaying the hotel merger over and over in his mind. He couldn't think of anything that he might have done wrong, especially something that would have caused the entire deal to collapse. Kelban's secretary, Sonia, would be arriving in a few minutes, and if Jake was about to get fired before he'd even been officially offered a permanent position with the firm, he decided he'd rather have it happen before anyone else was around to witness the carnage.

Jake knocked on the door and waited to hear Kelban's usual brusque response of, *Come in*. But the response never came. Instead, all Jake heard was a faint gargling and scratching sound. Already on edge from the cryptic e-mail message, Jake tensed up even further as he pressed down on the door handle and pushed it forward, entering the lavish office where he'd boldly made his first impression three months earlier.

The scene inside the office was the last thing that Jake expected to see. Kelban was lying on the floor in front of his desk in a large pool of blood. The position of his body and the direction of the dark red streaks in the carpet beneath him indicated that Kelban had been trying to move and had managed to prop up his head and upper back against the front of the desk. A large, metallic object was protruding from his chest, and Jake realized that it was a knife. Jake's first thought was that there was a massive amount of blood on the floor—Kelban was dying.

Just then, Kelban made a rasping sound as he coughed, and blood spurted from his mouth. Jake instinctively ran over to his mortally wounded mentor and knelt beside him. Kelban's head lolled to one side so that he was looking up at Jake, and then he tried to speak.

"Ch-check maay. Check maayl."

"I did. I checked my e-mail. I got the message," Jake answered hurriedly. "Is that why someone did this to you, because I screwed up the hotel merger?"

For a moment, Jake thought Kelban's eyes were glazing over and that he was losing consciousness, but then he realized that Kelban merely had a look of confusion on his face. All of a sudden, Kelban's eyes opened slightly wider with a jolt of recognition, and he began to slightly shake his head back and forth.

"Nooo, naaah e-e-maayl. Thah jus ki-kiddinn. Check n-nbaahcks."

As he spoke these last few words, Kelban's body heaved with a fit of coughing, and blood poured out of his mouth and nose as he struggled to breathe. Thinking that the knife could be causing more internal damage, Jake decided that he had to get it out of Kelban's chest if there was any chance of him surviving. Jake placed his left hand behind Kelban's head, and his right hand around the shaft of the knife. In one swift motion, he yanked the knife upward and out of Kelban's chest. For a split second the room was in complete silence as Kelban fell into unconsciousness with Jake kneeling beside him, supporting Kelban's head, and still holding the knife raised in his right arm above Kelban's body.

Then the silence was gone, shattered by a terrified scream from the doorway of Kelban's office.

CHAPTER 6

Sergei Ilanov, Friday, 8:46a.m.

Sergei sat at his desk rewinding and watching a video feed over and over again with great pleasure and excitement. The recording was from about five hours earlier and it showed Kelban foolishly pointing his empty gun at Sergei's men and Boris driving his knife into Kelban's midsection. Sergei knew that it would take some time for Kelban to bleed to death, and he'd instructed Boris to wound the attorney in this manner to ensure that his death would be slow and painful. Sergei did very little hands-on torture anymore and he definitely missed it. There was no feeling that could compare to having ultimate control over the life of another human being—determining when they would feel pain and how much, and also being able to provide them relief. Although for many of Sergei's victims, relief came only with death.

After Sergei watched Kelban being stabbed several times, he decided to switch back to the live feed from the camera that he'd had his top electronics man install in the ceiling of Kelban's office several days earlier. The camera had been inserted into a tiny hole drilled through the floor of the office above Kelban's, but completely hidden from view by the smoke detector installed in Kelban's office ceiling. Now that Kelban was dead, Sergei would send the same technician back into the building that afternoon to remove the high-tech camera. As he switched to the live feed, Sergei smiled in anticipation at the thought of

Kelban's secretary's reaction to finding his body upon her arrival at nine o'clock.

Sergei pressed a button to return to the live view from the camera, and he was surprised to see a young man going into Kelban's office instead of the secretary. But Sergei quickly recognized the man as Jake Hunter, and realized that he shouldn't have been surprised at all. Hunter had been the first person to enter Kelban's office every day that week. Sergei was transfixed as he saw Hunter go to Kelban, kneel down, and cradle his head. The audio on the feed was scratchy because the microphone attached to the camera in the ceiling was miniscule, but Sergei was able to discern Kelban saying something to Hunter about checking his mail.

Sergei had been amused by the images of Kelban being stabbed and suffering in agony on his office floor, but the smile disappeared from Sergei's face upon hearing Kelban tell Hunter to check his in-box. Why, with his dying breath, would Kelban tell Hunter to check his in-box? Sergei's mind began racing with the possibilities, and as it did, he watched Kelban's secretary enter the office and begin screaming.

In a flash of motion, Sergei's fingers started typing furiously on his keyboard as he rewound the video feed to approximately ten minutes before Boris and Ivan had entered Kelban's office. Sergei realized his mistake almost immediately. He'd missed it at first because the transmission from the ceiling camera was partially blocked by the computer on the center of Kelban's desk. Upon closer examination, Sergei saw that Kelban had inserted the disk procured by Boris into his laptop computer only after placing a flash drive and a note he'd written into an envelope and sending both down the mail chute on his wall.

Sergei knew that Kelban kept coded files on almost all of Sergei's activities, including his bank accounts and money laundering operations. Although Sergei hadn't allowed Kelban to maintain such records early on in their relationship, as Sergei's empire grew, Kelban convinced him that it was necessary to keep track of the numerous entities he owned and their various transactions. Sergei had insisted on the files being encoded, but the encryption was far from unbreakable, especially if the files fell into the wrong hands. If revealed, the information on that flash drive would cripple Sergei's operations and, more importantly, uncover his true identity.

While trying to decide how to proceed, Sergei turned back to the live video feed and saw that Kelban's secretary was using Kelban's phone to call building security. Hunter dropped the knife to the floor and was trying to explain the situation, but Sergei heard the secretary telling Hunter not to come near her. Hunter appeared to give up his effort to calm her down and walked unsteadily out the door of Kelban's office.

As Hunter left, Sergei heard Kelban's secretary speaking into the phone, telling security, "Jake Hunter just killed Michael Kelban."

Upon hearing the secretary's pronouncement, Sergei decided on a plan of action. He would need some luck to pull it off, but he'd survived his share of difficult situations before and had no doubt that he would escape this unexpected predicament as well. Sergei had plenty of law enforcement officials on his payroll at both the state and federal level. All he had to do was get that flash drive into the hands of one of his people and it was as good as his.

Sergei picked up one of several untraceable cell phones he kept handy, which he would destroy after using just to be completely safe. He dialed nine-one-one, and in a perfectly crisp American accent, with a believable trace of fear in his voice, Sergei said, "I just witnessed a murder. I saw Jake Hunter fight and stab a lawyer named Michael Kelban in his office on Sixth Avenue."

Picking up a second cell phone, which he would also discard after using, Sergei began dialing from a list of contact numbers for each of the city's major network television news affiliates. He gave each one of them an irresistible scoop to begin chasing down.

"A summer associate named Jake Hunter at the law firm Davidson Palmer & Wilcox just murdered a partner named Michael Kelban. The authorities are on their way to apprehend him at the firm's offices right now."

As he hung up with the last of the networks, Sergei took a deep breath and turned on several of the televisions in the entertainment center set up on the wall across from his desk. He knew that there would be a brief period of waiting before making his next move, and in the meantime, there was not much else to do except sit back and watch as the chaos he had set in motion ensued.

CHAPTER 7

Jake Hunter, Friday, 9:12a.m.

Jake exited Kelban's office and headed back down the hallway in a daze. Kelban's secretary, Sonia, had arrived just after Jake had pulled the knife from Kelban's chest, and she obviously misunderstood what she saw. She became nearly hysterical almost immediately and refused to listen to Jake's explanation about finding Kelban only moments before her arrival. Despite the confusion and shock that Jake felt, Kelban's strained, raspy voice kept repeating itself in Jake's head, telling him to "check his in-box." So that's what Jake figured he should do.

Still in shock, Jake entered his office and approached his desk, which was littered with documents, legal pads, and other supplies. He opened the envelope that was sitting on top of a pile of correspondence and interoffice memos in his in-box. Jake pulled out the contents of the envelope—one piece of paper containing Kelban's barely legible handwriting and a small metallic object about half the size of a standard cigarette lighter, which Jake recognized as a flash drive. Slipping the flash drive into one of the pockets of his khakis, Jake read the note.

Jake, I'm not sure, but I may be in a lot of trouble with the Russian mob. If anything happens to me, get the information on this drive to the FBI's International Organized Crime Unit—NOT the local cops. Also—Don't trust anybody! MK

The last line of the note was underlined, but it was the first line that Jake kept re-reading, disbelieving that it could be true. *Trouble with the Russian mob*—what the hell was Kelban involved in?

Jake's thoughts about the note were disturbed by movements behind him in his office doorway, and he turned to see two security guards that he recognized from the building's lobby. To Jake's right and facing forward was Alan, who had greeted Jake warmly all summer as he entered the building, often before seven o'clock. On Jake's left was Bobby, standing sideways with his arms folded across his chest and his right leg perched inside the doorway to Jake's office. Both men were less than five feet away and looked wary of Jake.

Afraid as he was, Jake knew that he could not let on how he was feeling. One of the lessons Kelban had taught him throughout the summer was that in a tense negotiation, it was critical to take control of the situation and defuse it before it disintegrated to a point at which no party could gain an ultimate advantage. Folding up Kelban's note and slowly putting it into the same pocket as the flash drive, Jake said to the guards, "Alan, Bobby, man am I glad you guys are here. Is Sonia all right? She was really shaken up when we found Mr. Kelban like that. It was awful. Sonia was so confused, I think she might have thought that I had something to do with it."

The guards looked briefly at each other, and seemed slightly confused by Jake's version of events. Finally, Alan, the older of the two, spoke.

"Jake, Sonia called us and said she saw you sitting next to Kelban holding the knife in your hand like you'd just stabbed him. I think we need to go talk to the police."

"Alan, Kelban was trying to pull the knife out of his own chest when I got there. I had just pulled the knife out for him when Sonia walked in."

Jake saw the skeptical looks on the guards' faces and knew that they didn't believe him. He thought of Kelban's note specifically instructing him not to go to the cops and not to trust anybody. Jake quickly decided to alter his plan for dealing with the security guards.

"Hey, you guys are right," Jake said, switching to a more conciliatory tone. "Why don't we go to the police and get this all straightened out."

At the mention of going to the police, the two guards were visibly relieved and relaxed their nervous stances in Jake's doorway. Alan spoke again.

"That sounds like a good idea, Jake."

"Just let me grab my coffee—I've got a feeling we might be a while."

Jake turned around completely, blocking the guards' view as he removed the lid from his now lukewarm cup of coffee. Jake then spun quickly, took a step forward, and threw the coffee directly into Alan's face. As Alan covered his face with both hands and yelled out in surprise, Bobby clumsily attempted to unhook his taser from his belt. Jake sprang toward Bobby, striding forward, turning his body sideways, and jumping off the ground. Leading with his right foot, Jake came down from his leap directly into the side of Bobby's right knee. Bobby crumpled to the ground, more stunned than truly injured, but nevertheless yelping in pain.

Jake sprinted between the two hobbled guards out of his office and toward the elevators. As Jake ran down the hallway, he heard Alan's voice shouting into his radio.

"We need help on the forty-third floor. There's a killer on the run!"

CHAPTER 8

Agent Stanton, Friday, 9:21a.m.

Agent Stanton sat in the passenger seat of a standard-issue black government sedan. Her partner, James Zarvas, occupied the driver's seat. They were parked on West Fiftieth Street between Sixth and Seventh Avenues in front of a large office building with the address 1251 Avenue of the Americas. Although Avenue of the Americas was more commonly known as Sixth Avenue, the agents figured that the law firms and other businesses residing among the building's fifty-three floors preferred the lengthier and more patriotic title in their mailing addresses.

Zarvas was in his late thirties, good-looking, and straight-laced. Though he was Greek, Zarvas's tangled dark hair, smoldering eyes, and quiet nature often earned him comparisons to a Hollywood actor of Spanish decent, Antonio Banderas. His rise through the ranks of the FBI had been steady and impressive, and both his patient nature and familiarity with foreign cultures had proved to be assets in his work with the IOCU.

Stanton and Zarvas had been getting along well since her promotion, usually passing the time on stakeouts by talking about any number of subjects. But today was different, as Stanton was caught up in her own thoughts. The past month had brought major changes in her life—a passionate, mysterious romance, her success and advancement at work as a result of the Pulachin bust, and finally, her recent realization that, for the first time in her life, she was in love. Despite this confluence of happy events, Stanton was deeply worried. The very person that she'd come to care for like no other was the same person who was providing her with inside information about the extremely dangerous people presently being targeted by the IOCU.

The tip about Pulachin's arms warehouse had been precisely accurate—right down to Pulachin's arrival time. Only a trusted gang lieutenant would have access to that kind of information, and trusted gang members who passed information along to the FBI did not have much of a life expectancy in the Russian mafia.

"You okay Stanton?" Zarvas asked. "You look like something's bothering you."

"Nah, I'm fine Jimmy. Just getting tired of waiting to hear back from the office about possible connections between the Russians and this building they were in last night."

The IOCU was well aware of the two major Russian gangs operating in New York City. Although Stanton's source had helped them take down Pulachin, the head of the other main Russian mafia organization was proving to be far more elusive. In the often thankless world of law enforcement, Stanton's kudos for arresting Pulachin were already being replaced by pressure to locate his counterpart in the rival gang. But the IOCU did not even have a name or a face to put to the man they were searching for, and the best lead they'd uncovered so far was a couple of thugs who were allegedly top lieutenants that occasionally made direct contact with their leader.

Another team of IOCU agents had followed these men, Boris Zagrev and Ivan Davydenko, to 1251 Sixth Avenue at around midnight the previous night and watched them as they appeared to be staking out some sort of law firm party or event at a restaurant located on the first floor of the building. The two suspected Russian mobsters were seen leaving several hours later, but they had merely gone back to the apartment complex where they lived, and the agents were unable to determine what the thugs had been doing at the restaurant or elsewhere inside the building. In response to an anonymous tip, the IOCU had been tailing Boris and Ivan off and on for weeks in an effort to find out more information about the leader of their organization, but had come up empty so far.

Zarvas and Stanton's commanding officer told them that morning that the IOCU research department analysts had some leads related to a handful of shell corporations that had been set up as possible fronts for the Russian mafia. They were in the process of tracking down the identity of a specific attorney who worked in the same building visited by Boris and Ivan, who they suspected was involved in setting up the fronting companies. Zarvas and Stanton had been instructed to head to the building, but to wait until they got a call with a name before heading inside to investigate.

Zarvas suddenly pointed in the direction of Stanton's open window and said, "Now, how come we never get lucky and see Boris come sprinting out of a building looking like that?"

Stanton turned her head and glanced out the window at a man in his early twenties running through the building lobby from the elevator to the front door and out into the street. The man looked in both directions, then darted down the street toward the entrance to the uptown subway line.

"Kid probably forgot his boss's coffee or something," Zarvas joked.

"Yeah. That or his briefcase."

"You know, it always cracks me up when I see lawyers or businessmen running around like that, as if it's a life or death situation if they don't make it to court or a meeting on time."

Stanton was about to reply to Zarvas when her cell phone rang, interrupting her response. She opened the phone and said, "Stanton here."

She listened for a few seconds and then shouted, in a tone of disbelief, "What! Okay, we're on it."

Stanton closed the cell phone and said to Zarvas, "Some big-shot lawyer was just found murdered in this building, and it looks like he may have been the guy connected to the Russians. The main suspect is a twenty-four-year-old summer associate."

"You don't think…that kid we just saw running?"

"Well, if it was him, he's long gone by now. I'll call in his description and location, and then let's get in there and check it out."

After briefly surveying the crime scene and confirming that the victim was dead, Stanton and Zarvas were surprised by how quickly several news vans and reporters heard about the murder and swarmed to the building. NYPD arrived on the scene as well, but the FBI agents took over for the time being due to the possible connection to their ongoing investigation. Stanton instructed the police to keep the news crews out of the building and to protect the integrity of the dead lawyer's office until the FBI crime scene unit arrived to process it. Zarvas interviewed the attorney's secretary and several other DPW employees, while Stanton met in Hunter's office with the security guards that were accosted by Hunter before he ran from the building. She was finishing up her interview with the older of the two security guards when Zarvas walked back into Hunter's office. He nodded toward Stanton, implying that he wanted to talk to her, and she said to the security guard, Alan, "Well, I think we're all done here. Thank you for answering my questions. You've been very helpful."

Stanton stood and extended her hand, offering her card to the somber-looking guard.

"If you remember anything else, please give me call."

Alan took Stanton's card, slowly collected himself, and began to depart the office. Zarvas, anxious to discuss the case with Stanton, turned to her and asked, "Did you get a good look at the knife that was used in the stabbing?"

"No. Why?"

"It's a Basko model."

"What's that?"

Before answering, Zarvas looked back at Alan, who had just crossed the threshold of Hunter's office door. Zarvas reached over and closed the door for privacy before speaking again to Stanton.

"It's a Russian hunting knife. They're custom-made there. It's a good bet that Boris and Ivan killed the guy. A Russian mobster would be a lot more likely to have a knife like that than some kid who's still in law school."

"What about the dead guy, maybe he was a collector or something," Stanton suggested.

"Anything's possible, but something about the kid killing the partner just doesn't add up. Everyone I've interviewed said that Hunter was a hard-working, friendly, generous person, and that he idolized the victim. Basically, the dead guy was the kid's mentor and worked with him all summer. Plus, the one security guard on duty in the lobby last night said that even though he couldn't identify Boris and Ivan from the picture I showed him, he did remember a couple of big guys wearing leather coats coming in and out of the building at some point last night. Problem is, the guy says it was a crazy night with lots of people in and out because of the end-of-the-summer party that was going on."

"But," Stanton replied, "if Hunter didn't kill him, why did he attack two security guards and race out of the office? And if Hunter did kill him, what was his motive?"

"I'm not sure. But one strange thing that came out when I interviewed the mail room guy—he said that he delivered an envelope from the victim to Hunter's office at about four o'clock in the morning. Unfortunately, he couldn't tell me anything about the contents except that it seemed to contain something other than just paper. Said he felt some kind of a hard, metal object in the bottom of the envelope. Only problem is," Zarvas continued, carefully picking up an empty envelope from the top of Hunter's inbox with his gloved hand as he spoke, "whatever was in here is gone now."

"The security guard I was just talking to said Hunter was holding that envelope and reading a note right before he went crazy and attacked them. So whatever was in there probably had something to do with Hunter's reaction."

While the agents talked over their interviews and theories, Zarvas sat down at Hunter's computer, which Hunter hadn't had time to shut down before running from his office. As Zarvas opened Hunter's most recently read e-mail, he cut Stanton off in the middle of a sentence.

"Stanton, I think I may have just found the kid's motive."

Stanton moved behind Zarvas and read the e-mail over his shoulder. At the end of the e-mail, she noted that it was signed "MK" and realized that she hadn't paid much attention to the victim's name while they questioned the staff about the suspect, Jake Hunter.

"M-K, are those the partner's initials?"

"Yup," Zarvas answered. "Michael Kelban. Why, does that name mean something to you?"

Stanton had been caught off guard by the name Michael Kelban, and Zarvas obviously had noticed her reaction. Stanton had heard the name before. Just a few days earlier, her source had mentioned an attorney named Michael Kelban as someone who might be in possession of information leading to the head of the largest Russian crime organization in the city. Stanton straightened up and quickly regained her composure.

"No, Jimmy. I've never heard that name before."

CHAPTER 9

Jason Carerra, Friday, 9:48a.m.

In a small office adjacent to a laboratory in the bowels of the Department of Veterans Affairs Medical Center, located on Twenty-third Street and First Avenue, Jason Carerra hunched over his desk reading charts containing data compiled during several experiments he'd run throughout the week. His research involved cataloguing the effects of the drug cocaine on the release of certain neurotransmitters in the brain. Much of Jason's work was with rats, but his supervisor, Doctor Greenwood, also had been granted approval to collect data on the effects of cocaine in human subjects. In order to find willing subjects for their cocaine study, Jason placed an ad in the Village Voice seeking individuals willing to be monitored while under the effects of small doses of cocaine. Although no money was paid to the subjects for participating in the study and the conditions of the cocaine intake were highly regulated, Jason's lab was very popular among the residents of the city's East Village.

Jason had majored in psychology and played varsity soccer at Binghamton University in upstate New York, but decided about a year after graduation that he wanted to go to medical school. Since he hadn't taken all of the prerequisite courses while at Binghamton, Jason spent the past two years taking classes at NYU, working in the lab at the VA Hospital, and studying for the MCAT. His hard work had paid off as Jason recently had been accepted to medical school.

As he reviewed data on the correlation between cocaine ingestion and increased serotonin levels in rat brains, Jason was half-listening to an early morning news broadcast on a small television set, which was perched on another desk behind him. One of the talking heads announced that there was a breaking story.

"A well-known lawyer was found brutally murdered this morning..."

What a shame, Jason thought sarcastically, as the announcer continued, "...at the prestigious firm of Davidson Palmer & Wilcox."

Jason immediately sat up in his chair and spun around to watch the news—his friend Jake worked at that firm. But as Jason turned to face his television screen, the last thing he expected to see was a full-screen, smiling photograph of Jake. The reporter provided further details of the murder as Jake's photo shrank in size and moved to the upper right-hand corner of the screen, the rest of which was now taken up by the reporter's face as she continued speaking.

"This man, Jake Hunter, a summer associate at the law firm, is wanted for questioning in connection with the murder. Several eyewitnesses saw Hunter running from the firm's offices earlier this morning. If you have any information about this crime or the whereabouts of Jake Hunter, the police have asked that you call the number on the screen below."

Jason immediately pulled out his cell phone, but not to call the number flashing on his television. He hit a few buttons and prayed that Jake would answer.

***

Jake's apartment building was only two subway stops from his office, and he was already out of the train and walking into his apartment when his cell phone rang, startling him. Jake saw that it was his friend Jason calling and answered.

"Hello."

"Jake, what the hell's going on?" Jason asked frantically.

"I found my boss dead in his office this morning, and the cops think I'm involved. Wait, how did you know something was going on?"

"Turn on your TV, Jake—you're on every channel. Where are you?"

"I'm in my apartment."

"Well, the cops are going to be there any minute. Are you going to turn yourself in? I mean, you didn't have anything to do with your boss's death, right?"

"I didn't have anything to do with it, but when I found the body, I pulled the knife that he'd been stabbed with out of his chest, and then his secretary walked in and thought that I stabbed him. Then the cops were at the office in like ten seconds, and now it's all over the TV already. Plus, my boss sent me a note last night that he was involved with the Russian mob and not to trust anyone—even the cops. I don't know what's going on, but I'm not sure turning myself in is the best idea right now. Something's just not right about this."

"Well, if you're not going to turn yourself in, then you've gotta get out of there quick. Can you get down here to the VA Hospital and meet me?"

"I think so."

"Good. Call me from the pay phone in front of the hospital, and I'll come out and get you."

Jake turned off his cell phone and raced over to the window leading to his fire escape. He climbed outside, removed the secret brick, grabbed the hidden plastic bag containing the cash and phone number, shoved the flash drive and the note from Kelban into the hiding place, and replaced the brick. Before leaving his apartment, Jake hurriedly removed his blood-stained shirt and changed into a navy blue long-sleeved t-shirt. He also grabbed a University of Maryland baseball cap from atop his dresser and put it on.

Just as Jake closed the door to his apartment, he heard the familiar *ding* of the elevator arriving at his floor. Jake was sure it was the police coming after him, so he darted up the stairs to his right before they could see him from around the corner. After ascending one more flight of stairs, Jake pushed open the door to the roof of his building as quietly as possible. He crept to the front part of the roof, leaning over the short wall at the roof's edge to look down on the cul-de-sac that made up West Sixty-third Street.

As Jake peered over the wall, he saw two police cars turn onto Sixty-third Street, joining the cruiser already parked in front of the building. Jake knew immediately what he would have to do. Starting from the middle of the rooftop, he began sprinting toward the western edge of the building, in the direction of West End Avenue. Reaching full speed after about ten yards, Jake planted his right foot atop the short wall at the roof's edge and launched himself forward. The eight foot distance between the two buildings did not appear very large, but the two and a half seconds that Jake was traveling across that space seemed to take a lifetime. His jump was slightly short of landing atop the roof of the next building, and his right foot slipped backwards as he teetered on the ledge. The awkward landing knocked Jake slightly backwards and he began to fall. He swung his right arm out wildly and was able to grab firmly on to the other side of the similar short wall of the neighboring building. For a few moments, Jake dangled precariously between the buildings, with only an eight-story drop onto the concrete alley below waiting to break his fall.

Jake mustered all his strength and, with his adrenaline pumping harder than it had during any college football game he'd played in, lunged upward and grabbed hold of the top of the ledge with his other arm. He managed to pull himself up and over the wall onto the rooftop, then stood with his hands on his knees and took a deep breath. Not having any time to spare, Jake took off again toward the western edge of the building he was now on, and made the much easier jump onto the roof of the supermarket that was on the corner of the block. The distance was about the same, but the roof of the supermarket was about ten feet lower, making Jake's second leap much easier.

Jake jogged to the far side of the supermarket's roof and climbed down the fire escape, which was on the side of the building facing West End Avenue. Pulling his hat down tightly on his head, Jake speed-walked up to Sixty-fifth Street and turned right, heading east. One block away, after crossing Amsterdam Avenue, he boarded a crosstown bus. As he sat alone in the back, Jake had the distinct feeling that everyone on the bus was staring at him. He tried to convince himself that he was just imaging things, but Jake felt unsafe and nothing could change that at the moment. At Lexington Avenue, he got off the bus and went into the subway entrance for the number six train, which would take him downtown to Twenty-third Street, not far from the VA Hospital.

Jake stood off to the side of the stone steps leading into the hospital. He'd just spoken to Jason on the pay phone in front of the building, and Jason was on his way outside to meet him. Jake suddenly became extremely nervous as he remembered Kelban's note—*don't trust anyone.* But Jake shook his head and dismissed the thought. If he couldn't trust one of his oldest and best friends, then there wasn't any hope for him to ever escape this mess anyway.

Jake had known Jason since they were four years old, when Jake and his family moved into a new house just down the block from Jason's family. The two boys started kindergarten together that fall and used to spend every day after school watching cartoons or playing outside in one of their backyards. The summer before Jake started third grade, his mother told him that his father had died. Jake was so upset that he'd run out of the house and sprinted down the block to where Jason lived. He spent the next week living with Jason's family, although his mother and younger brother came over every night for dinner and to talk. Eventually, Jake decided that it was okay to go home again, but every day after school for the rest of that year, and most days throughout their childhood and teenage years, Jake and Jason would walk home together after school and usually hang out until dinnertime or beyond. Although Jake only had one brother by blood and one true family, the Carerras were as close to a second family as could be, and Jake certainly considered Jason to be as much his brother as his friend.

Jake watched anxiously as Jason exited the front of the hospital, slowly looked around, spotted Jake, and began walking toward him. Jason was wearing a white laboratory jacket and holding a second lab coat in his hand. When he reached Jake, Jason said, "Here, put this on," as he handed the white coat to Jake.

"Am I supposed to pretend that I'm a doctor or something?" Jake asked.

"No. Everyone who comes into the hospital without clearance has to sign in at the front desk. The hospital doesn't like the fact that me and Doctor Greenwood keep bringing strung-out, disheveled addicts inside for our experiments, because they think that the junkies' appearance is unsightly and disturbs the other patients and employees. So, we compromised by meeting our subjects outside and having them wear lab coats into the hospital. Of course, the addicts love wearing them because it makes them feel important. So I guess everybody wins. Especially you. So just put this on, pretend that you're stoned, and make an X next to the fake name that I'll sign you in under. Got it?"

"Yeah."

Jason obviously had brought quite a few subjects into the hospital by this method because the nurse at the front desk hardly even glanced up from her magazine as Jason filled out the visitor blank on the hospital entry log and Jake scribbled an X on the signature line. When they got down to Jason's office, Jake explained everything that had happened—from the party the night before, to the note about the Russian mob, to jumping across rooftops to escape the police. After hearing Jake's story, Jason asked, "Do you think you'd be better off just going to the police, or to this IOCU branch of the FBI, and giving them the flash drive?"

"I'm not sure. Normally I would say that Kelban's note was just being overly paranoid, and of course I should go to the police. But, Jay, Kelban's dead. He wasn't paranoid at all. He was in trouble with the Russian mob, and it got him killed. These people obviously have some cops, and maybe even feds, on their payroll. How can I be sure of who to trust without at least trying to make sure that the people I'm giving the information to are the right ones? This morning has been so crazy, and now there's a manhunt going on throughout the city—looking for me. I think I just need to disappear for a few days, figure out who in the authorities I can trust, and then turn myself in and give them the flash drive. What do you think?"

"Well, on the one hand, you have to admit that it looks pretty suspicious for you to leave town when you're wanted for questioning in connection with a murder. But, there's no doubt that your life may be in danger, and keeping yourself safe has got to be your first priority. I think you're probably right. Your best bet is to get out of the city until things quiet down and you can decide on your next move. And I know where you can go."

"Where?"

"Remember last New Years, when we all went up to my uncle's ski cabin in Vermont?"

"Yeah. Feels like a million years ago."

"Well, I've still got the spare set of keys to the cabin, and no one is going to be anywhere near that place. You could crash up there for a couple of days. You could even take my car to drive up there, so you don't have to risk taking the bus or something."

"That sounds perfect. Are you sure you're okay with me taking your car?"

"Yeah, man. What are friends for, right? Let me just try to find those keys to the cabin."

Jason began pulling open desk drawers, looking for the spare set of keys. When he opened one drawer, Jake glanced into it and was surprised at what was inside.

"Jay, you've got a gun?"

Jason looked into the drawer that Jake was staring into before answering.

"No. Well, I guess so. I mean, it's not a real gun. It shoots tranquilizer darts. We have to have it as a precaution in case one of our human subjects ever gets out of hand while they are on the cocaine, or tries to threaten us to force us to give them more drugs. See those syringe-like things next to the gun—those are the darts. Supposedly, you could knock out a charging rhino by shooting him with two of those things. I've never had to use it on anyone though. Oh, wait, I remember now. The keys are in my locker. Wait here a minute. I'll be right back."

When Jason left the office to get the keys, Jake pulled open the drawer containing the tranquilizer gun. Part of him wanted to take the gun for protection, but he felt bad stealing it from Jason. Instead, Jake pocketed two of the darts, which did look like mini-syringes. The needle portion of the dart was covered by a hard piece of plastic, probably to prevent anyone from getting pricked accidentally. The back of the dart appeared to have a cap that could be screwed off, and Jake assumed that the dart could be used with another attachment that operated like a plunger, for injecting the dart manually, as opposed to shooting it from the tranquilizer gun. Jake wasn't sure what, if anything, he would ever use the darts for, but figured he could always give them back to Jason later.

Jason returned to the office with two sets of keys and handed them to Jake one at a time.

"These are for the car. I'll walk you down to the hospital's parking garage and tell you how to get up to the cabin. The garage is a small, self-service monthly lot, so there shouldn't be anybody around. These are for the cabin. If you run into any trouble on the way, just call me, and I'll do whatever I can to help."

"Jay, thanks man. You don't know how much this means to me."

"I know you'd do the same for me, Jake."

As Jake drove north out of New York and headed for the quiet skiing town of Killington, Vermont, he again grew concerned about his precarious situation. It had been good to talk to Jason and to have someone helping him, but it seemed too risky to continue getting other people involved in the mess Jake found himself in. The more he thought about it, the less he could believe that he was actually on the run—from both the cops and the Russian mob. But there was no doubt that Jake was caught in the middle of an extremely dangerous situation. The only question was, how in the world was he going to get himself out?

CHAPTER 10

Peter and Nicholas, Friday, 2:30p.m.

In the back of the Russian Vodka Room, talking quietly at a small table, sat two men wearing dark leather coats and shiny, expensive wristwatches. In both attire and behavior these men blended in seamlessly at the club, which made sense since both of them were born and raised in Russia. However, blending in was a specialty that these men had perfected, and they could do it just as easily whether their business took them to an exclusive East End country club or an infested downtown crackhouse.

Directly next to the two Russians sat a group of men who did not blend into their surroundings at all. They spoke with thick Texas accents and wore large ten-gallon hats and leather cowboy boots with their suits. From their loud conversation, it was clear that one of the men had just sold several large oil fields in his home state for multiple millions, and had begun celebrating immediately, with straight bourbon being his drink of choice. The Russian Vodka Room was an odd location for these businessmen, but the driver who had picked them up from the airport the night before told them that many exotic and attractive women could be found there. That was all the Texans needed to hear, and they had made their way to the bar after the completion of their business dealings that morning.

When the men lit up a round of cigars, the smoke quickly drifted toward the two Russians at the next table. One of them got up from his seat and politely addressed the Texan who had been doing the majority of the talking.

"Excuse me, sir. Your cigar smoke is bothering my friend and me. We would appreciate it if you would put them out."

The silver-haired cowboy paused for a moment and looked the Russian man over before responding.

"Well, son, the way I see it, you and your friend over there are bothering me and my cigar smokin'. So why don't you just go ahead and mosey yourselves on out of here if you don't like it."

The Texan then took several deep puffs on the end of his cigar and blew a large plume of smoke directly into the younger man's face. He and his fellow cowboys then busted out in a fit of laughter, as the Russian turned away and slowly headed back toward his table. His friend stood up and they walked away, but, although they could no longer be seen by the obnoxious Texans, they did not leave the bar.

Less than twenty minutes later, the offensive oil tycoon got up from his seat and headed for the restroom. He was standing in front of a urinal, still smoking his cigar, when he heard the door creak open behind him. Turning around, the Texan saw the familiar face of the young Russian enter the bathroom and a smile crept over his lips as he spoke over his shoulder.

"What's a matter, son? You get a little upset that I blew smoke in your face? Made you look bad in front of your boyfriend out there? Well, let me just finish up my business here and we can have it out if that's the way you want it."

As he finished speaking, the older man's hands moved in front of his body, presumably to zip up his pants. Much to the Russian's surprise, however, the Texan wheeled around to face him, and pulled a revolver from a holster beneath his suit jacket. Equally surprising as the Texan's gun was the portion of his anatomy that was still exposed and also pointing directly at the Russian.

In spite of this awkward and precarious stand-off, the Russian was completely calm. He knew that his training and physical abilities would momentarily overwhelm the Texan, despite the presence of the firearm that the man was currently holding. In fact, the Russian was actually somewhat amused, thinking to himself that he would rather be shot by the Texan's gun than hit with whatever might come out of his other protrusion.

In an instant the Russian's thoughts turned much more serious and he focused on the Texan's breathing pattern, his grip on the weapon, and the placement of his finger outside the trigger block. Moving so suddenly that the older man barely had time to be surprised, the Russian lunged forward and wrapped both of his hands around the Texan's wrist. In one swift, powerful motion, he rotated his hands and snapped the bones connecting the man's hand to his arm and the gun dropped harmlessly to the bathroom floor.

As the pain from his broken wrist set in, the Texan's mouth flew open and the cigar he'd been chomping on fell toward the floor. The Russian removed one of his hands from his victim's wrist, reached out, and caught the cigar at around waist level.

"I told you that the smoke was bothering me," the young man said in a voice that eerily registered almost no emotion. "Now, I'll put this out for you."

The Russian pressed the lit end of the cigar down hard onto the only area of exposed flesh on the Texan other than his hands and face. As the Texan howled with pain, the Russian applied pressure to the broken wrist, effectively freezing the larger man from making any movements other than a vain attempt at bucking his lower body in response to the agonizing burning of the cigar against his skin.

The door to the restroom opened, and the Russian's friend entered and surveyed the situation. Without speaking, he bent down and retrieved the Texan's gun, placing it into his waistband in the small of his back. Then the two men grabbed the whimpering, in-shock Texan beneath his arms and carried him out of the bathroom. Instead of heading back toward the bar, they turned toward the rear exit, opened the back door, and deposited the old cowboy on the pavement in the alley running behind the establishment.

In a different era, there would have been one simple word to describe Peter and Nicholas's occupation—spies. But spies usually had an allegiance to one side of a dispute and maintained their loyalty to that group, even when pretending to work for the enemy. Peter and Nicholas, on the other hand, had no allegiances whatsoever, and their only loyalties were to each other. Although they favored solely the client who offered them the most money, their skills were often in high demand because Peter and Nicholas were masters of disguise, cunning thieves, and, for the right price, cutthroat killers.

They could have easily murdered the rude cowboy and left him for dead behind the bar without a drop of remorse, but the one rule that Peter and Nicholas attempted to abide by was not to kill unless it was absolutely necessary. Many of their contemporaries enjoyed the murder of others, but Peter and Nicholas firmly believed that unless it was required to complete a job, or if death was the assignment itself, that they were talented enough to complete any of their assigned tasks without killing anyone. Although leaving victims alive occasionally left open the possibility of revenge, most of the people that came into contact with Peter and Nicholas had no desire to ever cross their paths again.

After the group of Texans discovered their severely wounded boss and rushed him to the nearest hospital, these dangerous men returned to their table and sat chatting idly when they were approached by an old friend.

"I thought I might find the two of you in here."

"Well, when we're not working we like to relax where we know we will be surrounded by familiar faces," said Peter, who usually did the talking for both of them. Nicholas merely gave a slight nod hello as Peter continued speaking.

"But yours is a face we have not seen for quite some time. To what do we owe the honor?"

"I have a job for you. And I need you to start right away."

"Well, you have always been good to us in the past, and lucky for you, we happen to be between jobs at the moment."

"One thing about this job—it might get messy before it's all done."

"If there's one thing you know about us," Peter responded with a sly half-smile, "it's that there's nothing that we can't handle."

After receiving their assignment, Peter and Nicholas spent the next few hours gathering information and deciding upon the best method to approach their first target. Although they always planned ahead, the two men had a unique ability to adapt on the fly to any situation they found themselves in. This ability had saved their lives on more than one occasion.

Peter and Nicholas located their subject's address, and learned that he lived alone. They planned to follow him home from work and accost him there, where they would have plenty of time to get the information they wanted out of him. But when their target left the office building where he worked at around six forty-five, he headed in the opposite direction from where he lived and across the street into a bar called the Playwright Tavern. Peter and Nicholas were close behind the man, but he never would have noticed them. They were average in height, weight, and appearance, with no scars, markings, or any characteristics to make them stand out. They wore dark pants and plain shirts with no writing. Even their hair was entirely ordinary. Peter and Nicholas were just two guys walking into the bar for a drink, blending in perfectly.

At first they sat and watched him, though it appeared that they were deeply immersed in their own conversation. In truth, one of them had his eyes on their mark at all times. When he'd first arrived, the man had ordered a beer and a shot of whiskey. After the first round, he'd ordered another. Although the bar was somewhat crowded and many people chatted affably, happy to have reached the end of another work week, the man Peter and Nicholas watched sat quietly alone and his silence caused the people around him to shy away. Seeing an opportunity, the two Russians nodded at one another and stood up from their seats.

***

Unlike many of the security guards he worked with, Alan did not believe in the notion that they were some kind of glorified "rent-a-cops." He took a lot of pride in his work, and it had been eating away at him all day that he'd let his guard down and allowed Jake to escape from the building after possibly murdering Mr. Kelban. After a few drinks in the bar across the street from his office building, Alan realized that he wasn't feeling any better, and that it would probably be best to just go home and get some sleep. He was about to drink the last swallow of his second beer when two men suddenly approached behind him on either side. The man on his right spoke over Alan's head to his friend.

"Hey, Johnny, what are you drinking?"

"How about a shot of Jack and a beer," the other man responded.

"Sounds good," the first man answered, and then turned to address Alan. "Hey pal, you wanna join us for a round?"

"No thanks," Alan answered, surprised at the offer. "I should be getting home."

"Why, what do you have to go home to?" Peter asked, knowing full well that Alan had nothing to go home to except for a microwave dinner and some *Law and Order* reruns.

"Come on," Peter continued, "have a drink with us. Bartender—three Buds and three shots of Jack." Turning again toward Alan, he asked, "So, what's your name, pal?"

"Name's Alan. And I appreciate the drinks." Alan thought that it was lucky for him that these guys were drinking the same thing he'd been drinking. Not that he would have turned down the free drink if it had been something else.

"Alan, good to meet you. I'm Mark. And that chatterbox over there is Johnny. We work security over at the McGraw-Hill building around the corner."

"No kidding. I'm on the job too—right across the street at 1251 Sixth Avenue."

"Small world," Nicholas chimed in, and the three men clinked their shot glasses together and drank.

Peter and Nicholas had seen their opening to get information from Alan and had fallen right into the roles of Mark and Johnny, two friendly security guards out for a drink. A couple of hours and several rounds later, Peter asked, "Hey, Alan, you said you work in the building across the street, right? Wasn't there some big shot lawyer who got killed in that building last night? I saw something about it earlier on the news, they think another lawyer may have done it."

"Well, he's not actually a lawyer. Not yet anyway. His name's Jake Hunter, and he's a summer associate. Although from what I heard, he was at the top of the summer class—at least until today."

"So did you see this kid today? It sounds like there's a city-wide manhunt looking for him right now."

"Yeah, I saw him." Alan's head sunk into his chest as he thought back to the morning's events. "We had him cornered in his office, me and my partner, but the kid surprised us and got away. I shoulda been more prepared, but he always seemed like such a nice kid."

"Hey, you can't blame yourself for that, Alan. That kid could have been a psychotic murderer. They don't pay us enough to deal with those kind of people, right Johnny?"

"Right," said Nicholas, choosing not to embellish his response any further.

"So," Peter kept pushing for more details, "did the cops show up and talk to you?"

"The cops were there, but they weren't running the show. It was the FBI. They were the ones who interviewed me." Alan was feeling much better since Mark and Johnny showed up to keep him company and buy him drinks. He decided he could share a little more about what he'd seen earlier, and maybe even impress them. "But the feds didn't have any more of a clue than I did about the connection between the kid and the dead partner. Although I think it must have something to do with whatever the partner sent him in the mail this morning."

"What do you mean? What could he have sent him?"

"Well, I know for a fact he sent the kid a note, because he was reading it when me and Bobby showed up at his office. But that wasn't the only thing he sent him. I talked to the guy from the mail room, Ricky, and he said that there was definitely something else in the envelope, and that it felt like a small computer drive, or something like that."

Alan was now getting excited at retelling the story and he could see that Mark and Johnny were hanging on his every word.

When he paused, Peter asked, "Did the feds say anything else to you about the kid, or the dead guy?"

Alan racked his brain to come up with any more details from the morning, and he remembered one last thing that he'd heard before leaving Hunter's office.

"They did say something about the murder weapon. It was some kind of special knife I think."

"Special how?"

"I'm not sure, but the FBI guy said it had a special name, something with a "B." Oh, I remember now—Basko!"

Peter and Nicholas kept their faces expressionless, but inside they knew that the brand of knife had a particular significance.

"Never heard of it," was all Peter said in response.

Within a few minutes, Peter and Nicholas had paid their tab and left Alan alone at the bar. Alan wondered why they had left so suddenly after it seemed like they were all having a good time together, but then figured that they probably had families to get home to. Feeling a little bit drunk, Alan decided he'd take a cab home from the bar. As he left, he thought to himself that if the cab drove fast enough, he could catch the start of the ten o'clock episode of *Law and Order.*

***

A few blocks away from the bar, Peter and Nicholas placed a call to their client from a pay phone. As soon as he heard the familiar voice on the other end, Peter said, "We've got news. Kelban definitely sent Hunter some kind of information, and maybe even sent him a computer disk or a mini hard drive. Also, there's an excellent chance that Kelban was killed by a Russian."

"And how do you know that?"

"The murder weapon was a Basko knife."
"Well then, you know what you have to do next."
"Yes," Peter answered. "Find Hunter."

CHAPTER 11

Jake Hunter, Friday, 5:14p.m.

Jake had always enjoyed driving, and the uneventful ride to Vermont had relaxed him somewhat. He was now heading east on Route Four through the heart of Killington, past Pico Mountain and a number of inns, restaurants and shops. Jason's uncle's ski house was located about half a mile outside of town, and Jake almost missed the small mailbox with the address indicating that he needed to make a right turn into the long driveway leading to the cabin at the top of a small hill. Even though the house was about one hundred yards from the main road, and was enclosed by trees on all sides, Jake pulled the car off the driveway and around to the back of the cabin so it would be completely out of sight even if someone ventured up to the front of the house.

After exiting the car, the first thing Jake noticed was how quiet and peaceful the cabin and the surrounding woods seemed. The only sound was the flowing water of a small brook nearby. Jake unlocked the back door using Jason's keys and entered the first floor of the house, which was essentially one large, open room. To the left was a thick wooden table with benches on either side, which Jake remembered he and his friends had used for both dining and playing drinking games when they'd stayed there for New Years.

Immediately to Jake's right was a staircase leading up to the cabin's second floor, which had three bedrooms and a bathroom, all situated off a long central hallway. Past the dining area on the first floor was the living room, which consisted of three non-matching couches flanking a small coffee table in the center of the room. In the very front of the house, next to the door, was a large stone fireplace. Jake recalled how much Jason had enjoyed stoking the fire and adding wood to the blaze whenever it was in danger of going out. Off to the side of the living room and fireplace, on the other side of the front door, was a small kitchen. The kitchen had been used on the New Years trip to cook breakfast once or twice, but the refrigerator and freezer had been stocked with far more beverages than food products on that particular weekend.

After all that he'd been through that day, the cozy little cabin in the middle of the woods felt safe to Jake. He had happy memories of being there with his friends, and with Jen, the previous New Years Eve. They had celebrated, drank, laughed, and hugged—life had seemed so good at the time. Now the cabin was silent, and Jake realized that he had no idea whether he was truly safe there or not. Partly to distract himself and partly for protection, Jake began searching the cabinets and closets for anything that he might be able to use as a weapon. As he came across some tools, games, and other random items, Jake decided that he would rig the entrances to the cabin to alert him if anyone tried to get in, and also prepare some ways to defend himself if he was attacked.

In the back of his mind, Jake knew that his booby-trapping of the cabin was simply a way to keep from thinking about his situation. Still, he managed to put those thoughts aside, and actually chuckled at his creative handiwork, deciding that his efforts fell somewhere between those of MacGyver and the Macaulay Culkin character from the *Home Alone* movies. On the rear wall of the house was a small shelf with hooks for coats below it. The shelf was only about six inches away from the back door and five feet from the floor. Jake filled a plastic cup with seven or eight marbles that he took from the game *Hungry Hungry Hippos* and balanced the cup right on the edge of the shelf. He then took a ruler that he'd found in a drawer in one of the bedrooms and nailed it to the door, positioned so that it was almost touching the precariously balanced cup. If anyone opened the back door, no matter how silently, the ruler would tip the cup and knock the marbles to the floor.

Jake used a much more rudimentary alert system near the front door and hoped that it would, at the very least, give him a chance to get out of the house if someone tracked him there. At the far end of the upstairs hallway, Jake placed a large mirror that he took from the master bedroom, thinking that he might be able to use it from one of the other bedrooms or the bathroom to see someone coming up the stairs. Jake also planted some items he could use as weapons throughout the house. He would take the hammer he found to bed with him, as it was the best thing he could find to defend himself with, in case he was attacked while sleeping.

After his primitive efforts at home safety were complete, Jake searched the kitchen for something to eat. He cooked some Kraft macaroni and cheese in a pot on the stove, but it didn't taste very good without any milk or butter. Jake found a can of green beans that he cooked and seasoned with salt and pepper, and which were sufficient to satisfy what little appetite he had. With nothing else to do to keep his mind off his predicament, Jake thumbed through a stack of novels that people had left behind in the house over the years. The pile of mostly older books contained everything from the first *Harry Potter* to several of John Grisham's earlier novels, but Jake was drawn to a story from a much more distant past, which he'd read once before back in high school.

Homer's *Odyssey* was a classic, and did not seem to fit in with the other light reading materials that surrounded it. Jake thought that there was something fitting about reading the tale of a man who ventures far from his home, and must overcome great struggles to return. Jake recalled that Odysseus eventually did get back to his homeland, but once there, he encountered further strife. Jake's only wish was that whenever he was able to go back home, he would have a much easier return than the mythological hero. Jake had no way of knowing at the time that he would be lucky to get home at all.

CHAPTER 12

Agent Stanton, Friday, 5:47p.m.

Stanton and Zarvas hadn't left the law firm offices until almost one o'clock that afternoon. After scarfing down a couple of hot dogs from one of the vendors outside the building, they proceeded to Hunter's law school to interview some of his classmates and professors. Although classes would be starting up again in a week, the school was still fairly deserted and ended up being a dead end. There were a handful of students there participating in some sort of moot court competition, but none of them knew Hunter very well, and those that did had little to say other than that he seemed like a really nice guy.

The two agents decided to split up in an effort to track down more leads in less time. Zarvas headed to Hunter's apartment building to follow up on what had apparently been a near-miss of catching him by the NYPD. Stanton pulled Hunter's cell phone records and went to interview Jason Carerra, a friend who had been the first to call Hunter shortly after news of the murder broke. During their conversation, Carerra admitted to Stanton that he had alerted Hunter that news reports said that police were heading to his apartment, but claimed not to know Hunter's present location. Stanton wasn't sure if Carerra was being entirely truthful about not having any idea where Hunter might be, but one thing he was adamantly clear about was his belief that Hunter was innocent and would be exonerated.

Zarvas was equally unsuccessful at Hunter's apartment building and the two agents decided to meet up back at the FBI forensics lab to see what kind of evidence the crime scene techs had discovered. A quick visit to the "latents" lab, where fingerprints were catalogued and run through various databases for identification, confirmed that Hunter's prints were the only ones on the knife. Evidence like that was sufficient for many prosecutors to convince a jury that the person who left the prints was the killer, but most law enforcement officers had seen enough contaminated crime scenes to know that such evidence actually established only one thing—that Hunter had held the knife at some point. The prints alone did not prove that Hunter was the person who had stabbed Kelban.

The "trace" lab, where all of the smallest, otherwise unidentifiable materials found at a crime scene were sent, had surprisingly little to offer. Perpetrators of crimes usually were unable to completely remove every piece of evidence that they left at the scene. The smallest piece of hair, fiber, or any other substance with unique characteristics sometimes could be traced back to specific locations or, on rare occasions, even to specific people. The present case, however, was devoid of evidence linked to anyone other than people who were known to have been at the scene. This was especially strange in the case of a stabbing, because in many violent crimes where a knife is used, the perpetrator often cuts himself and leaves traces of his own blood at the scene.

"What do you think it means?" Stanton asked her partner, who had more experience with homicides.

"Well," Zarvas answered, "it could mean that Kelban was drugged or unconscious at the time of the stabbing, so it was easier to stab him without the killer cutting himself."

"But we won't be able to tell that until after we get the toxicology results back on Kelban."

"Right. And the truth is, there's a much more likely explanation that makes particular sense in this case."

"What's that?"

"Usually, when we come across a stabbing with no defensive wounds and no secondary source of blood from the doer, it means that the person using the knife was very good at it. Probably even an expert—possibly one trained in using weapons like large, Russian-made hunting knives."

"So you do think the Russians killed Kelban."

"I'm not saying I'm certain about anything yet. Especially until we find this Hunter kid and figure out how he's involved in all of this."

The agents final stop was the electronics lab, and it was the last place that they expected to find anything useful. The technician who worked electronics was a young, redheaded, freckled man that everyone called Sully. His full name was Mike Sullivan, but he hadn't been called that since his freshman year mechanical engineering class at MIT, where Professor Hazeltine had refused to call anyone by a nickname.

Sully was always telling stories and playing practical jokes on the other techs, but he was excellent in his field of communications, and had even patented a new wireless earpiece transmitter that was being phased into use for agents throughout the country and overseas. As he saw Stanton and Zarvas approaching, Sully had the usual glimmer of mischief in his eyes, but he also seemed excited and began speaking as soon as they were within earshot.

"You guys are not gonna believe what we found in that dead lawyer's office!"

Sully was holding a tiny, round device between his thumb and forefinger, and could barely take his eyes off it long enough to look at Stanton and Zarvas, as they tried to get a better view of whatever he was holding.

"Calm down, Sully," Zarvas commanded the excitable technician. "Just tell us what the heck it is."

"Man, this is a crazy, super-new, fresh on the market listening device. I mean, we're talking cutting-edge, high-end, top-of-the-line eavesdropping equipment here."

"Okay. We get the picture," Stanton said. "Someone was bugging Kelban's office with a high-tech listening device."

"No. You don't get it," Sully explained. "This isn't just a high-tech listening device. I've never even seen anything like it before in this country. Whoever was listening to this guy has some serious technology at his disposal. First of all, the techs who processed the scene only found this thing by accident. They were checking the lawyer's phone for standard taps and didn't notice it at all. Then, one of the klutzes working the scene drops the phone on the guy's desk, and this little sucker pops out onto the floor. Another tech on the scene actually picked it up and sent it to trace instead of to me. It was lucky I was in there leaving a stinkbomb under Jensen's chair and noticed it on his desk before he started dissecting it."

"Why would they send a listening device to trace?" Zarvas asked.

"Here, feel it," Sully answered, as he placed the small, round bug into the palm of the agent's left hand.

Zarvas pressed the top of the device with his right index finger and immediately noted that it was soft, almost squishy. It felt like a piece of *Skittles* candy that had been left out in the sun all day.

"I don't understand. How exactly is this thing a listening device?"

"The actual device is miniscule, and it's housed inside that soft outer shell. This recorder is placed inside the phone, but all it actually does is send the voices coming across the phone line to a nearby transmitter, which is what really sends the signal to whoever is listening in much farther away."

"So, did the techs find the transmitter?"

"No. That's why I went out there myself to look for it. I searched every inch of that office and the surrounding areas, but the transmitter was nowhere to be found."

"Maybe there was no transmitter," Stanton offered. "Maybe whoever got a hold of this device didn't understand how to use it."

"Highly unlikely. I said the transmitter wasn't in the office when I got there. I didn't say it was never there. The ceiling of the lawyer's office has a standard smoke detector in the middle of it. Unlike the techs who were first on the scene, I removed it from the ceiling and noted that a hole had been drilled through the floor above. Now, there was nothing in that hole by the time I got there, but the opening was certainly big enough to house a transmitter, and possibly even a mini camera and microphone setup. Also, before I came back here, I stopped in on the Forty-fourth floor and found out that an employee from the building was in the conference room directly above the lawyer's office this afternoon supposedly working on the air conditioning system. I bet when you guys check with building maintenance you'll find out that there was no work done or scheduled to be done on the Forty-fourth floor today."

"Impressive, Sully," Zarvas said, as Sully glowed with pride at the compliment. "The fact that this thing is so rare should make it easier to trace."

"Yeah, well, I really hope you guys catch whoever is behind this one."

"Really?" Stanton asked. "Since when do you take such an interest in whether or not we nail the bad guys?"

"To tell you the truth, I just want you to catch this guy so I can find out where he gets his equipment. I would love to get my hands on some more of these devices and do a little reverse engineering."

The agents were not at all surprised by Sully's true motive for wanting them to apprehend Kelban's killer, but they were slightly taken aback when he extended his hand toward Zarvas and said in a serious tone, "You know, it really is a pleasure working with you guys."

Zarvas, sincerely touched by Sully's kind words, and proud of the initiative the young technician had taken, reached out and firmly gripped his hand to shake it. The toy buzzer that Sully had secreted in his palm made a loud whirring noise as it jolted Zarvas with a painful, but ultimately harmless, electric shock. Zarvas pulled his hand away angrily as Sully doubled over with laughter, cracking himself up at his juvenile prank.

"Man, you agents are so easy to fool," Sully said, as Zarvas and Stanton strode away down the hall. "You're lucky I'm not a criminal."

CHAPTER 13

Sergei Ilanov, Friday, 7:09p.m.

The excitement from earlier in the day had died down, and Sergei turned the sound off on the last of the evening news reports that he was watching. He'd assumed that Hunter would be taken immediately into police custody, but the young attorney-to-be had escaped his office building and then seemingly vanished. The news media took the bait that Sergei offered them, and all of the networks had led with the story of Kelban's murder and the disappearance of Hunter—the authorities' main suspect.

Minutes later, Sergei glanced at the video screen linked to the security camera at his building's front door and saw that a package he was waiting for had arrived. He pressed a button on the intercom in his apartment, which unlocked the door and allowed the delivery man upstairs. Sergei proffered a twenty dollar tip as the man handed over a package containing the disk that Boris had removed from Kelban's computer before infecting the hard drive with the virus that Sergei had commissioned. Sergei inserted the disk into his computer and, for the first time in years, he was actually slightly nervous about the uncertainty of what he would find on the disk, and where Hunter had disappeared to with a flash drive containing the same information.

At first, all the disk revealed was a number of coded files, but Sergei had the best decoding software on the market, which immediately began breaking through the encryptions. Soon, all of the information on the disk was readily available to him. Although the files were well-protected, Sergei knew that it would only be a matter of time before the FBI would crack the encryption if they ever got hold of the flash drive in Hunter's possession. As each successive file opened on his computer, revealing aliases, account numbers, and potential threats to expose him, Sergei grew more and more enraged. Although he was angry at Kelban for creating and keeping these files, Kelban had been eliminated and no longer posed a threat. The majority of Sergei's fury was now directed at the only person capable of using the files against him—Jake Hunter.

If the information recorded on the flash drive in Hunter's possession were ever discovered, Sergei would be forced to fold most, if not all, of his operations and go back into hiding. Kelban was remarkably intelligent, and in helping Sergei set up front businesses and false identities, he had also been able to create a massive flow chart of names, corporations, accounts, and payoffs, all of which linked back to one person—Sergei Ilanov.

Sergei knew that evidence like this would be a federal prosecutor's wet dream. Not only would it bring down him and his gang, but it would also end the careers of numerous police officials, federal agents, and even a few high-ranking politicians who had received payments, bribes, contributions, and many other illegitimate gifts from Sergei and his organization over the years. Of course, Sergei was not really afraid of being caught and going to jail. He would always be one step ahead of the authorities and would be long gone and living off money stashed in accounts that no one else knew about. But the thought of having to run, of having to admit defeat and turn his back on everything that he'd built, made Sergei's blood boil. He had been forced into hiding once before in his life, and there was nothing he would not do to keep it from happening again.

Sergei picked up the phone and dialed his most trusted lieutenants. Boris answered after the first ring.

"Yes, boss."

"I have instructions for you and Ivan. Are you ready?"

"Yes. I'm listening."

"First, have Ivan stake out Hunter's apartment. Tell him to watch it from somewhere he won't be seen and to figure out if the feds or the cops are watching it as well. If he sees them, he has to stay out of their sight. If no authorities are there, I don't care who else sees him, as long as he doesn't tip off Hunter. I doubt that Hunter will go back there, but if he does, make sure Ivan brings him to me alive."

"Understood. What about me?"

"You will contact our connections inside the FBI and the NYPD and get as many details as you can about their search for Hunter. I want to know about any leads they have on his location, and any ideas they have about where he might be, no matter how farfetched. If he is taken into custody, make sure that you are notified immediately. As soon as either one of you has any useful information on Hunter, contact me right away."

"It will be done, boss."

Once he finished instructing Boris, Sergei's thoughts turned to another matter that needed to be dealt with. It was not something Sergei was looking forward to, and he did not trust anyone to handle it for him. He prepared himself for the trip he was about to make by washing his hands and face, and then putting on a light-weight windbreaker and a thin pair of leather gloves. Before leaving the apartment, Sergei grabbed one more item that would be required during his short excursion. It could not be traced to him, but he would not be bringing it back to the apartment anyway.

Sergei exited his building onto West Forty-ninth Street and headed east. He passed a small diner, a supermarket, and a CVS store before coming to Ninth Avenue, where he turned right and headed downtown towards Times Square. Several blocks further south, Sergei crossed over to Eighth Avenue and found himself surrounded by the early evening weekend crowds getting ready to go to the theater, or just heading out for dinner or to a bar. Tucked away between two establishments offering twenty-five cent peep shows was a small storefront with lettering on the glass stating its name—*Drew's Pawn Shop and Electronics Superstore.* It struck Sergei that only in New York could a six hundred square foot bandbox call itself a "superstore" and get away with it.

The small sign hanging on the inside of the front door listing the store's hours of operation said that it was open until ten o'clock on Friday night. But as Sergei entered the store, he flipped over another, larger sign in the window from *Open* to *Closed,* and also turned the deadbolt lock on the door so that no one could come in even if they thought that the store was still open for business.

Like most pawn shops, the front area of the store was cluttered with random goods, ranging from an old electric guitar, advertised as having once been played by Jimi Hendrix, to a lamp whose base was a woman's leg. The walls were glass cases, housing everything from jewelry, to weapons, to assorted electronic devices. In the deepest recesses of the store, a large metallic grate separated the customers from the proprietor of the establishment, a greasy looking man in his late thirties or early forties with too-long, brown hair poking out from beneath a well-aged Mets baseball cap. The man wore a pair of work overalls and his attention was focused on a miniature camera that he was tinkering with on the desk in front of him. Although the man never looked up at Sergei, he seemed well-aware that someone had entered the store and spoke in a slow, heavy voice.

"Hello, Sol."

Drew Wasserman addressed Sergei by the fake name that Sergei had used when he was first introduced to the man, whom he'd been told was an electronics genius. Drew believed that "Sol" was an extremely wealthy recluse who had a Nixon-like compulsion to keep tabs on the people closest to him by recording their conversations. Using this cover story, Sergei had easily persuaded Drew to bug a number of different people and places without questioning the purpose for the eavesdropping. When it was necessary, Drew also was able to provide video surveillance.

"It's nice to see you again, Drew."

"How did everything work out with the latest equipment I provided for you?" Drew asked, referring to the camera and listening devices he'd planted in Kelban's office weeks before, and removed earlier that day.

"Very well actually. I was able to eliminate some very distressing leaks regarding my business interests. I am intrigued by one thing though. Tell me, how did you get your hands on the equipment you used. Everything worked so well, I assume the technology must be quite unique."

"It's unique all right. They don't even make that stuff here in the states yet. I get 'em from Germany. That's where all the latest advances are coming from. Fortunately for me, this line of work is a family trait. My brother, Grant, he's working over there in Germany right now. Lots of top-secret stuff going on where he's at. Don't worry though. It's all run by the U.S. They just set up shop overseas because the government would get too much heat over here if people knew what was going on."

"So, your brother—Grant—he is able to smuggle you some of the things he is working on over there?"

"Yup. Usually only in pieces though. Actually makes it more fun for me. I get to figure out how to put 'em all together.

Never takes me too long though. Just always had a knack for putting things together."

"Do you have any more of your brother's gadgets in there with you? I'd love to see some." Sergei actually couldn't have cared less about seeing any more of Drew's, or his brother Grant's, high-tech toys. But he knew that the glass behind the grate separating him from Drew was bulletproof. Sergei would not be able to accomplish what he'd come here to do unless Drew was willing to buzz him inside.

Drew rarely let anyone through to the back of his store, but Sol had been an excellent customer over the past couple of years. As Drew took a closer look at the curious man, wearing his silly windbreaker and gloves on this warm August night, he decided that the guy was harmless. Plus, Drew didn't usually get to show off his expertise in putting together the advanced devices that he worked on. It would be fun to wow the old guy by showing him how smart he was when it came to machines and electronics. He reached under the desk in front of him and pressed the button that opened the door in the grating. Sergei eagerly strode through, closing the grate door behind him.

Drew led the way through a wooden door into the cramped back office where he worked on his secret, and illegal, projects. Spread out on a small bench were numerous wires, tools, and other small devices, including cameras and transmitters. A pair of headphones was hooked up to a stereo unit, but it appeared to be turned off at the moment. Sergei's eyes immediately were drawn to a wall containing four video monitors at the rear of the tiny work space. He realized that there were cameras hidden throughout the store, and his face had been recorded on tape. Fortunately for Sergei, this was the first time he'd ever met Drew at his store.

"Drew, I am curious," Sergei began to ask what he believed to be a critical question. "Most pawn shops I have been to prefer to keep their video cameras exposed, out in the open, to discourage people from stealing. Yours are obviously well-hidden. Are these monitors linked to the only cameras hidden in the store?"

"Yup, just these four that you see here. Fact is, I wouldn't even care if people stole most of the stuff in the front of this store anyway. I hide the cameras specifically to test whether people notice them or not, and also to experiment with different resolutions, shadows at certain times of day, and certain angles. People don't realize that it's not just the quality of the equipment you use that makes for good spying, it's how well you can deploy that equipment that makes all the difference."

Sergei knew that it would be difficult to find another electronics man as good as Drew. But the fact remained that Drew might have been seen going in and out of the conference room on the Forty-fourth floor above Kelban's office. It was only a matter of time until he was tracked down, along with his brother in Germany. Although Drew knew next to nothing about Sergei's true identity, he possessed plenty of knowledge about the electronic devices he'd planted over the past few years and, more importantly, the places he'd planted them at Sergei's behest. Sergei could not afford to leave this loose end alive.

"So, Grant sends me this camera, right," Drew began sharing a story with Sergei. "Except when it gets here it's in about fifteen tiny pieces."

Drew thought that the serious expression on his customer's face was due to his deep interest in the story he was telling. However, when he turned back to face the older man and continue his tale, he was shocked to see the man's arm extended and pointing a gun directly at his chest.

Before Drew could utter a sound, Sergei pulled the trigger three times, firing a tight circle of bullets into Drew's heart. His body was driven backwards and crashed over a chair and onto the ground. Sergei walked forward and, with his gloved fingertip, pressed the eject button below each of the screens that was receiving a feed from the video cameras hidden throughout the store. One by one, four videocassettes popped out of the machines and Sergei placed them all in a small plastic bag. He was slightly amused at the thought that anyone who passed him on the street probably would confuse him for a dirty old man who had just made a purchase at one of the many X-rated video stores in the area.

Sergei looked down at Drew's body, which was already beginning to reek from the expulsion of waste that occurs with being fatally shot. Drew's eyes were blue, and as they stared up at Sergei, still wide with fear and surprise, they reminded him of Jake Hunter's eyes. In a wave of anger, Sergei aimed his gun at the dead man's forehead and pulled the trigger two more times before dropping the gun and leaving the store. As he walked out the front door, Sergei's own eyes narrowed as he thought about what he would do when he was alone with Hunter. One thing was for sure—Hunter's suffering and death would not be over nearly as quick as Drew Wasserman's.

CHAPTER 14

Jason Carerra, Saturday, 7:45a.m.

The hospital was always quieter on the weekends, and Jason was thankful for the relative solitude as he entered the building that morning. He'd barely gotten any work done on Friday, between helping Jake get out of town, and then the surprising visit from the female FBI agent. Jason knew that Agent Stanton doubted his assertion that he didn't know anything regarding Jake's whereabouts, but she hadn't pushed too hard when he'd adamantly proclaimed Jake's innocence and admitted that he told Jake that he should leave New York City until he was sure that it was safe to return.

The lowest level of the hospital, where Jason's lab was located, ordinarily was accessible only by certain hospital personnel and lab technicians. Before eight in the morning on a Saturday, there was not a single other person around as Jason got off the elevator and headed toward his office. Everything about Jason's lab and office looked exactly as he'd left it the night before, and he calmly opened the door and walked into the bare, clinical space just as he did most every morning. His thoughts were still on Jake, hoping that his close friend was sitting safely in his uncle's cabin, and wondering whether there was anything else that he could do to help. Jason took two steps into the office and was about to turn on the table lamp on his desk when there was a sudden flash of movement from the corners of the room.

***

After leaving the Playwright Tavern, Peter and Nicholas spent the remainder of the previous evening gathering intelligence on Hunter. Their primary objective was to determine his present location, or where he might be headed. They researched his background, family, and friends, checking whether Hunter was close to anyone that was connected in any way to law enforcement, because they knew that civilians caught up in criminal investigations often turned to people they knew in the authorities with questions or for help. But this was a dead end in Hunter's case.

Whenever Peter and Nicholas were charged with locating a subject, they started developing leads by simply accumulating as much information as possible to see if any particular names or places came up on multiple occasions or from various sources. While using their resources to pull Hunter's cell phone records, Peter and Nicholas discovered their first common cross-reference. One of Hunter's closest childhood friends had called him shortly after the news broke of Kelban's murder.

Peter and Nicholas had gone to the hospital where Jason Carerra worked the previous night and managed to sneak a look at the visitor log entries from Friday. At ten thirty-five in the morning, Jason had signed in a patient named "A. Smith," whose signature was nothing more than a large, scribbled X. Although it was possible that this visitor was a legitimate subject for Jason's study, Peter and Nicholas asked a few questions of the evening hospital staff and found out that the researchers did not usually conduct live-patient studies on Fridays. In fact, patient "A. Smith" was the only subject that Jason had signed in all day.

Peter and Nicholas often employed a typical technique used in espionage of turning the tables on the person they were following by surprising him at a place that was a part of his customary routine. They had observed over their many years in the business that even the most paranoid members of the intelligence community could not completely eliminate the basic human tendency to feel more comfortable or relaxed in what they perceived to be a safe, familiar environment. When Peter and Nicholas saw Carerra leave his apartment that morning and begin walking uptown, they sped ahead of him in their van and went to the hospital, surmising that he was heading to work. Getting into Carerra's office had been simple, and the surprise on his face was evident as the two men leaped out from the dark corners of his office and easily subdued him.

Jason now sat in his desk chair, his arms and legs bound to the arms and legs of the chair with vise-like plastic restraints. His mouth was covered with tape, but Jason knew that these men wanted information from him and the tape would have to come off. Jason assumed that his captors had something to do with the death of Jake's boss, and that they had found out about his phone call to Jake yesterday morning, just like the FBI. The stockier of the two otherwise average-looking men stood off to the side, seemingly watching both Jason and the hall outside his office door at the same time. The slightly smaller, thinner man was perched in front of Jason, bent at the knees so that they were almost at eye level, but showing no sign of physical strain from the awkward position, despite having maintained it for several minutes. The man was saying Jason's name as he prepared to take the tape off his mouth, and Jason began to consider the chance of anyone hearing him if he were to yell for help.

"Jason," Peter spoke more forcefully now, attracting his full attention. "If you are thinking of trying to shout for help when I pull this tape off, let me tell you exactly what will happen if you do. As I pull the tape off with my left hand, if you so much as begin to speak, my right hand will instantly strike your larynx with great force, leaving you temporarily unable to make a sound. Then, as you are hunched over, trying to recover from absorbing the painful blow to your throat, I will remove this knife from my side," Peter pointed to a knife attached to his belt on his left hip, "and I will stab you through your lower torso, slashing through your small intestine. You will be in unbearable pain, but you will have plenty of time left alive to tell us what we want to know before you bleed out in agony. Your other option is to remain quiet when I remove this tape, and you will probably live to see the results of your interesting drug research. I think you know which is the correct choice here, am I right?"

Jason merely nodded his head slowly up and down one time. The tone of Peter's voice made clear that the picture he'd painted was not one created by his imagination, but was in fact an all-too-real description of a scene he'd enacted before and would have no problem performing again. The tape was yanked from Jason's mouth in one swift motion, and Jason exhaled reflexively.

"Now," Peter began, "we know Jake Hunter was here in this office yesterday and we know you know where he is. Tell me now, or I'm afraid things will get extremely unpleasant for you."

"I swear I don't know where Jake is," Jason responded, trying to speak quietly. His voice was raw with fear and emotion, and he prayed to himself that it made his lie sound believable.

Peter's head dropped slightly at Jason's response and he finally stood from his crouched position. He reached toward the desk behind him and when he turned back around, Jason could see that he was holding a syringe containing a cloudy solution.

"You study the effects of this drug, cocaine. You have seen the tortured and tormented souls who deal with the daily addiction to a needle just like this one. It must be hard on their families, don't you think? But your family must be proud of you, Jason. Doing research studies designed to help people. Heading off to medical school soon to become a doctor. I wonder how sad your family will be when they find out that you died of a drug overdose here in your office. They will have no choice but to believe that you were no better than the junkies you used in your studies. That will be hard on them I think. But you could save them from all of that pain and sorrow by just telling me where I can find Hunter."

As he finished speaking, Peter lunged forward and gripped Jason's left arm, rotating it almost effortlessly so that his palm was facing up. Between struggling against the restraints and Peter's painful grip, Jason could see the veins in his arm practically bursting through the skin in the crook of his elbow. Peter held the tip of the syringe just millimeters away from the bulging bloodlanes. Gritting his teeth in fear and desperate anticipation, Jason spoke again.

"I already told you and the cops that were here yesterday everything I know. I saw Jake on the news and I knew he didn't have anything to do with killing that guy. I called him on his cell phone. He said he was in his apartment, and I told him the cops were on their way over there, but I have no idea where he could be now. I can't tell you what I don't know."

A single tear formed in the corner of Jason's left eye, and he wondered as it rolled down his cheek if that was the last sensation he would remember feeling before the prick of the needle that would inject a fatal dose of cocaine into his bloodstream. There was something ironic about all of the studying he'd done to get into medical school, because Jason knew exactly how the drug would overload his heart, causing it to go into arrhythmia and lead to the heart attack that would kill him. Worse yet, he would die in a hospital where the personnel and equipment that could have saved his life were so close, yet impossibly far away. Jason had no appreciation for the irony, however, and he was almost wishing that his captor would just get it over with, when he noticed the second man reentering the office. Jason hadn't heard him leave, but he now grew even more distressed as he saw what the man held in his hand.

Peter was no longer holding Jason's arm, and he hadn't injected him with the syringe. In fact, Peter was somewhat impressed that Jason appeared willing to take his chances at overdosing rather than give up his friend's location. The Russian spy had more than enough training in body mannerisms, tone, and facial response to know that Jason was lying to him. But unlike most human beings, self-preservation hadn't made him divulge the truth. So Nicholas had searched Jason's locker for another way to force him to talk.

"I have to admit, Jason," Peter's tone was as flat as it had been throughout their entire conversation, "it is very rare to find someone who would risk his own life to protect a friend. I commend you on your resolve. Now, unfortunately, we have no more time to continue getting to know each other's strength of character. You recognize this picture of your family. Tell me where Hunter is right now, or they will all be dead before the sun sets today. I won't frighten you further with the details of how it will be done. I don't think it's necessary because a man of your character does not let his entire family die to protect one friend, no matter how close that friend might be. Again, I think you know that you have no choice. Where is Hunter?"

In the moment after Peter finished speaking, Jason's eyes turned from the man's face to the picture he held of Jason's parents and his younger sister. He'd known Jake for a long time, and he loved him like a brother, but he had to protect his own flesh and blood first. It was with deep and painful sorrow that Jason finally spoke.

"My uncle owns a ski house in Killington, Vermont. Jake took my car there yesterday when he left here. I don't care what you do to me, but please don't hurt my family."

Tears were now streaming from both of Jason's eyes, and he did not even struggle as Peter knelt beside him, again directing the syringe toward his arm. The needle poked through Jason's skin, and he prepared for the exuberant rush that had been described to him on many occasions from the high dose of cocaine he believed he was being injected with. But then he heard Peter's voice one last time.

"Jason, you aren't going to die of a drug overdose. This syringe is filled with flunitrazepam, not cocaine. You will be knocked out for quite a while, and you won't remember very much about our visit to your office, but you and your family will be fine. Unfortunately, I can't guarantee that the same will be true for your friend. You shouldn't feel bad about that though. You did everything you could to protect him."

By the time Peter finished speaking, the powerful sedative was already taking effect, and Jason was about to be rendered completely unconscious. One final thought went through his mind before the room faded into total darkness—*I'm sorry Jake.*

CHAPTER 15

Jake Hunter, Saturday, 1:52p.m.

After reading the *Odyssey* until after four o'clock in the morning, Jake managed to sleep until almost eleven on Saturday. Still not sure what to do about getting the flash drive to the authorities, Jake went for a run along a trail through the woods behind the cabin in an effort to clear his mind and come up with a plan. The running path traveled away from the house for almost three miles over some hilly and rocky terrain, which forced Jake to slow his pace at times to maintain his footing. When the trail ended at a roadway, Jake turned around and followed the same route back to the cabin. The run took him a little over an hour, and he was famished upon returning. Jake searched the kitchen cabinets again and found a couple of cans of soup, which he heated up on the stove. After eating, he went upstairs and took a shower.

Jake was still in the bathroom after showering and dressing in some old clothes that had been left in the cabin's closets, including a plain white t-shirt, blue jeans, and sneakers. He could not find a toothbrush in the house that he was comfortable using, so he was squeezing toothpaste onto his index finger to brush with, which he figured was the best he could do under the circumstances. But as Jake reached out to turn on the cold water, he heard a sound that sent chills up his spine.

***

Peter and Nicholas spent the morning driving up to Killington, hopeful that Hunter would still be hiding out in Jason Carerra's uncle's ski house. When they reached the address, they left their van parked on the road and silently made their way up to the house through the woods that bordered the driveway. Through the front windows of the house, they could see that Jake was not downstairs, but there were signs that the house was occupied, such as a saucepan sitting on the table and a can of soup on the kitchen counter. The two men agreed that Nicholas would keep watch on the front of the house while Peter went in through the back door, next to which they could see the stairs leading to the second floor.

After scoping out the area behind the house, Peter easily picked the simple lock on the cabin's back door without making a sound. His eyes peered through the glass pane of the door and toward the stairs as he began to gently push the door inwards. Peter's instincts kicked in as he began opening the door, and his eyes roved back to where the door was about to crack open. Surprised, but not shocked, Peter saw the shadow of the thin piece of wood nailed to the door and the hint of red from the plastic cup that the ruler was dislodging from a shelf next to the door. Acting without thinking, Peter swung the door open wider and had a clear view of the small, white marbles that were tumbling from the clever warning apparatus that Hunter must have constructed.

With lightning quickness Peter's right hand slid off the door knob and into the opening between the door and its frame. His hand darted back and forth through the air, catching the first two marbles in mid flight, a third an inch or two lower down, and then two more just a foot above the floor. As he caught all of the visible marbles, Peter swung his left hand into the doorway and felt it close around the plastic cup, falling at a slightly slower rate than the marbles, and which Peter could only have seen out of the corner of his eye. Just when he thought that he'd prevented announcing his entrance to the cabin, the last two marbles rolled out of the cup in Peter's left hand. He noticed their movement, but was too late to react and catch them before they struck the wooden floor of the old house. The sound of the tiny pellets hitting the ground certainly was not loud, but there was a noise as they each bounced and landed a second time before Peter finally corralled them.

The sound caused no visible or audible reaction from upstairs or anywhere else inside the house. Still, Peter planned on proceeding with extreme caution as he began climbing the stairs to the second floor. Perhaps Hunter had left the house, or maybe he was sleeping in an upstairs bedroom. But Peter hadn't survived and excelled in his chosen profession by underestimating his opponents.

***

Jake stood frozen in the bathroom, unsure if he could believe what his ears had just heard. The sound was extremely distinct—marbles hitting the floor—but it sounded like only two or three at the most, not the seven or eight that Jake had placed in the cup the day before. It didn't make any sense, but Jake figured that he could not be too cautious. He slowly and quietly wiped the toothpaste from his finger with a towel and then reached out and noiselessly switched off the bathroom light. He did not think it was a good idea to leave the room and try to get back to the bedroom where he left the hammer he'd slept with the night before. Fortunately, he'd planted another makeshift weapon in the bathroom, although the possibility that he would actually have to use it had seemed remote at the time.

Jake now stood with his back pressed to the bathroom counter, staring out into the hallway, but not toward the top of the stairs. Instead, Jake's eyes focused intently on the dungy mirror he'd placed at the far end of the hallway. Just as he was wishing that he'd cleaned the surface of the mirror so that he could see better, Jake saw the reflection of a man climbing to the top of the stairs and holding a gun. The only problem with Jake watching the man approach in the mirror was that the closer he got, the less visible he would be in the mirror from Jake's angle. If the man hugged the wall leading up to the bathroom door, which was the first door along the hallway, Jake would be unable to see him at all just as he reached the bathroom.

The man paused at the top of the stairs and noted the presence of the mirror. Jake thought he actually saw the man smile for a moment, but the reflection was too cloudy to be sure. With his gun raised in front of him, the man began slowly moving down the hallway, sticking close to the near wall as Jake had feared. When he was about three steps away from the bathroom door, Jake knew that he was about to lose sight of the man. Once he disappeared from view, Jake decided that he would count to three and then put his weapon to use. He figured that he would only have one shot, and he prayed that it would work.

***

Peter reached the top of the stairs and immediately wondered if the younger generation of Americans had an undeserved reputation as being lazy and weak-willed. Earlier that day, he'd dealt with Jason Carerra's valiant efforts to protect his friend and his family, and now Hunter was proving to be much more resourceful than Peter had expected. He smiled as he reached the top of the stairs and saw the mirror at the end of the hall. It did not bother him, however, knowing that Hunter could probably see him approaching. In fact, Peter had used his foes' presumed advantages against them on multiple occasions. As he crept along the hallway toward the first doorway, Peter's senses were on full alert. Just one step away from the door, he heard something that caused him to immediately dive to the floor.

The sound was the striking of a lighter, probably an old cigarette lighter that someone had left in the cabin. Jake started the flame with his left thumb and then pressed down with his right index finger on the nozzle of an aerosol can of hairspray. The fluid mist hit the lighter and ignited a fireball that blew out into the hallway precisely where Peter's face would have been had he not dropped to the ground a moment earlier.

Peter reached out from the floor with his right arm into the bathroom and clamped it tightly around Jake's right leg. He squeezed hard on Jake's calf muscle and then yanked forward forcefully. Jake realized too late his mistake in aiming high with the fire spray. He saw the man on the ground in front of him just as he felt a sharp pain stinging through his leg, and then a powerful force pulled his right leg out from under him. Jake fell backwards to the floor hard, but his upper back took the brunt of the fall, and he was able to keep his head from cracking back into the floor with too much force.

With only a second to react as the man's gun was swinging around toward him, Jake managed to flick the lighter a second time and shoot a spray of flame directly toward the gunman's outstretched hand. As the fireball engulfed his arm and his jacket sleeve caught fire, Peter yanked his hand backwards, releasing the searing-hot metal gun, which flew behind him. The gun skidded across the hallway floor and through the wooden slats of the railing that ran along the length of the hallway and looked down on the living room below.

Peter turned and saw the gun fall through the railing to the first floor and then quickly covered up and patted out the flames on his jacket. In that moment, Jake got to his feet and jumped over Peter's still prone body. He thought that he was going to make it to the stairs, but Peter's leg shot out, tripping Jake, who crashed to the floor on his stomach. Peter was instantly on top of Jake, and his powerful arms locked around Jake's shoulders and neck in a painful stranglehold.

Peter lifted Jake onto his feet, maintaining his chokehold from behind, and leaned back against the waist-high railing for support. With only air behind his back, Peter was able to lean backwards over the railing to apply more pressure as he spoke to Jake, who was desperately clawing at Peter's arms.

"Well, Jake, that was a very creative display of planning on your part. Unfortunately, it wasn't nearly enough to save you. My employer has a few questions for you, and I am going to deliver you mostly unharmed. But for your own good, I'm going to put you to sleep first."

Jake could sense his air being cut off and knew that he would soon black out. Once that happened, he had no doubt that he would eventually end up like Kelban, even though this man said that he was going to deliver him to his boss unharmed. As Jake's mind raced to come up with one last chance to escape, his body went completely limp and his head sagged to his chest.

Peter had executed the "sleeper" hold dozens of times before and was not surprised when Hunter passed out relatively quickly. He began to release his grip, and was preparing to support Hunter under his armpits and carry him downstairs. But just as Peter was expecting to bear the burden of Hunter's presumably dead weight, he received a surprise that truly shocked him.

***

Jake had pretended to be knocked out before he actually lost consciousness. In the split second when Peter loosened and then readjusted his grip, Jake bent low at his knees and swung his head and body backwards with all the strength he could muster. Jake's skull crashed into Peter's nose, breaking the bones and splattering blood everywhere, but instead of reaching up to his face for protection, Peter grabbed Jake around his chest tightly. Realizing that he could not get out of his assailant's hold, Jake tried the only thing left he could think of. With one more crouch and violent push backwards, Jake propelled both himself and Peter over the railing and down to the floor below.

The twelve foot drop stunned both men, but Peter, landing on the bottom with Jake on top of him, bore the brunt of the punishing fall. Although he was only semi-conscious, Peter still fought to keep hold of Jake, grabbing at his t-shirt and jeans to keep him from getting away. Nicholas, who had been waiting outside the front of the house, came barging through the front door with his gun raised. But as soon as his right foot hit the wooden floor inside the house, onto which Jake had emptied an entire bottle of Crisco cooking oil the night before, both of his feet flew out from under him and he landed with a thud on his back.

Jake knew that it would only be a matter of seconds before Nicholas righted himself and started shooting at him. Peter was still holding on to Jake by the front pocket of his jeans when Jake noticed the knife that Peter was wearing on his hip. Jake pulled the knife from its sheath and slashed Peter's left arm, which the Russian then yanked back toward the floor. As Jake sprinted out the back door, still gripping Peter's knife in his hand, the first shot from Nicholas's gun smashed into the door frame and the second whistled by Jake's ear.

Thankful that he'd parked Jason's car around back, Jake pulled open the driver's side door, jumped behind the wheel, threw the knife onto the passenger seat, and started the engine with the keys he'd left in the ignition. The car peeled out as Jake directed it around the front of the house and toward the driveway. Nicholas ran outside and fired at the car as it plowed down the blacktop, shattering the rear windshield and causing Jake to duck and swerve wildly toward the woods on his left. Jake regained control of the car and sped down to the bottom of the driveway. He spotted the white van parked on the road across the street and realized that the man shooting at him from the house would be down the driveway in about fifteen seconds and following him in the van. He slammed on the brakes and Jason's car screeched to a halt almost directly behind his pursuer's vehicle.

Jake grabbed the knife off the seat next to him and hopped out of the car. He drove the knife deep into the van's front driver's side tire and heard an immediate hissing sound as air began to rapidly seep out of the shredded rubber radial. Jake wriggled the knife back and forth briefly, finally ripping it from the tire with great force. A moment later, he was back in Jason's car and heading down the road toward the main village of Killington.

Jake was nervous as he drove through the sleepy skiing town with a shattered rear windshield and a face that had been all over the news. He felt slightly better as he traveled further west out of Killington on Route Four toward the town of Rutland. But when Jake noticed a bridge up ahead where the road crossed the Clarendon River, an idea occurred to him. If the people chasing him believed that he was dead, perhaps he could buy himself some time to figure out what to do.

Near the end of the bridge, Jake veered the car sideways and set the emergency brake, locking the vehicle's wheels. He used Peter's knife to rig the accelerator pedal so that it was almost completely pressed to the floor. Although the emergency brake prevented the car from moving forward, the car bucked in place, its engine revving with the flow of fuel it was receiving. Standing outside the car, Jake reached in through the driver's side window and pulled the lever that released the emergency brake. With the wheels unlocked and the accelerator still depressed, the car screeched forward, crashed through the wooden barrier running along the side of the bridge, and fell down to the banks of the river below.

No one witnessed the wreck that Jake engineered, but he had no doubt that someone would be along eventually. As soon as the car crashed into the embankment, he began jogging the remaining half-mile into Rutland, staying close to the woods on the side of the road and ducking into them for cover each time a vehicle drove by heading toward the bridge. As Jake entered the outskirts of the town, he passed several homes, a high school, and a McDonalds. In the center of town, Jake found two buildings located directly across the street from each other, one of which he hoped might offer him salvation—a church and a bus station. In his present circumstances, Jake believed that although the church might help save his soul, a bus might save his life.

CHAPTER 16

Agent Stanton, Saturday, 2:51p.m.

Stanton and Zarvas had spent much of the previous evening as well as Saturday morning trying to track down the manufacturer of the cutting-edge listening device that Sully had so proudly discovered. The agents' efforts to compile a list of people working on the secret technology overseas had been met with surprising resistance—even from their own government. Just when their frustration was about to boil over, they received a call on Saturday afternoon that they hoped would prove to be their first lucky break in the case.

"Stanton," Zarvas called out to his partner as he held a phone to his ear but away from his mouth. "We got a report of a vehicle going off the road on a bridge in Vermont about half an hour ago. Local cops up there ran the plate and guess who the car came back registered to."

"Who?"

"Jason Carerra. The same guy who called Hunter yesterday morning and then swore that he didn't know where Hunter was."

"Damn it! I knew he was lying to me. He must have lent Hunter his car. Was there anyone in the wreck when the cops got there?"

Zarvas held up his hand as he listened to someone on the other end of the line. He wrote something down on a piece of paper and then thanked whoever he was talking to before answering Stanton's question.

"No. No bodies. If anyone was in the car when it went off the bridge, they either got thrown from the car and into the river, or were miraculously unharmed. The cops will search the river, but they said they might never find a body, even if there was one to find. They did find a knife with blood on it in the car, but it was a no-frills hunting knife that the cops think could have been bought anywhere. They're sending the evidence they collected down to our lab, and we're going to have a truck pick up the vehicle and bring it back here too."

"So," Stanton began, "if Hunter was on the run in Carerra's car, and we hadn't tracked him down yet, why would he run the car off the road?"

"Well, it wouldn't make sense for Hunter to draw attention to himself like that if nobody was on to him. But what if somebody got to him before we did? Hunter could have been forced to ditch the car because whoever was chasing him knew what he was driving. Or, someone might already have taken Hunter and didn't care about pushing his car off a bridge. Which would not be a good situation for us."

"Yeah, but it would be an even worse situation for Hunter."

"Well, let's go have a second interview with Carerra. Maybe he knows how someone might have tracked Hunter down."

Upon arriving at the hospital and heading down to Jason's office, the agents were surprised to find the young researcher semiconscious and strapped to a chair. They called upstairs for medical help, and Jason was taken by stretcher to a private room in the hospital where doctors started him on an IV and administered smelling salts. Once he was able to talk and cleared by the doctors, the agents entered his room and began questioning him.

"Jason," Agent Zarvas asked, "do you know who did this to you?"

"No," Jason replied quietly. He appeared traumatized and struggled to maintain his composure. "Can you call my family please? Make sure they're okay?"

"We've already spoken to them. Your parents are on their way to the hospital now. You'll see them as soon as they get here. But in the meantime, we really need to know anything you can tell us about whoever attacked you. Do you remember what they looked like?"

"There were two guys, but all I can picture is fuzzy faces. I think the drugs distorted my memory. One of them did all the talking, and I feel like I can still hear the sound of his voice. There was no emotion in it at all, even as he talked about killing me."

"How about an accent?" Stanton asked. "Anything distinct that you could place?"

"I wouldn't swear to it, but they sounded Russian to me. I know that might just be in my head because Jake said his partner was involved with the Russian mob. But that's who these guys seemed like to me."

"Was there anything else that they said, Jason? Anything about Jake? Or any other specifics you can remember?"

"Just the last thing he said when he injected me with the flunitrazepam. He told me that I wasn't going to die. But he couldn't make the same promise about Jake."

As he said this, Jason broke down in tears and told the agents that he didn't want to talk anymore. A nurse came into the room and told them that Jason needed some rest and they would have to wait until tomorrow to ask him any more questions.

Stanton looked back at Jason as she left the hospital room and chastised herself for not being more forceful with him during her first interview. If she had, there was a chance that Hunter would be safely in their custody right now. Stanton worried that they would never find Hunter alive, and that if someone else found him first, her source's identity would no longer be a secret. This latter concern weighed on Stanton's mind far more heavily than the former.

CHAPTER 17

Peter and Nicholas, Saturday, 3:16p.m.

Nicholas planned on following Hunter in the van, but by the time he reached the end of the driveway and saw Hunter's car speeding away down the road, the van's front tire was almost completely flat. Realizing that it would take too long to change the tire to try to catch up to Hunter, Nicholas went back to the house to check on Peter.

As usual, Peter appeared completely calm as Nicholas carefully entered through the front door, stepping around the makeshift oil slick that Hunter had used to waylay him earlier. Peter had re-set his own broken nose, and shoved balled-up paper towels into each of his nostrils to staunch the bleeding. His eyes, despite showing slight signs of swelling, were resolute and clear as he spoke.

"Let's search this house quickly for something that looks like a disk or a mini drive, or anything else that our client might find useful. Then we go get Hunter. He'll be delivered alive, but I wouldn't mind paying him back a little first."

"But how will we know where to find him?" Nicholas asked.

"Before he slashed me with my own knife, I managed to shove a tracking device into the pocket of his jeans. Hunter can run all he wants, but once we get back in the van and turn the receiver on, we'll find him wherever he goes."

***

Jake stood inside the front of the church, staring at the bus station across the street. He knew that he needed to figure out a way to get out of town as soon as possible, but getting on a bus wouldn't do him any good if the person selling the tickets either recognized him or could tell anyone who asked about him what bus he was on. Jake noticed a bank of pay phones in front of the bus station and thought about all the people he wished he could call—his mom, his brother, Anna, even the secret number that was only supposed to be used in a life-or-death emergency. He reached into his jeans pocket for a quarter, but the only object his hand made contact with was much smaller—it had to be a dime or a penny. Jake knew that it didn't make sense for him to call anyone from where he was now anyway. No one would be able to help him, and he would only be putting whoever he contacted at risk. He was already worried about Jason since he couldn't figure out any way that the Russians could have found him without going through his friend first. Jake was so caught up in his thoughts that he didn't even notice the man approaching him from behind.

***

Peter and Nicholas searched the cabin but found nothing useful. They changed the flat tire on the van and drove back through Killington. On the way, they crossed the bridge over the Clarendon River, and were waved around an accident scene by a local policeman. There were several police vehicles and a tow truck at the site, but the Russians noted the absence of an ambulance. Nicholas looked out the passenger side window and confirmed that the car was the one that Hunter had driven away from the ski house a short while ago.

"Why would he get rid of the car?" Nicholas asked.

"He must have had another way of getting out of town. All the better for us anyway. It means he can't have gotten too far."

Peter examined the receiver that was linked to the tracking device he'd placed in Hunter's pocket. The signal remained strong, and as long as Hunter didn't disappear into an underground cave, it would lead them directly to him.

As they continued through the town of Rutland, Peter suddenly slowed the van down beside a large church on the side of the road.

"Why are you stopping?" Nicholas asked. "The receiver says that Hunter is still miles away from us."

"Look across the street, my friend. Hunter may be riding a bus out of town. If we stop in there first, we might find out where he's going. Our employer would probably appreciate the advance notice."

The two men exited the van, crossed the street, and entered the bus station. A single, teenaged employee sat behind a thin glass pane. The girl had curly black hair and pink-framed glasses, which kept falling down her nose as she attempted to read Charles Dickens' *A Tale of Two Cities*.

"Excuse me," Peter politely interrupted her reading and held up a picture of Hunter in front of the glass. "Has this man come in here today?"

The girl scrunched her nose up as she examined the picture.

"Nope. Haven't seen that guy. Sorry."

She quickly buried her head back in her book, and Peter looked at Nicholas, who shrugged. They knew she was telling the truth and didn't know what else to do, so they turned to leave. But something occurred to Peter, and he turned back to ask one more question.

"I'm sorry to bother you again. But I just need to know one more quick thing. Has anyone else come in here and bought a ticket in the last hour or so? Maybe paid for it in cash?"

The girl looked up, again scrunching her nose. Apparently, this action went hand-in-hand with thinking for the young woman.

"Actually, yeah. Father Murphy bought a ticket to New York about forty-five minutes ago. He paid for it in cash."

"Father Murphy?" Peter responded with an inquiring tone.

"Uh, yeah. You know, works in the church across the street."

Peter was amused by the girl's display of attitude toward him and thought about how easily he could have snapped her neck if he wanted to. But he simply smiled and mouthed the words *thank you* to the top of her head, as she was already immersed once again in her Dickens.

Just to be sure that Father Murphy was not planning a trip to New York for himself, Peter and Nicholas stopped in the church and approached the gray-haired, straight-backed man in the familiar black clothes and white collar.

"Hello, gentlemen," the priest greeted them cheerfully. "What can I do for you today?"

Peter held up the same picture of Jake and, in a perfect New York accent, asked, "Have you seen this man today?"

"Yes I have. And he told me to expect that you might come here and ask me about him."

"And now here we are," Peter replied. "So, he asked you to buy him a bus ticket to New York and probably to call the police or something, right?"

"Well, no. He did ask me to buy him the bus ticket, but he didn't say anything about the police. He actually told me his whole story about how he lived around here with his father, who'd always told him that his mother had died when he was a baby. But he recently discovered that his mother was actually alive, and he'd been kidnapped by his father. He'd just run away from his father and needed the bus ticket to New York to go find his mother. Now, which one of you two is that boy's father, because you've got some explaining to do."

"Actually, Father," Peter responded, "neither of us is that boy's father. In fact, we're with the NYPD, and we're up here investigating a homicide. The story he told you was nothing but lies, and that kid is wanted for questioning in connection with a murder yesterday morning in New York City. You've probably seen his picture on the news."

"Oh my. I don't watch too much television. But I do recall hearing some of the parishioners talking about that murder this morning. So you're saying this boy tricked me into buying him a ticket to New York?"

"It appears that way, Father. Don't feel bad though. He's been fooling the New York police and the FBI for the past two days. We've got to get back on the road and track that bus down. Thanks for your time, and if you remember anything else, please give us a call."

Peter handed Father Murphy a fake business card, identifying him as Detective Sal Romano of the NYPD. The priest apologized again and wished the officers good luck on their search.

It took over an hour for Peter and Nicholas to overtake the Vermont Transit Lines Bus that Hunter was riding to New York City. After discussing their options for getting Hunter off the bus, they decided to use the same ruse they'd pulled on Father Murphy. After all, it was easy pretending to be cops when the person you were chasing was wanted for murder. Peter pulled the van up along the left side of the bus, and Nicholas placed a blue flashing light on the dashboard where the driver of the bus could see it. Nicholas held a fake badge out the van window and indicated to the bus driver that he needed to pull over onto the shoulder. Looking quite nervous, the driver did as he was told.

Peter and Nicholas boarded the bus, holding guns and a handheld receiver, which beeped with greater frequency with each step they took into the vehicle. Peter looked at the passengers closely as he passed them on his way to the back of the bus. He nodded reassuringly, and held a finger up to his lips when it looked as if one particularly frightened woman might begin to cry. When the two men reached the door to the bus's bathroom, the beeping of the receiver became a single solid whine, indicating that the tracking device was less than three feet away.

Hoping that Jake was standing close behind the bathroom door, Peter reared back and kicked the door in with his right leg. He expected to draw down his gun on a confused and terrified Jake Hunter. Instead, he saw nothing but an empty bathroom. Sitting on the floor was the small, round tracking device that Peter had placed in Jake's pocket back at the ski house. Peter gritted his teeth as he and Nicholas trudged back down the aisle and off the bus, apologizing to the riders for the inconvenience as they knew that real cops would have done.

When they got back into the van to continue the drive to New York City, Peter vowed to himself that he would not underestimate Hunter again.

CHAPTER 18

Sergei Ilanov, Saturday, 5:29p.m.

Sergei was extremely displeased that Hunter's whereabouts remained unknown. All of the reports he'd been receiving from his various sources contained nothing but unreliable or unconfirmed information.

He knew that Hunter's friend had been injured at the hospital where he worked, and that Hunter was in the hospital the day before. There was an investigation going on at a ski house in Vermont, and the friend's car had been run off a bridge, but no bodies were found. The authorities had been receiving hundreds of tips from people claiming to have seen Hunter, or who supposedly knew his location. But these leads ranged from an airport in San Diego, to a bus terminal in Boston, to a trendy Manhattan ice cream parlor. Even with the combined resources of the NYPD and the FBI, only so many of the tips could be investigated.

Ivan was staking out Hunter's apartment but, not surprisingly, there had been no sign of him there. The FBI also was rotating agents inside Hunter's building just in case he was foolish enough to return home. Sergei had a handful of good sources within the Bureau's New York office, and several more inside the NYPD. But none of his people were directly involved in the search for Hunter, and Sergei was growing frustrated by the lack of progress.

Worse than his frustration was the small, yet clearly present, sensation of fear that Sergei now felt. Knowing that Hunter possessed the flash drive with its incriminating contents was worrisome enough, but hearing that someone else had tracked Hunter down in Vermont scared Sergei more than anything. He was reminded again of his friend Pulachin's recent downfall, and was wondering about the loyalty of his own lieutenants, when one of them happened to call.

"Boris," Sergei greeted his second-in-command as he picked up the ringing phone, "do you have news about Hunter?"

"Not so much about Hunter, boss. But I do have some information about the people who are looking for him."

"Go on."

"One of the lead agents working the case for the FBI is a woman named Charlene Stanton. She's the one that has been following me and Ivan around for the past two weeks."

"Did they see you go into Kelban's law firm last night?"

"I don't think so, but I can't be sure."

"So, what else does this Stanton woman have to do with us? Can we get information from her about Hunter?"

"I think we might be more interested in who she is getting her information from. It seems that Agent Stanton was the undercover agent who cultivated the source that led to Yevgeny Pulachin's arrest."

"That is interesting," Sergei replied, as his mind began to race with thoughts about who could have been feeding information to the female FBI agent. Sergei had known about Pulachin's weapons deal and when and where it would occur, but that information was provided by his former protégé to ensure that Sergei's gang would stay clear of the location. Sergei had discussed Pulachin's deal with several of his own closest associates, but they were people he'd believed he could trust—until now.

"How would you like me to follow up on this information?" Boris asked, interrupting his boss's thoughts.

Sergei knew that his men were often the subject of police and FBI surveillance, but he rarely permitted them to interact with the authorities in any way, much less confront them directly. Yet the lack of information on Hunter was of great concern to the Russian gangster, and he decided that it was time to take a risk.

"Boris, I want you to pay a visit to Agent Stanton. Make sure she is alone when you approach her. If she possesses information that would be valuable to us, do whatever you have to do to get it. Understood?"

"It will be done."

CHAPTER 19

Jake Hunter, Saturday, 8:35p.m.

About four hours earlier, just past four thirty in the afternoon, Jake had been riding the Vermont Transit Lines bus to New York that Peter and Nicholas eventually pulled over. Not long after leaving the depot in Rutland, the bus made its first scheduled stop in a town called White River Junction, which served as a hub for the bus company. The driver announced that they would remain there for ten minutes before departing for the express trip to New York.

Jake had watched most of the other passengers exit the bus and head into a large mini-mart located right next to the bus station. Feeling anxious at being one of the few remaining people on the bus, and realizing that he was hungry, Jake got off the bus and walked into the store. He grabbed a bottle of Coke and a cellophane-wrapped turkey sandwich to bring back to the bus, and the cashier rang up the total of his items, which came to exactly five dollars.

As Jake pulled a five dollar bill out of his wallet, he noticed a clear plastic tub of *Bazooka Joe* bubble gum sitting on the counter with a handwritten sign on a piece of tape indicating that the price of the gum was five cents per piece. Thinking that it had been a while since he'd had a piece of the famous gum, Jake remembered the lone coin in his pocket and pulled it out, hoping to find a dime and not a penny. What he'd discovered instead made his heart skip a beat.

Jake did not have a background in electronics or tracking devices, but the memory of the Russian man grappling with him and grasping at the pockets of his jeans convinced Jake that he needed to get far away from this thin, round piece of metal as quickly as possible. Jake was still holding the device as he picked up his sandwich and soda and left the mini-mart. Just as he walked outside, another bus pulled into the depot, and Jake noticed that the sign on the front of the bus said *Boston*.

Jake watched as the bus to Boston pulled up alongside the bus headed for New York. He then glanced back at the tracking device in his hand and hastily began walking toward the two buses. Jake boarded the bus to New York and moved all the way to the back where the bathroom was located. He deposited the device on the floor of the bathroom, and then returned to the front and got off the bus. With his head down, hoping that the driver did not recognize him or ask to see his ticket again, Jake boarded the bus bound for Boston. He took a seat far in the rear of the vehicle and scrunched himself down low, with his knees pressed up against the seat in front of him. Although the position was not entirely comfortable, Jake didn't mind at all as the bus pulled out of the depot with him safely aboard.

Jake hadn't been to Boston since a trip to Fenway Park several years earlier. As a Yankee fan, he'd been rooting against the Red Sox that day, but Pedro Martinez had pitched a two-hitter, striking out sixteen batters. By the end of the game, even though Jake still didn't want the Yankees' main rival to win, he couldn't help but appreciate the impressive performance that Pedro had authored. After the game, Jake went out to several bars in the area with friends from college and crashed on a couch in one of their apartments.

On his current journey to Boston, Jake found himself in a dingy hotel room a few blocks from the bus station, where he'd paid for his room in cash. The clerk had barely looked up before handing him the key to room two-oh-eight. After his harrowing day, Jake was exhausted and the last things he wanted to think about were the Russian mob, dead lawyers, and secret computer drives. Instead, as he laid down in the creaky hotel bed, Jake managed to force his thoughts back to the dazzling sunshine at Fenway Park, the delicious sausage hoagie he'd eaten, and Pedro's mesmerizing pitches. Jake could still see the baseball fluttering through the brilliant sunlight in his mind as he drifted off to sleep.

CHAPTER 20

Agent Stanton, Saturday, 10:17p.m.

Every time the FBI caught a break in the search for Hunter, it only led to further questions. Zarvas and Stanton's supervisor was getting impatient and chewed them out, demanding that they find Hunter and get some answers. It hadn't helped when Stanton reported that by the time they traced the high-tech listening device to a pawn shop in Times Square, the owner had been found executed in the back of his own store. So far, forensics had come up empty on their search of that crime scene. Although they'd found the murder weapon on site, the gun was untraceable, and probably would never be linked back to the shooter. The last words that their boss had screamed before throwing the agents out of his office were, *"Find that Hunter kid while he's still alive!"*

But Stanton believed that Hunter was already dead. Since she and Zarvas had seen him running from his firm's office building, and the NYPD had just missed him at his apartment, a day and a half had gone by and there had been no sign of him, except for the appearance of Jason Carerra's wrecked car in Vermont. To most everyone else outside the FBI, Hunter was a murder suspect on the run who would be caught sooner or later. But Stanton was convinced that Hunter's disappearance was somehow tied to the Russian mafia. And when people involved with the Russian mafia disappeared, they usually were never seen or heard from again. In fact, Hunter's disappearance provided a perfect cover if Kelban was killed by the Russians because Hunter served as an ideal scapegoat. Stanton decided not to share her theory that the Russian mob had set up Hunter as Kelban's killer because she didn't want to reveal that her source had provided her with Kelban's name shortly before his murder.

The one thing that Stanton could not deduce was how Hunter had been fingered so quickly as Kelban's murderer. She'd found out about the anonymous call naming Hunter as the killer and supporting the secretary's version of events. But Stanton did not understand why an anonymous tipster would be helpful enough to call the cops, but then proceed to contact not one, but four, news stations—unless it was to attract attention to Hunter as the killer and divert the authorities from the actual perpetrators. Although Stanton could not confirm that the caller was the same, all of the calls had been made from untraceable cell phones—an unlikely coincidence.

Another aspect of the investigation that turned out to be a dead end was Kelban's laptop computer. Even the Bureau's whiz-kid techno-geeks weren't able to retrieve anything from the laptop's hard drive, although they were thoroughly impressed with the virus program and were attempting to replicate it for future use. Other than the motive-providing e-mail from Kelban, Hunter's computer contained nothing unusual.

The medical examiner estimated that Kelban was stabbed sometime between three and four o'clock in the morning. Several attorneys told the police that Hunter had left the restaurant hosting the law firm event at around one a.m. on Thursday night, but none could say for sure that he'd actually left the building. Stanton concluded based on the witnesses' timeline that it was possible for Hunter to have been in Kelban's office at the time of the murder.

Stanton knew that Boris was a much more likely suspect for Kelban's murder, but the media was heavily promoting the idea of the "Summer Associate Slasher." The local cops also considered Hunter the prime suspect based on the facts that his fingerprints were the only ones on the murder weapon, he'd exhibited violent behavior in fleeing the scene, and his whereabouts remained unknown.

Stanton and Zarvas had spent a good portion of the prior thirty-six hours interviewing Hunter's coworkers, friends, and relatives, and had gotten to know and understand him fairly well. Everyone they talked to seemed to sincerely like Hunter, calling him smart, funny, and friendly. No one believed that it was possible that Hunter could have murdered someone. One neighbor mentioned the fact that Hunter's father had passed away when Jake was about seven or eight years old, but then quickly dismissed the notion that his father's death could have led in any way to Jake committing a crime, much less murder.

Hunter's mother and his eighteen-year-old brother, Bret, were distraught by Hunter's disappearance. They were certain that Jake was innocent, and were extremely worried about his safety. Stanton tried to allay their fears while interviewing them, but she had a hard time believing that Jake was going to turn up unharmed, if at all. Still, when she'd finished interviewing Hunter's family, Stanton wanted them to know that they would be protected.

"Mrs. Hunter," Stanton said as she stood up to leave, "we're going to station a few agents at your house in case Jake decides to return here. For his own safety, it will be best if our men are here to take him into custody if he comes back."

"You mean *when* he comes back." Bret may have been half her age, but Stanton felt herself grow red with embarrassment under Jake's brother's accusing glare after her insinuation that Jake might not be found.

"Of course," Stanton responded quickly. But she wasn't able to look Bret in the eyes as she said it.

After two days straight on the job, investigating Kelban and Hunter and trying to glean any clues about Hunter's location, Stanton finally stepped back into her apartment. Although she was exhausted, Stanton needed to unwind before going to bed, so she put *Van Morrison's Greatest Hits* on her CD player, turned the volume up, undressed, and got into a steaming hot shower.

Facing forward, Stanton stood with her head bowed, the hot water beating down on the back of her neck. The CD player blared from her living room, as Van the Man sang about a girl named Gloria. Between the music and the water, Stanton did not hear the door to her apartment open, and remained unaware as the sliding door of her shower slid softly open a minute later. She was so lost in the massaging heat of the shower that Stanton did not sense the powerful arms wrapping around her midsection until they were completely around her.

Before she had a chance to jump or scream, Stanton was spun around and kissed deeply and passionately, moaning gently as her lover's arms massaged her back and continued rubbing down her entire body. As had become their routine, Stanton's source knelt down in front of her, always ensuring that Stanton would be the first one to feel pleasure when they were together. Of course, Stanton was only too happy to return the favor, and often did just that. But now, Stanton simply leaned her head back under the steaming water, arching her back and feeling her body grow flush and shudder, knowing she would be kept safe from falling in the wet shower by the firm grip of the hands tightly holding on to Stanton's hips, as her own hands gripped the towel bar and shower door. Just as she felt as if she were going to explode, Stanton realized she was being lifted up out of the shower and carried to her bed, still dripping wet, but feeling too good to care. Their lovemaking continued for over an hour before both were spent and Stanton passed out, exhausted but feeling wonderfully fulfilled.

Stanton awoke alone the next morning—not an unusual occurrence. There was a note on the table next to Stanton's bed, which was also common after these late night trysts. Excited to see what was written on the note, Stanton grabbed it off of the table, but was disappointed to find that the message was all business and no pleasure. It read:

Hunter is alive. But he's as good as dead unless you find him first.

CHAPTER 21

Santo Alampi, Sunday, 9:07a.m.

He just wanted the noise to stop. Still half asleep in the rumpled suit he'd worn the day before, Santo Alampi rolled over on the couch in his office and pressed one of the cushions to the side of his head in an attempt to cover his ears. But the noise would not subside, and Alampi's eyelids finally squeezed open, allowing in a light from the sun that was as painful to his eyes as the incessant ringing was to his ears.

Alampi was a private investigator and, when sober, he was damn good at his job. He'd been somewhat of a loner throughout high school in northern New Jersey, and fell victim to the pitch of an Army recruiter on the day of his graduation. After his time in the service was up, he'd moved back home and was hanging out at a local bar with some old wrestling buddies when one of them mentioned that he thought his wife was cheating on him, but he hadn't been able to catch her in the act. Later that night, Alampi privately offered to follow his friend's wife for a few days and find out if she really was being unfaithful.

Alampi ended up following the woman for less than half of the next day before she took her lunch break at a motel on the outskirts of town. Minutes later, one of Alampi's other wrestling buddies who had been out with the group the night before showed up and went to the same room as his friend's wife. As Alampi photographed the two in bed together through the motel room window, he knew that he'd lost at least one friend, but had found a new career. Within weeks he had his private investigator's license, and shortly thereafter a fairly successful business. The only downside of the job was that it was often lonely staking people out, and depressing seeing how many of them were lying, cheating, and stealing from their loved ones and business associates. Whenever he felt particularly lonely or depressed, Alampi would have a few drinks. But he didn't only drink when he was feeling down. In fact, he often drank even more when he was feeling good, and the night before had been a very good night.

After receiving a large payment the previous day for taking some outstanding digital photos of a philandering wife, Alampi had celebrated a little too hard. As he stumbled off the couch and toward the blaring telephone ringing on his desk, Alampi suddenly felt like he was going to vomit. He steadied himself by grabbing the edge of his desk, and the wave of nausea passed as he finally reached out and grabbed the phone, mumbling in a barely audible whisper, "Hello."

"Mr. Alampi," said the familiar voice of one of his occasional clients, "another late night I take it?"

"Yeah, something like that," Alampi answered, closing his eyes as he spoke in an effort to stop the room from spinning.

"Well, get yourself some coffee and get your act together. I've got work for you, and it's important."

"What do you need, surveillance, information, pictures?"

"No. Nothing like that. I need you to find a missing person that half the city is looking for. Do you think you're up to the task?"

"How much we talkin' if I find him first?"

"Depending on how reliable your information proves to be, how does fifty thousand dollars sound?"

Alampi paused at the mention of that kind of money, which was more than he'd made all year up to that point. He'd done a handful of jobs for this client before and payment had always been quick and in cash. Alampi had no reason to doubt that he would get the fifty thousand if he located the missing person.

"That sounds like an acceptable fee. Who's this guy that I'm supposed to find?"

"His name is Jake Hunter, and he's wanted for murder. I need to find him before anyone else gets to him. He's got something that I want. Do you still have that computer expert working for you?"

Alampi had worked alone for his first twenty-five years as an investigator. About a year ago, he'd been hired by a wealthy financier, whose father had created a trust fund for his grandson, the financier's son. The financier noticed from the monthly statements that the principal of the trust had been steadily decreasing even though his son was only in high school and was not allowed to access the fund until he turned twenty-one. The bank's investigators and several accounting specialists were able to confirm that small sums of money were being siphoned away from the trust on a regular basis, but they couldn't ascertain who was taking the money or where it was going. Suspecting that his own son might be responsible, the financier hired Alampi to keep an eye on him.

After a cursory investigation at the bank, which he knew would get him nowhere, Alampi began tailing the financier's son. He followed him to school, to his afternoon football practice, and to his girlfriend's house, where the kid had the girl's parents wrapped around his little finger, and their daughter wrapped around something else. On the third day of trailing the son, Alampi watched him heading into the school building after lunch. A skinny younger boy was sitting on the steps leading to the school eating a sandwich and reading a book. As the financier's son walked by with his posse of football buddies and their cheerleader girlfriends, he knocked the book from the other boy's hands, and kicked over the can of Coke that he'd been drinking with his sandwich. As his friends laughed and they walked past, Alampi noticed two things—the look of utter hatred on the thin boy's face as he watched the bully walk away, and the title of the book that he'd been reading, *Advanced Programming Code.*

That same day, after school let out, Alampi followed a student into the school library, but it wasn't the financier's son. He watched from behind the bookshelves as the boy from the steps logged on to one of the library computers with his book propped open on the desk next to him. The teenager was fiercely focused on the screen as he typed commands on the keyboard, bypassing encrypted files and firewalls until he'd hacked into his final destination at the bank's mainframe. Although he had the access and ability to move any amount of money from any account, the kid only selected one account, and only chose to move a few hundred dollars into an account at another bank. The boy was so focused on the task at hand that he didn't even notice Alampi standing behind him until the older man clamped his hands down onto his shoulders.

"That guy's not very nice to you, is he?" Alampi said softly, both because he was in a library and because he didn't want to frighten the kid any further.

"What guy?" the boy responded warily.

"You know," Alampi answered, "the rich kid. Football player. The jerk who picks on you, kicks over your soda, tosses your book."

As he said this, Alampi gestured toward the book on the desk, the same one the kid had been reading on the steps earlier.

"What's your name, son?"

"Jesse. Jesse Halpern. Are you a cop?"

"No. I'm not a cop. I'm a private investigator, hired by the jerk's dad to figure out who was stealing his kid's money, because none of the fancy bankers or computer guys could track you down."

"Are you going to tell them it was me?"

Something in the sad look on Jesse's face triggered a memory of Alampi's own lonely days in high school, and he suddenly found himself feeling overwhelmingly terrible about turning the kid over to the authorities. On the spot he came to a decision.

"Listen, kid, I know you have it rough with these guys bustin' your chops all the time, but you're a smart kid—too smart to be risking your future by taking money out of Richie Rich's trust fund. Let me ask you one thing, have you been spending the money that you've taken out of that account?"

"No. Not a dime. It's all just sitting in another account. I could move it back right now if you want."

Jesse sounded eager to put the money back right away, and Alampi believed that he hadn't spent any of it, but he wanted to make sure that he collected his fee from the financier before the money magically reappeared. So Alampi told Jesse the plan he'd come up with to make sure that Jesse would stay out of trouble and Alampi would get his fee.

The next day, Alampi watched as the financier wrote him a large check in anticipation of his son's money being returned. Alampi had told his grateful client that his son had nothing to do with the missing funds. Alampi also claimed to have found the responsible parties and roughed them up just enough to ensure that the trust fund would be fully reimbursed at precisely three o'clock that afternoon. At exactly three, Jesse transferred the funds back where they'd come from, and two minutes later, Alampi walked out the front door of the financier's house with his check in hand. That night, Alampi had taken Jesse out to dinner to celebrate, but he did not have any alcohol during the meal. The reason for staying dry, he told himself, was that it was a business dinner. After the meal, Alampi asked Jesse if he'd like to work with him on weekends and after school, doing some of the more high-tech computer searches that Alampi often struggled with, and maybe even riding along on some surveillance jobs. The kid's eyes had opened wide at the thought, and he quickly agreed. Alampi thought that it would be nice to have a partner after working alone for so many years. And they had proved to be a good team. Now, for the first time, one of Alampi's clients was specifically requesting that Jesse's computer and hacking expertise be used on a case.

"Jesse, yeah, he's still here." Alampi paused to look down at his watch before continuing. "In fact, he's usually here by nine on the weekends."

"Good, have him start searching by putting together a list of possible locations where Hunter might be—anyplace he's used a credit card in the last five years, out-of-town family members, you know the drill. And tell Jesse that I want him on call in case I need him to look into any leads on a moment's notice. Got it?"

"Yeah, I got it. We'll get started right away."

As Alampi placed the phone back in its cradle, a tall, gangly teenager wearing thick glasses walked through the office door carrying two large cups of Starbucks coffee.

"What'll we get started on right away?"

"We got a case, Jess. And it could be a big one."

CHAPTER 22

Jake Hunter, Sunday, 10:15a.m.

It was Sunday morning when Jake woke up in the seedy Boston hotel with the television still on, as he'd left it when he fell asleep the night before. The room was cold from the air conditioning pumping through a vent above the bed. As Jake began pulling a blanket up around his shoulders, his eyes focused on the TV, and he figured that he must be either dreaming or delirious because the two people on the screen looked exactly like his mother and brother. Jake shook his head and rubbed the sleep out of his eyes. Sure that he was, in fact, awake, Jake focused on the words being spoken by the television reporter that was interviewing his family.

"Mrs. Hunter, if you could say one thing to Jake right now, what would it be?"

Jake's mom was trying hard not to cry, but with the camera panning in for a close-up of her face, the tears were already flowing down her cheeks.

"Jake, honey, we love you so much and we're so worried about you. We just want you to come home. I need to know that you're safe. Please, please come home."

With that, Mrs. Hunter's eyes squeezed shut and her shoulders started heaving up and down. She began crying even harder and could not continue speaking. Standing behind her, Bret put his hands on his mother's shoulders to calm her, and was whispering to her that everything would be all right, when the interviewer chimed in again.

"Bret, before we go, is there anything you'd like to add that you want your brother to know, assuming that he's out there watching right now?"

Bret's face looked up into the camera, as he continued to hold tightly to his mother's much smaller frame. There was pain in his eyes, but resolve in his voice as he spoke.

"Jake, whatever the deal is with this mess you're involved in, I know we can work it out when you get back here. But you have to get back here first so we can figure everything out together. We need you to come home, Jake, and we'll help you get through whatever trouble you might be in. You've always been there for me, and I'll always be there for you, brother."

As the images of his family faded out, Jake's picture appeared on the screen along with a phone number, which anyone with information as to his whereabouts was instructed to call. Jake's body sank away from the television, and he began to cry. The tears came slowly at first, but eventually began streaming down his face, as his body shook from the emotional trauma he was feeling. After several minutes of heaving, hysterical sobs, Jake's tears ran dry. He felt sick about what his family was going through, and all he wanted to do was rush home and let them know that he was okay.

At that moment, Jake was somehow reminded of another lesson that Kelban had taught him over the course of the summer—never let your emotions cloud your reasoning. Jake realized that going home at this point would not necessarily solve anything, and might even put his family in danger. Instead, Jake knew that he had to shift his mindset from sadness to determination and clear thinking. Having discovered this new focus, all of the thoughts and ideas that had been running through Jake's mind over the past two days suddenly came together into one clear plan. Jake was still upset, but the only way he could make things right was to channel those feelings into a resolve that he would need to carry out his goal of getting back to his family safely.

Jake threw off the blanket that was covering him, got dressed, and went downstairs to the convenience store on the corner to buy a few necessary items. Upon returning to his hotel room, he headed straight to the bathroom. Using a newly purchased pair of scissors and a bottle of five minute hair coloring, Jake gave himself a haircut and then dyed his hair a light shade of dirty-blond. It was certainly not his best look, but Jake definitely resembled a new person, and with a baseball hat pulled down low over his face, he would be difficult to recognize.

Jake left the hotel, not bothering to check out, and headed back to the bus station where he planned to catch a bus to the Port Authority in New York. Jake knew that taking the bus back into New York was somewhat risky, but he figured that, if anything, the police would be looking for him on transportation heading out of town, not buses coming into New York from Boston.

Even though going back to his apartment was sure to be dangerous, in order to clear his name and get back to his family, Jake knew that he was going to have to get the flash drive that Kelban had sent him, which currently was sitting behind a brick wall next to the fire escape outside of his apartment. Despite thinking that he was prepared for the worst possible outcomes, Jake had no idea just how bad things were going to get once he arrived back in New York.

PART TWO

THE RETURN

CHAPTER 23

Agent Stanton, Sunday, 11:12a.m.

Stanton had spent most of the morning in the IOCU offices working the phones for leads on Hunter's whereabouts and following up on the evidence gathered at three separate scenes. The findings from the pawn shop owner's murder were minimal at best. The weapon provided no leads, and the only fingerprints in the back room, or behind the locked metal grating, belonged to the victim. By tracing some envelopes they'd found in the trash, the agents tracked down the victim's brother, who was working in Germany on some kind of confidential project for the U.S. government. Although there appeared to be some smuggling of high-tech electronics equipment and listening devices between the brothers, the FBI was unable to make any link between them and either Hunter or the Russian mafia.

The scene at the Clarendon River, where Jason Carerra's car had been totaled, provided a few interesting clues, none of which gave any indication of where Hunter might be or who had tracked him down in Vermont. Hunter's fingerprints were on the steering wheel and a few other places inside the car. Notably, his prints were found on the emergency brake release lever. Stanton thought this was a curious, but good, sign. If Hunter had set the car up to go off the bridge by himself, then maybe there was a chance that whoever located him at the ski house had failed to capture him.

Hunter's prints were found on another piece of evidence at the site of the car wreck—the bloody knife. The DNA lab found that the blood on the knife did not belong to Hunter, but it did come from another male. If the agents could find someone to provide a sample to test it against, the lab could confirm whether or not there was a match. But at this stage of the investigation, they didn't even know who they were looking for to attempt the comparison.

The last location from which evidence was collected was the ski house. The techs had found dozens of fingerprints, most of which were getting no hits in the FBI's computerized databases. Hunter's prints were discovered throughout the house, as it seemed that he'd searched the cabin in an effort to find food, potential weapons, and a change of clothes. Another blood sample was found in the upstairs hallway near a broken railing, which separated the second floor from the ground level, and this sample was matched to the bloody knife. In attempting to recreate the sequence of events, the crime scene investigators surmised that Hunter was involved in a fight with an unknown assailant in the upstairs hallway just outside the bathroom door. The fight ended when one or both of them broke through the railing and fell to the first floor below. Hunter escaped out the back door and into Carerra's car as a second assailant rushed through the front of the house and slipped on a puddle of cooking oil. Either before or after this fall, the second assailant fired at least one round, which was embedded in the frame of the back door.

As with the blood evidence, the firearms lab would be able to compare the bullet to a test shot, but only if the agents could locate a weapon to test it against. The investigative team's final observation was that the two assailants had performed a thorough, professional search of the ski house before leaving. But there was no way to tell if they'd found whatever they were searching for.

Stanton was getting frustrated with the lack of progress on the case, and decided to take a walk outside the office to clear her head and get some coffee that didn't resemble diesel fuel. On her way toward the local barista on the corner, Stanton passed an alley between two stores and was surprised to hear someone whisper her name.

"Agent Stanton," said Boris, his voice characterized by his thick Russian accent.

Stanton peered into the alley and immediately recognized the man she'd been following for the past two weeks. Attempting to act unfazed that he knew her name, she responded coolly.

"Something I can help you with, Boris?"

"Perhaps. Maybe I am just curious as to why you keep following me around everywhere I go."

"Well, that's pretty simple. I follow you around because you are a cold-blooded killer working for the Russian mob, and I plan on catching you in the act and arresting you."

"Agent Stanton, I am offended that you would think such a thing."

"That you are a cold-blooded killer?"

"No. That you could ever catch or arrest me." Boris smirked as he spoke, but he was less amused by Stanton's response.

"I'll bet Yevgeny Pulachin didn't think I could catch him either. And he'll be spending the next decade in jail. Which is the same place I plan on putting you, as soon as I prove that you killed Michael Kelban."

Although Boris grew concerned at the mention of Pulachin's arrest, he could not help but laugh at the agent's bold assertion. He felt that her inexperience and early success must have gone to her head, and decided to deflate her ego a bit.

"Yes, you did catch Pulachin. But you didn't do that by yourself, did you? A little rat told you where to find him doing bad things, and all you had to do was show up. You know what happens to rats like that, who don't know how to keep their mouths shut? They end up getting their necks broken."

Boris was practically snarling as he spoke, and Stanton grew fearful—not for herself, but at the suggestion that her source was in danger. She needed to find out what else Boris knew, so she switched to a more conciliatory tone.

"All right, so we've both proved we can act tough. You didn't approach me just to make threats. Why don't you tell me what you want to know and why."

Boris was surprised that the agent was suddenly willing to be so forthcoming with him. She hadn't appeared scared, and he had yet to offer her money or favors, or threaten her loved ones, in exchange for information. So it was with a wary tone that he next spoke.

"I would like to know any information your investigation has turned up about where Jake Hunter might be located. Can you provide that information?"

"Maybe. But you still haven't told me why you want it."

"Unfortunately, Agent Stanton, why I want that information will have to remain my business. But I can tell you that your help in locating Hunter would not go unrewarded. You have done well for yourself in the Bureau so far, but further promotions could be arranged if I get the information I need about Hunter. Or perhaps you would prefer to have enough money to never have to work again at all. Of course, if you ever tried to double-cross me, you and everyone close to you might suddenly be in grave danger."

"I said you don't need to keep making threats. I'm not sure that I can get you the information you want, but I'll keep your offer in mind."

Stanton pulled a business card from her pocket and wrote her cell phone number on the back.

"Call me at this number in twenty-four hours and I'll let you know if we have a deal."

"I'll be in touch," Boris answered, as he placed the card in his inside jacket pocket. "And good luck with your investigation of Kelban's murder." Smirking once more, the large Russian disappeared down the alley in the opposite direction.

If Boris wanted to keep an eye on Stanton's investigation, she would have no problem keeping an eye on him as well. If he got the information he wanted from Hunter and it included the name of her source, Stanton hoped that having an open line of communication with Boris would provide her with enough of a warning to make sure that he never got the chance to carry out his threats. As she watched him walk away, Stanton was reminded of something she'd been told a long time ago in one of the first foster homes she had lived in—*Keep your friends close, but your enemies closer.*

CHAPTER 24

Santo Alampi, Sunday, 3:30p.m.

Over the years, Alampi's work had put him in contact with several members of the New York Police Department. None of the connections he'd made were with anyone at the higher levels of the force, but sometimes the best information came not from the top, but from the street-level beat cops. These were the officers that Alampi had fostered relationships with.

One of these relationships even blossomed into a brief romance a long time ago when Alampi was just starting out in the business. A cop named Susan Smith was the first officer on the scene of a homicide, where the victim was a female teenage runaway that Alampi had been hired to find. He'd tracked her to a building in lower Manhattan where she was staying with her boyfriend and several of his drug-addict friends. But by the time Alampi busted down the door of the apartment, the boyfriend had strangled the young girl during a drug-induced hallucination.

After Officer Smith interviewed a clearly upset Alampi at the scene, he thanked her for her efforts at comforting him. She smiled and told him to call her Sue, and then asked if he wanted to get a cup of coffee when her shift ended later that night. Alampi agreed, and they'd talked all the way through to the following morning, when Sue cooked them both breakfast at her apartment.

They dated for a while after that, but neither ever grew to have serious feelings for the other, and they ended up close friends. Sue put in her twenty years on the force and then retired from active duty, but still worked in law enforcement as a 911 operator. Because so many calls had been coming in about Hunter on the tip-line, phone operators, like Sue, were pulled in to help handle the volume. When she recognized Alampi's number on her cell phone, Sue was happy to hear from him.

"Hey stranger," she greeted him in a throaty, sing-song voice. "It's been a couple of weeks since I've heard from you. How are you doing?"

"Not bad," Alampi answered, and she could picture him smiling his usual crooked smile. But then his voice turned more serious.

"Listen, Sue, I need a favor, if you can help me out. I know the whole city is looking for this Jake Hunter kid, and I've got a client who wants to be kept up to date on the kid's whereabouts. I wouldn't normally ask you about an ongoing investigation like this, but there could be big money in it for me if I can just provide a little information."

"Wow, Sant, I don't know. Like you said, it's an active investigation. Plus, all I'm doing is answering calls from every crackpot in town who thinks they're gonna get a reward for claiming to have seen this kid."

"I know. But I also know that you guys all talk to each other while you're working and on breaks. You have to, because if a couple of people get calls about the same location, it makes the lead that much more of a priority. I'm not asking you to pinpoint the kid for me. I just need someplace to start. Whatta you say, can you help me out?"

"All right, all right. You always could talk me into doing anything you wanted. Listen, truth is, there haven't been too many legitimate calls or leads to follow up anyway. From what I've heard, there's only been one tip we've passed along that the feds deemed worthy of checking out with the local authorities in another city."

"What did the calls say? What city?"

"Well, we had one caller last night say she saw Hunter at a *Bonanza* bus station in Boston. Then, we get a call from another guy this morning—also from the *Bonanza* bus station—and he says he saw a guy who looked just like Hunter, except with blond hair. Not really the strongest leads in the world, but it's the closest thing we've had so far to multiple hits at one particular location."

"I appreciate it. Maybe I'll head into the city and hang out at the Port Authority for a while. See if the kid gets off any of the buses coming in from Boston. Whether this tip leads anywhere or not, I definitely owe you dinner for helping me out."

"How about dinner, and then a nightcap at my apartment afterwards?" Sue asked, thinking that it had been a while since she'd had an overnight guest, and remembering her brief fling with Alampi fondly.

"You know I love you, Sue. But I don't think that's the best way for me to patch things up with my wife."

"I guess you're right. Well, you can't blame a girl for trying. One more thing, Santo, be careful with this case—there's something strange about it."

"You know me. I'm always careful."

CHAPTER 25

Jake Hunter, Sunday, 4:27p.m.

Jake had plenty of time to think on his bus ride to New York. He knew that he needed to retrieve the flash drive, but his apartment was surely being watched—maybe by several parties. He finally arrived at the Port Authority at around four thirty on Sunday afternoon. The terminal was fairly crowded, and Jake did his best to keep moving within the crowd, with his chin tucked to his chest and his eyes surveying everyone around him. He avoided walking near any police officers or transit cops, but was stunned for a moment when he noticed that there were actually posters with his picture on them stapled to several beams and walls of the building lobby. Jake froze as he heard a man's voice say, "Hey, you see that kid from the posters?"

Jake thought that he'd been spotted and quickly ducked behind a newsstand. He glanced around the corner and saw a young couple, maybe nineteen years old, wearing backpacks and holding hands. The man was pointing at one of the posters with Jake's picture on it. The girl was shaking her head from side to side in response to his question. Jake realized that the man wasn't asking if she had actually *seen* Jake, but just whether she'd heard about him.

"Yeah, well, apparently, the guy snapped from the pressure of working at some big law firm. He killed his boss, and right now he's probably on his way to Mexico."

The man's erroneous version of events was almost enough to make Jake smile, but instead he lowered his head and headed toward the Eighth Avenue exit. As he approached the exit, Jake noticed a man in an ugly Hawaiian shirt who seemed to be staring at him from a bench about fifteen feet away. The man yawned, absently looked away from Jake, and then glanced down at the newspaper that was open on his lap. Although the stranger seemed innocuous, Jake couldn't afford to take any chances, so he turned back in the opposite direction away from the exit to the street.

***

Alampi looked up from his newspaper and watched Hunter begin walking into the heart of the bus terminal, unsure whether he'd been made or not. He got up from the bench he was sitting on, folded the paper he was using as a prop in half, and tucked it under his arm. Alampi strolled toward the middle of the terminal, pretending to check one of the monitors for departure or arrival information, but keeping Hunter in his line of sight. He saw Hunter heading into the men's room and slowly wove his way through the throngs of people, positioning himself against the wall directly across from the bathroom door. Alampi noted the heavy police presence at the Port Authority and he didn't want to risk making a scene by confronting Hunter in the restroom. He figured that he would be better off letting Hunter get out to the street before grabbing him. Alampi carried a gun, but the weapon he planned on using was a simple electric taser that would shock Hunter and temporarily immobilize him. Alampi would play the role of a concerned parent and rush Hunter into a cab, purportedly to take him to the hospital. Instead, Hunter would be heading back to Alampi's office. The private investigator was already planning on asking for double his initial fee on this case for actually producing Hunter, rather than mere information as to his whereabouts.

As Alampi stood outside, he carefully monitored all of the patrons entering and exiting the bathroom. A tall black man in a sharply tailored business suit went in shortly after Hunter. He was followed moments later by a scruffy looking, possibly homeless white man in a hooded gray sweatshirt and blue jeans. Another minute went by and two young Latino boys wearing Derek Jeter replica baseball jerseys chased each other toward the door, which was held open for them by the black man in the suit on his way out. About twenty seconds later, the man in the sweatshirt ducked out of the bathroom and skulked off into the crowd.

It had been almost five minutes since Hunter went into the bathroom, and Alampi decided to go inside and see what was taking so long. He entered the bathroom and walked a few steps forward down a short entry hallway before taking a right-hand turn into the main section of the restroom. Directly to Alampi's right was a wall of seven or eight urinals, none of which was presently in use. In the center of the room was a circular basin-like structure with several spigots for people to wash their hands. The two Jeter fans were using the spigots for a different purpose, as they took turns splashing each other with the running water. The basin was about waist high and ran almost the length of the room, so Alampi was unable to see if anyone was hiding behind the far end, but he doubted Hunter would be sitting on the floor of a public restroom—especially one in the Port Authority.

To Alampi's left were the stalls. There were six of them, all with the doors closed, and he began moving down the line quietly pushing open each door and looking inside. One by one, Alampi opened the doors of the first five stalls and found them empty. He was nearing the end of the row when something caught his attention on the floor to his right, behind the large oval basin in the center of the room. It was a shoe, sticking out from the rear of the structure, as if someone were crawling away on the other side.

Alampi leaned over toward the basin, placed his right hand on the edge, and lunged out with his left hand, grabbing the back of the ankle attached to the still-visible shoe. The scream was not unexpected, but its pitch certainly was. Rather than the mature voice of a man in his twenties, Alampi heard a squealing shriek. When he looked around the other side of the basin, he saw that he was holding on to the leg of one of the two young Latino boys. The boy had gotten down on one knee to tie his shoelace, and Alampi had scared him half to death. The private investigator released his grip, and the two boys scurried out of the bathroom, looking over their shoulders in fear.

Alampi was cursing himself and wondering how Hunter had gotten out of the bathroom without him noticing, when he heard a sound directly behind him. He turned around and realized that he'd never checked the final stall. Somewhat angry and embarrassed at his mistake, Alampi kicked the door open and saw a cowering young man standing crouched on the toilet, holding his hands in front of his face.

"Come on, Hunter," Alampi said to the terrified young man. "If you come with me quietly, I promise I won't turn you in to the cops."

At the mention of the police, the man lowered his hands from his face, and Alampi was met with his second surprise in the past minute. The man was not Jake Hunter.

"Hey, man," the stranger addressed Alampi, "you can't turn me in to the cops. All I did was sell my sweatshirt to some dude for fifty bucks. I found that thing in somebody's garbage, man.

But that guy wanted it bad. Told me he'd give me another fifty if I hid out in this stall for a while. Pretty good deal, huh?"

The man held up and waved a crinkled hundred dollar bill in the air. Alampi was so mad at himself for letting Hunter get away that he grabbed the bill out of the bum's hand and threw it into the toilet. Before walking away, he pressed the handle to flush the money, but the scruffy man almost instantaneously held up his wet arm, stinking of urine and brandishing the retrieved hundred dollars.

"Hey, man. That's attempted robbery, man. I should call the cops on you!" the man shouted at Alampi's back as he exited the restroom, still seething at his missed opportunity.

Like any good investigator, Alampi knew that he had an obligation to report in to his client, even if the report contained mostly bad news. On the bright side, he was hired to find Hunter, and he'd accomplished that. He'd just been so close to doing so much more. Alampi realized that he probably would have noticed Hunter leaving the bathroom in the other man's clothes if he hadn't been distracted thinking about the hundred grand he would get from his client for handing the kid over. Then again, Alampi thought that it might be for the best that Hunter had gotten away from him, because turning him over to his client instead of the cops might have gotten Alampi into trouble.

When he called his client to check in, Alampi reported that he'd located Hunter in New York City, but had lost him in the Port Authority. Rather than being upset by this news, Alampi's client seemed quite pleased.

"Excellent job finding Hunter. I have to make a quick call, but I'll get back to you with further instructions. You may get another chance to confront Hunter sooner than you think."

When the client called Alampi back very early the next morning, he was given an assignment that was more unusual than anything he'd ever been hired to do before.

CHAPTER 26

Jake Hunter, Sunday, 4:47p.m.

After tossing the filthy gray sweatshirt that had allowed him to safely exit the Port Authority, Jake walked uptown to Sixty-fourth Street and Amsterdam. He entered the park next to his apartment complex from the corner farthest away from the entrance to his building. As usual, Ollie was sitting on a bench in the park, seemingly staring off into space. Jake approached his friend, desperately hoping that he could trust him, and sat down on the same bench. Without turning to look at Jake, Ollie spoke first.

"How you doin', Jake?"

"I've been better, Ollie. I'm actually in a pretty big jam right now."

"I know. I've seen it in all the papers. Anything I can do to help?"

Upon hearing the sincerity in Ollie's offer of help, Jake was relieved and decided that he could trust him.

"I need some information Ollie. You spend most of the day in this park, and you've got a pretty good view of my apartment building from here. Can you tell me if anyone's been watching the building, or my apartment in particular?"

Ollie's head tilted slightly downward, and when he spoke again, it was in a low voice that only Jake could hear.

"There's two of them switching on and off every twelve hours. They dress like those characters from the *Matrix* movies—you know, same dark suit, ugly tie, and sunglasses. First guy watches your place from six a.m. to six p.m. The night guy will be coming along to replace him in a little less than half an hour."

"Thanks, Ollie. That's good stuff. I knew you had a good eye for detail, but that's even more impressive than I thought."

"Yeah, well, like I think I've told you before, it used to be my job in the service to keep lookout for my team. At least it was until that day."

It was the closest Jake had ever heard Ollie come to talking about why he'd left the Army, and despite everything that was going on in his own life, Jake had the feeling that Ollie was finally ready to talk about his secret.

"What happened on that day, Ollie?"

Ollie turned and looked Jake directly in the eye. He held his gaze for a few moments and then lowered his head and began to speak.

"I didn't do my job, that's what happened. It was near the end of the first Gulf War in Iraq. Things had quieted down and the word was that we were all going to be sent home in a few more weeks. My unit hadn't seen any live action in over a month, and except for the fireworks in the sky on a few nights here and there, it seemed like the fighting was just about over. And I think I must have lost my edge because things were so quiet. Lost my edge and got a bunch of boys killed when I didn't pick up on a device buried in the road my unit was traveling on.

"I was walking ahead of the group, like always, with the boys rolling up behind me in the truck. And I had to keep to the side of the road, you know, to keep a good view of all the ridges and dunes to make sure they weren't providing cover for an ambush or hiding the enemy. But I was also supposed to watch the road itself for IEDs—improvised explosive devices—that could be buried in the dirt and go off under the pressure of a vehicle. And I walked right by one of them, probably thinking about how close I was to getting back home to my wife, and eating a slice of her delicious sweet potato pie.

"I was about a hundred yards up the road when the truck rolled over the bomb, and the blast was strong enough to throw me to the ground. By the time I got back there, six men were dead and four others were severely burned and screaming in agony. They was just boys, Jake, most of 'em younger than you. I could never get over it. The Army cleared me of any wrongdoing, but after I left the service, I could never stop thinking about it. My wife eventually left me, I couldn't keep a job, and for a while I turned to booze and drugs. That's why my memory ain't what it used to be. But I finally got some help from an old buddy of mine from the unit who helped me sober up and see that I was disrespectin' the memory of those boys by slowly killing myself the way I was. I'm not exactly back on my feet yet, but I'm working on it. Because if I don't use the rest of my life to do something good to help other people, then I'll never make it up to those boys that lost their lives because of me.

"You remind me of them, Jake. Maybe that's why I kept an eye on you all summer, and also made sure I checked out the people watching over your place since you've been gone. I just hope it helps you out somehow."

Jake wasn't sure what to say in response, but he knew that Ollie needed to hear something encouraging after revealing his story.

"I think it's going to help me a lot, Ollie. If it wasn't for you, I probably wouldn't have noticed the men watching my place, and they would have caught me trying to get back into my apartment. The guys in your unit would have been proud of how you're helping me out. As long as they didn't think that I was a murderer, like the rest of the city does."

Several minutes passed and neither man spoke, both seemingly lost in their own thoughts. Finally, Ollie broke the silence.

"So, Jake, did you do it?"

"No. I would never kill anybody."

"Never say never Jake. Sometimes people don't know what they're capable of doing until they get put in a position they never expected to be in."

It dawned on Jake that Ollie was probably right—if anyone ever threatened to hurt his family, Jake knew that he would do whatever was necessary to protect the people he loved.

"Hey, Jake," Ollie nodded his head to the left as he spoke, "there's your boy now."

Jake saw a dark, late-model sedan pull into the cul-de-sac of West Sixty-third Street. The driver was exactly as Ollie described, right down to the sunglasses. He parked the car and entered Jake's building. About five minutes later, a very similar looking man, except a few inches shorter than the first, walked out of the building, got into the car, and drove away.

"Cheap bastards," Ollie muttered, "won't even splurge for two cars to stake out your place, Jake."

"That's because they don't really believe that I'd come back here."

"The U.S. government—wrong again."

As Jake stood up to leave, Ollie asked, "Anything else I can do to help?"

"Not right now, Ollie. I'll let you know though."

"You know where to find me."

Jake exited the park the same way he'd come in, onto Sixty-fourth Street. Only instead of heading to the right, toward Amsterdam, he turned left toward West End Avenue and the apartment buildings that were connected to his building on

Sixty-third. Jake milled around by one of the entrances, as he didn't have a key to get into the buildings on this side. After a few minutes, a woman taking her dog for a walk exited, and Jake grabbed the door before it closed and went inside. He walked to the end of the first floor hallway and out a door, which led into the small courtyard running between the Sixty-third Street and Sixty-fourth Street structures. Jake went into his building through a back door entrance on the opposite side of the courtyard similar to the one he'd just exited.

Underneath the stairwell near the back door were several bins full of recyclables, including newspapers, bottles, and a few cardboard boxes. Jake sifted through one of the bins and found a long, thin box that had contained the pieces of an entertainment center that someone must have recently built for their apartment. There was no sign of anyone in the first floor hallway, so Jake carried the box to the elevator and pressed the button with the arrow pointing up. The elevator made its familiar *ding* as it arrived on the first floor, and Jake entered the small space, keeping his head down and using the box to shield him from the camera in the upper right-hand corner as he pressed the button marked seven.

Jake got off the elevator on the seventh floor, which was one floor above his apartment, and leaned the box against the wall outside. He walked down the hallway toward the stairs and peeked over the railing down to the sixth floor below. The agent watching Jake's apartment was sitting on the steps reading a newspaper. He had a thermos next to him, and had poured a cup of what smelled to Jake like some kind of French Roast coffee. The agent's head suddenly snapped up from his paper, and Jake whisked his head away from the railing just in time before the agent looked up to where Jake had been standing the moment before.

Tiptoeing back to the elevator, Jake pressed the down button and the doors opened immediately. Reaching inside, he pressed the button for the sixth floor, which lit up as he touched it. Jake then stepped halfway out of the elevator and, as the doors began to close, he positioned the cardboard box inside the elevator so that it was leaning against the now closing door. Jake stepped out of the elevator, moved back to the end of the hallway where the stairs were located, and listened closely to determine whether his plan would work.

The elevator dinged, announcing its arrival on the sixth floor. Jake heard the elevator doors open and, after a few moments, begin to close. For a second, Jake thought his plan had failed, but then he heard the familiar *ding*, and the sound of the doors opening again on the sixth floor. When the doors first opened on six, the long cardboard box that Jake had left leaning against the elevator door fell to the ground and was now preventing the elevator from moving because the doors could not shut when there was an object in the way. Instead, they would keep opening and closing, followed by the annoying bell sound, until someone moved the box.

When the elevator doors reopened for the third time, the agent finally stood up and peered around the corner. He could vaguely see that something was blocking the doors. After drawing his gun, and briefly looking back at Jake's apartment, the agent turned the corner and headed down the hallway toward the elevator.

Jake reached into his pocket and pulled out the two tranquilizer darts that he'd taken from Jason's lab on Friday morning. He unscrewed the backs of the darts and carefully held the open containers in one hand. Jake scurried down the flight of stairs, dumped the contents of the two tranquilizer darts into the agent's coffee cup, and rushed back up to the seventh floor.

In his haste, Jake slipped slightly near the top of the stairs, and when he put out his hands to break his fall on the seventh floor landing, they made a slapping sound against the ground.

Jake stood up and jogged as quietly as he could down the hall, flattening his back behind a cut-out where the hallway walls widened about halfway between the stairs and the elevator. The agent would not be able to see Jake unless he walked all the way down the hall, and Jake was beginning to think that the agent hadn't heard him fall, when he recognized the clear sound of footsteps slowly climbing the stairs. The sound grew louder as the agent got closer, and Jake thought that he could actually smell the agent's coffee on his breath. Just when Jake began to think his heart was beating so loudly that the agent could hear it, the sound of a radio transmission crackled in the distance. After a brief pause, the radio crackled again, only this time it was followed by the sound of the agent's footsteps heading in the opposite direction along the hallway and down the stairs.

Jake noiselessly exhaled and listened to the agent speaking into his radio.

"Ruddy here."

The radio crackled again, as someone said something that was unintelligible to Jake. But Agent Ruddy responded immediately.

"Nope. Nothing going on. Same as the last two days. Everything's quiet."

Jake counted to three hundred and then eased back toward the stairs. He looked over the railing just in time to see the agent gulp down the last of his coffee and screw the cup back onto the top of the thermos. Within two minutes, Agent Ruddy was groggily shaking his head back and forth. About ten seconds after that, he keeled over onto the floor in front of Jake's apartment.

Jake hurried down the stairs, pulled out his keys, and unlocked his door. He dragged the unconscious Agent Ruddy into the apartment, used some duct tape to bind his hands and feet, and left him in the bedroom with the door closed. The apartment clearly had been searched, as everything was somewhat out of place, although not as bad a mess as Jake had expected. He opened the window and hopped out onto the fire escape, praying that his hiding spot hadn't been discovered.

After removing the secret brick, Jake reached into the hollow space behind it and grabbed the flash drive. His hand brushed against something else, and he discovered that he'd shoved his cell phone into the hole as well after speaking with Jason on Friday morning. Jake pocketed the phone and the flash drive, replaced the brick, and climbed back into the apartment, shutting the window behind him. He turned away from the front door and looked toward the bathroom, wondering if there was anything else in the apartment that he might need or could use.

Jake almost jumped out of his own skin when he heard a familiar voice whisper from the doorway behind him.

"Hello, Jake."

CHAPTER 27

Neha Arora, Sunday, 4:54p.m.

Neha had been having a fun and exciting summer working at a midsized law firm in midtown, where the people were nice, the work was interesting, and the money was good enough that she was able to make a dent in the credit card debt she'd been piling up since the start of law school. Still, the excitement of the past few days made the rest of the summer feel incredibly tame in comparison. When Neha first heard that Jake was suspected of murder, she didn't believe it was possible, and she'd told the FBI agent that interviewed her and the rest of their neighbors exactly that. But with each day that passed without Jake's return, Neha was finding herself both more worried about his safety and more uncertain about his potential involvement in the killing.

She went for a run in Riverside Park along the West Side Highway, which temporarily cleared her mind of Jake, and everything else for that matter. But as she exited the elevator in her building and reached the end of the hallway, she saw the familiar FBI agent perched on the steps outside the door to Jake's apartment. He smiled kindly at her and mumbled a greeting, though Neha could not help but feel a bit spooked by his presence. She nodded back politely and quickly unlocked the door and entered her apartment, turning the deadbolt again as soon as she was inside.

Neha dropped her keys on an end table in the living room and walked into the bedroom to get out of her sweaty clothes before showering. As soon as she cleared the threshold of the bedroom doorway, there was a flash of motion and Neha felt as if she was being smothered and held down at the same time. Before she could even think to scream, a thick piece of tape was pressed over her mouth and, moments later, her wrists were bound in front of her by some sort of plastic wire handcuffs.

Neha realized that there were two men in her bedroom. The first had grabbed and subdued her expertly, while the second had been ready with the tape and the ligature used to bind her. Although she was terrified and wanted nothing to do with being put onto her bed, the man behind her easily moved Neha from the doorway and forced her into a seated position on the bed's edge. Her fear rose as she considered what these two men might want with her in her bedroom, but Neha felt slightly relieved when the second man slipped another plastic binding over her ankles, forcing her legs to remain tightly together. In this brief moment of relaxation, Neha also noticed that the first man was speaking to her and calling her by name.

"Neha. Neha, listen to me."

Observing that the girl was focusing on his voice and had recognized that he knew her name, Peter explained to her what was happening.

"Listen, Neha, I'm quite certain that you don't know anything about Jake Hunter's whereabouts or what he's involved in. But you do know that the FBI is looking for him and they have an agent sitting outside his apartment. Well, I'm here to tell you that the FBI are not the only ones trying to find Jake. We work for someone else who wants to find him, and we need to use your apartment for a little while in case he decides to come back here. That's why we had to use the fire escape and break into your apartment through your window.

"Now, listen very carefully, Neha," Peter continued, "because I want you to understand me—the last thing we want to do is hurt you while we are here waiting to see if Jake returns to his apartment. And I promise you that if you sit quietly watching television while we're here, no harm will come to you. But if you even think of running for the door or a window, or trying to make noise so someone hears you in here, I may not hurt you then either. But the only reason you won't be hurt is that you will be dead before you ever have a chance to feel any pain. Do you understand me?"

Neha looked at the man's face, which was really quite ordinary. She glanced up at his partner, who had disappeared into the other room briefly, but now stood in the doorway looking slightly bored yet menacing at the same time. When she looked back at Peter's face, she thought about how matter-of-factly he'd spoken about why they were there and what would happen to her if she didn't comply with his requests. Finally, Neha considered how quickly she'd been subdued and realized that these men were serious professionals who would carry out the threat against her exactly as Peter described it if she tried anything funny. She had no choice except to hope that his promise not to hurt her could be trusted.

Neha looked into Peter's eyes and nodded intently, desperately trying to convey that she understood him perfectly.

"Good," Peter said. "I can see that you are a smart girl. Unfortunately, we cannot trust you enough to take the tape off your mouth, but come into the living room with us and we will put the television on for you to watch while we wait for Jake. If he hasn't shown up by tomorrow, we will have to try another way to find him, and you'll never see us again. If he does show up, we'll be gone that much sooner."

Peter and Nicholas led Neha to the living room, where Nicholas sat beside her on the couch and turned on the news. Peter moved over to the front door and stood silently beside it, periodically staring through the peephole at Jake's apartment and the agent sitting outside. Neha found that she was watching Peter more than she was watching the television, and she wondered who these men were and what they wanted with Jake. There was one thought that Neha could not get out of her head—she sincerely hoped that Jake did not come back to the building while these men were here, because she did not think that he would survive an encounter with them.

CHAPTER 28

Richie Butler, Sunday, 6:44p.m.

Ever since he was a little kid, Richie Butler always had big dreams. From the first time he saw the movie *Top Gun,* with Tom Cruise playing an elite Navy fighter pilot, Richie wanted to fly jets. But in his teens, when Richie first looked into how to achieve his dream, he found out that almost all Navy pilots graduate from the Naval Academy at Annapolis, rather than coming from the ranks of the enlisted men. Since there was no chance that he would ever get into the Academy, Richie made some adjustments to his life's plan.

Realizing that he would never achieve his goal of becoming a jet pilot via the military, Richie figured he would have to get rich enough to buy his own plane. Then he could fly it whenever and wherever he wanted. And he could still buy one of those cool leather flight jackets that the pilots in the movies always wore. After finishing high school, Richie enrolled in night school at Queens College. His plan for getting rich was to graduate college, get a job on Wall Street, and make a killing in the stock market. Richie was not exactly sure how the market worked, but he would figure it out eventually, and then it would be just a matter of time until he was flying the friendly skies in his own private plane.

In the meantime, to pay his tuition bills, Richie worked part-time as the concierge for the apartment buildings on West Sixty-third Street. There was some excitement on Friday morning when the cops came looking for a kid named Jake Hunter, who lived on the sixth floor and was suspected of killing his boss at some big law firm. But after Hunter got away from the cops, things quieted down for the rest of that day. The following morning, on Saturday, Richie was approached by a large, ugly man, who had offered him the chance to make some money.

Richie had been instructed by the FBI that there would be an agent sitting outside Hunter's apartment in case he came back, and they ordered him to phone the agent and the cops if he happened to see the suspect anywhere in or around the building. The feds explained that Richie might have the best chance to spot Hunter because of the security cameras in the elevators and foyer area, which played back on monitors located at the concierge desk where Richie sat. At the time, he said he would be happy to help, but Richie soon wondered to himself what he would get out of helping the cops do their job. The answer, he knew, was simple—nothing.

So when the big guy with the foreign accent and the shoulder holster, which was barely visible beneath his unfastened black overcoat, offered Richie two hundred dollars to watch the same monitors and let him know if Richie saw anything unusual, Richie thought it was a no-brainer. In fact, the guy promised to throw in an extra three hundred bucks if Richie actually spotted Hunter and told the foreigner first before calling the authorities. For the past two days, the big man with the gun sat in his car across the street from the front of the building throughout Richie's shift, except for a few minutes around six o'clock, when he would drive away and return shortly thereafter.

At first, Richie diligently watched the monitors for any sign of Hunter. But after a full day with no sign of him, Richie left when his shift ended at eight o'clock on Saturday night. By eight a.m. Sunday morning, when his next shift started, Richie dismissed as hopeless the thought that Hunter would actually come back to the building. At a little before seven o'clock on Sunday night, Richie was deeply immersed in a science fiction novel and was barely paying any attention to the camera monitors at all.

Just as he reached the end of a chapter and was going to take a bathroom break, Richie happened to glance at the video screens and noticed something odd. One of the elevators was stuck on the sixth floor, and its doors kept opening and closing. Richie watched as the FBI agent approached the elevator with his gun drawn before realizing that there was nobody in there. The agent removed the object blocking the doors, which turned out to be a large cardboard box, before heading back down the hallway and moving out of the elevator camera's range.

Richie didn't think that the obstruction stopping the elevator on Hunter's floor was a big deal, but the idea of possibly earning another three hundred dollars was enough to make him decide to report it. Richie figured he would tell the guy sitting in his car across the street what he saw, and if the large man went inside to check it out, Richie would keep a close eye on the monitors and be ready to call the police right away if there was any sign of trouble. As he walked toward the foreigner's car, Richie was already wondering how many flying lessons he could get for five hundred dollars.

CHAPTER 29

Jake Hunter, Sunday, 7:05p.m.

Jake spun around and, for what felt like the tenth time in the past three days, felt completely disoriented. He realized that when he'd dragged Agent Ruddy into his apartment, the door hadn't closed, and there was now someone standing in the doorway, staring at him intently.

"Anna?" Jake said, unsure of how to react to her presence.

"Jake, I'm so glad you're all right. I've been so worried about you," Anna responded in her soft southern accent.

Realizing by her response that she was happy to see him, Jake felt a wave of emotion come over him because it was good to feel that someone still trusted him and believed that he was innocent.

"Anna," Jake replied, "you have no idea how great it is to see you."

As he spoke, Jake strode over to the doorway and hugged Anna tightly. He felt her wrap her arms around him and hug him back, but then her grip began to loosen and she broke away from him slightly and back out into the hallway.

"Jake, I don't understand. Why does everyone think that you had something to do with murdering that man at your law firm? And why did you disappear for three days? And what did you do to your hair?"

"Anna, I know it seems like there are a million questions for me to answer. But the short version is, I didn't have anything to do with killing anyone. Kelban, the partner who was killed, was involved somehow with the Russian mafia. I know it sounds crazy, but it's true. I found his body and he sent me a note about what he was mixed up in, and I think he wanted me to get something to the FBI, but I'm not sure who I can trust. I've got to figure it all out before I turn myself in, to make sure that I don't make a mistake and put the information into the wrong person's hands."

Seeing that Anna looked somewhat skeptical, but desperately wanting her to trust him, Jake asked, "You believe me, don't you?"

"I don't know, Jake. It all sounds so unreal. I mean, the Russian mafia, and some kind of secret information. Do you even know what this information is all about?"

"No, I don't. And I can't stay here while I'm trying to figure it out. I've got to leave now. But you have to promise me that you won't tell anyone you saw me. If you do, it could be dangerous for both of us."

Jake stepped out into the hallway with Anna and was pulling the door to his apartment closed when he heard the elevator's familiar *ding*, signaling the arrival of someone else on the sixth floor. Jake grabbed Anna's hand and began to pull her toward the steps leading down. As they crossed the hallway, Jake looked back, saw a large man exiting the elevator, and was shocked when the man's face registered a look of recognition upon seeing Jake. The next thing Jake knew, the man was reaching beneath his heavy leather jacket and pulling out a gun.

"Run!" Jake shouted at Anna as he urged her down the steps.

The man behind them pulled the trigger of his gun twice in rapid succession, and the shots struck the wall directly above Jake and Anna, who were now quickly descending the stairs together, attempting to escape from the shooter whose footsteps they could hear lumbering down the hall in their direction.

CHAPTER 30

Peter and Nicholas, Sunday, 7:09p.m.

Nicholas was watching through the peephole in Neha's door as Hunter made a brief appearance on the stairwell outside his apartment and drugged the FBI agent that was stationed there. Although he was ambivalent about the fact that there would be no need to deal with the already subdued agent, Nicholas was pleased that Hunter was within his sights. He signaled to Peter, who used another set of the plastic cuffs to bind Neha to the couch so that he could join Nicholas by the door.

Peter and Nicholas continued looking on as Jake dragged the agent into his apartment, but the door to Jake's apartment had closed almost completely behind him when he went inside, obstructing their view. They spoke to each other in whispered tones and agreed to wait until Hunter exited his apartment before restraining him, in the likely event that he was retrieving something important that was stashed inside. But before Hunter came back out of his apartment, someone else showed up and walked in.

As Hunter came into view and spoke to the unknown girl, Peter and Nicholas quietly discussed the pros and cons of taking both Hunter and his visitor. But before they could come to a decision, the elevator opened and Hunter and the girl bolted down the stairs as two gunshots rang out. Peter looked at Nicholas and made a split-second decision, directing his friend and partner, "Whoever it is, take him out."

Nicholas swung open the door to Neha's apartment just as Ivan went running by, chasing after Hunter and Anna. The sound of the door opening behind him made Ivan pause, but before he had time to turn around, Nicholas cracked the butt of the pistol he was holding down on the side of Ivan's neck. The blow temporarily stunned Ivan, who wobbled forward and then crashed down the short flight of stairs and onto the landing below.

While Nicholas was detaining Ivan, Peter grabbed a portable phone from its cradle in Neha's living room. He placed it into her still bound hands and looked her straight in the eye as he said, "I told you I'd keep my promise."

Just as quickly as they'd entered her life, Peter and Nicholas were gone, and Neha never saw them again.

CHAPTER 31

Jake Hunter, Sunday, 7:18p.m.

Jake and Anna heard the man who was chasing them fall on the steps above them, but they did not slow their pace as they raced down the stairs and out the front door of the apartment building. They ran toward West End Avenue and when Jake saw an unoccupied cab heading north, he flagged it down, pulled Anna in beside him, and yelled, "Drive! Drive! I'll tell you where in a minute."

The cab driver merged back into traffic and gunned the engine, speeding up in response to the urgent tone of Jake's voice. They had traveled about twenty blocks in silence, with Jake and Anna too stunned and breathing too heavily to speak, when Jake noticed the driver staring at him in the rearview mirror. The cabbie's eyes moved to something laying on the passenger seat, and Jake shifted slightly to see what he was looking at. Jake realized that the driver was looking at a newspaper with a picture of Jake on the front cover and came to an immediate decision.

"Stop the car! We're getting out here."

The cabbie dutifully pulled over, but barely took his eyes off Jake as the car came to a stop on the corner of West Eightieth Street. Although the fare was only four dollars and ten cents, Jake handed the driver a ten dollar bill and told him to keep the change. Anna didn't understand why they were getting out of the cab, but she was still in shock after being shot at back at the apartment building. Jake hurried her along the street and they headed east on Eightieth toward Broadway. Their cab continued driving north on West End, but Jake saw the driver talking on his radio as he drove away. Worrying that he'd been recognized and that cops were being called to the area, Jake wanted to get out of sight.

"I think we need to get off the street for a little while. We've got to figure out someplace to go—maybe duck into a store or something. There's a huge Tower Records down on Sixty-sixth and Broadway."

"Jake," Anna replied, "I'm not sure I can walk that far right now. I need to sit down for a little while."

As they reached Broadway, Jake turned south and thought of a perfect place nearby where they could sit down and get out of sight. And it was a place where he couldn't imagine anyone would ever come looking for them—a tiny hole-in-the-wall restaurant called *Big Nick's,* which was located only two blocks away between Seventy-seventh and Seventy-eighth Streets. The restaurant had been one of Jake's favorites ever since he discovered it shortly after moving to the city, and he and his friends had made many late night excursions to the eatery, which was open twenty-four hours a day.

The décor inside *Big Nick's* was completely outdated, and obviously had never been redone in the three decades that the restaurant had been open. The walls were covered with black and white photographs and headshots of mostly D-list celebrities. But that was all part of the charm. Also, the food was so good, none of the customers cared how the place was decorated. *Big Nick's* was particularly famous for its hamburgers, and their specialty was called the Sumo Burger, advertised as "one full pound of beef, perfect for sharing." Jake and Anna sidled into a secluded booth in the back of the restaurant and, as they looked at their menus, realized that they were both ravenously hungry.

After agreeing that the least conspicuous thing they could do would be to order food and eat, Jake and Anna decided to split a Sumo Burger and a side of waffle fries.

After placing their order, Anna quietly asked Jake, "Who was that man shooting at us?"

"I don't know," Jake answered. "But if I had to guess, I'd say he was with the Russian mob, and maybe he was the one who killed Kelban."

"And now he wants to kill you. My god, Jake, how the heck did you get involved in this? And now I'm involved too—I mean, that guy, that Russian mobster, he was shooting at me too, wasn't he?"

As Anna spoke, she covered her face with her hands, overwhelmed with the situation and the thought that she had almost been shot. Jake wanted to comfort her, and he reached out and took one of her hands in his.

"It's going to be okay, Anna. I promise. Tomorrow morning, I'll make some calls, figure out who I should be talking to at the FBI, and we'll both be protected from whoever these guys are."

Noticing that his soothing words had calmed Anna down a little, Jake continued.

"Listen. There's nothing we can do about this mess right now, so why don't we just try to act normal and enjoy the fact that at least we're together. I've been so scared and alone for the past few days, I'm just glad that you're with me right now. How about we talk like we've been meaning to—you know, get to know each other a little better. What do you think?"

Anna dropped her other hand from her face, took a deep breath, and looked at Jake with a half-smile.

"I think I could try that. You have to ask first though. What do you want to know about me?"

Jake thought about this for a second and then asked, "Well, why did you move to New York?"

"Did you ever have a place that you went to or heard about as a little kid, and it became kind of like a dream to go back, or to get there?" Anna answered Jake's question with one of her own.

"I guess so."

"Well, for me," Anna continued, "that place was always New York City. I'm an only child, born and raised in North Carolina. When I was nine years old, my parents took me on a trip to New York, and I was amazed at the size of the buildings, and the crowds of people. We went to an evening show of *Cats* on Broadway, and I remember thinking that there were so many lights in Times Square lighting up the sky, that it was like daytime in the middle of the night."

"You think it's like daytime at night in Times Square, you should see what it's like in Las Vegas."

Anna smiled, but her expression had grown melancholy. Jake noticed the sudden change in her demeanor and didn't want to pry, but he knew there was more to Anna's story.

"So, what took you so long to get back to New York?"

Anna hesitated for a few moments, but then she looked up at Jake and stared directly into his eyes.

"I was supposed to come back with my parents after my high school graduation. The trip was going to be their present to me."

Anna's eyes began to water, and a single tear rolled down her cheek as she continued.

"They died in a car crash a month before graduation. I went to live with my grandmother for the summer, and then went off to college at UNC Charlotte. I wanted to come back here sooner, but the memories were too painful. When I finally realized that my parents wouldn't want me to be holding my own life back because of them, that's when I knew I had to move here."

"Wow, Anna, I'm so sorry about your parents."

Jake reached across the table and brushed the tear from Anna's cheek. She smiled shyly, slightly embarrassed by her emotional display.

"It's okay, Jake. It's been five years. And the fact that I'm here now is a good thing. So, what is your special place from when you were a kid?"

Now it was Jake who grew quiet and hesitant, as he had a sensitive tale to share as well—although Jake would have to leave out some of the details of his story.

"Well, I first went to my favorite place when I was a lot younger than you were when you first came to New York. I was only six months old. I don't remember that trip, of course. But I've seen the pictures—me, my mom, and my dad, standing in front of some hotel on the boardwalk in Atlantic City. I guess my family couldn't afford to take any fancy vacations when I was young, because my mom was just out of law school and my dad was bouncing around between jobs, so we'd always take our vacations down in AC. My dad loved to gamble, and after my mom and I would go to sleep in the hotel room, he would stay up all night playing blackjack. He always came back to the room right around the time the sun was rising. He would wake me up and take me for walks on the boardwalk while my mom was still asleep. I remember when I was younger that he would put me up on his shoulders, and when the sun started to rise in the sky, I felt like I could reach out and touch it. Eventually, we'd go back to the room and my mom would take me out for breakfast and to the beach while my dad slept for a few hours."

Jake's eyes had fallen toward the table as he told his story, and now it was Anna who reached out and took hold of his hand as she spoke.

"Jake, you said your dad loved to gamble. Is that because he doesn't gamble anymore?"

"Honestly, I don't know. My father disappeared when I was seven years old."

"Disappeared? What happ—"

Anna was cut off by the ringing of her cell phone. She looked down at the phone and then back up at Jake.

"I'm sorry, Jake. It's my roommate and she's been having problems with her boyfriend. I should take this."

"It's okay. Go ahead. I understand. Just be careful."

Jake was relieved that Anna's roommate had called. He didn't really want to discuss his father's disappearance, but he felt like he couldn't lie to her after she'd just told him about her parents dying.

Anna walked outside the restaurant to talk to her roommate, and the waiter appeared at Jake's table with a large plate holding the enormous Sumo Burger and a side of crispy, golden brown french fries, and two smaller plates, so that Jake and Anna could divide up their hearty meal. A minute later, Anna returned to the table and gasped at the size of the hamburger.

"Oh my God! That's the biggest burger I've ever seen. And I've been to some pretty crazy barbecues."

"I told you this place wouldn't disappoint. Hey, is your roommate okay?"

"Yeah, she's fine. In fact, she made up with the boyfriend and asked me if they could have our apartment to themselves tonight. I told her that I already had plans to sleep out tonight anyway. I guess that means we'll have to find someplace to stay, maybe check into a hotel or something."

Jake didn't know if it was a good idea to let Anna stay with him for the night. He wondered if he would be putting her in danger. But as long as they were careful, there wouldn't be any way for the Russians to find them. Jake again found himself thinking about something that Kelban had taught him—sometimes you have less than ten seconds to weigh the pros and cons of an offer before it's going to be pulled off the table, so you've got to be able to think fast and respond quickly. Jake went over the advantages of his current situation in his mind: staying with Anna provided good cover from cops or anyone else looking for a man traveling alone; going to a hotel would be a safe place to clean up and get some rest; and a gorgeous girl had just invited him to spend the night with her.

The only negative Jake could think of was that he'd have to wait a little longer to call the authorities and figure out how and where to turn himself in. But the delay was fine with Jake because he wanted to determine what he should do to make sure he could trust whoever he was going to contact about turning over the flash drive. About ten seconds had passed since Anna had floated the hotel idea, and Jake was sure that the pros outweighed the cons. She was looking at him expectantly, and his answer made her break out into a demure smile.

"I think I like your hotel idea. Let's do it."

CHAPTER 32

Agent Stanton, Sunday, 9:41p.m.

After what felt like a wasted weekend, due to the complete lack of any helpful leads in the case, Agent Stanton finally got some potentially good news late Sunday night. Hunter was alive, or at least he had been a few hours earlier. He'd returned to his apartment and somehow managed to drug Agent Ruddy. Stanton began to think that, based on his actions and the other suspicious events that had been unfolding, maybe Hunter was more involved with the Russian mafia than she originally believed.

By the time Stanton and Zarvas arrived, the FBI's forensics team was going over Hunter's apartment for a second time. The head technician reported in to the two agents.

"First off, we pulled two bullet frags out of the wall behind the stairwell outside. We've already sent them to ballistics to see if they can match them to a specific weapon. Second, after someone, presumably Hunter, drugged Agent Ruddy—with what, we don't know yet, we sent a sample of his blood to the lab to find out—he dragged the agent into the apartment, put him in the bedroom, taped his wrists and ankles, and closed the bedroom door. Other than the doors and the cabinet under the sink where the duct tape was, the only other place we found fresh prints was on the window frame and ledge. The positioning of the prints indicates that Hunter opened the window and then closed it."

"Why would he open the window?" Zarvas asked.

"I don't know," the forensics technician responded. "This isn't some TV show where the techs collect the evidence *and* solve the crimes. I just tell you guys what I find, and it's your job to figure out what it all means. Good luck."

Zarvas looked at Stanton and shrugged, dismissing the technician's bitterness. He pulled on a pair of white latex gloves, opened the window, and climbed out onto the fire escape. Looking around, he asked Stanton, "Why do you think Hunter would come back to the apartment?"

"It had to be to get something. He's a smart kid. He knew we'd be watching this place. He wouldn't have come back unless there was something here that he really needed."

"Maybe something that whoever killed his boss would be interested in?"

"Like evidence relating to Kelban's murder?"

"Anything's possible at this point," Zarvas answered.

While he was talking to Stanton, who was looking around inside the apartment, Zarvas remained outside on the fire escape. After he finished searching the window ledges, all the other surfaces within reaching distance, and the grated fire escape floor, he began running his hands along the brick wall immediately to his left. As his fingertips moved down the wall, Zarvas's right index finger caught the corner of a brick, which shifted slightly as his finger applied pressure to the edge. He grabbed each side of the loose brick with his hands and slowly pulled it out of the wall.

As he removed the brick, Zarvas knew that he'd found the hiding spot in which Hunter had stowed whatever he came back to his apartment for. But Zarvas was surprised to find something still sitting in the hollowed-out space behind the brick. Bending his head toward the open window, Zarvas shouted to his partner, who had moved into the bedroom, "Hey, Stanton, I think I just found something that explains Hunter's connection to this case."

Stanton and Zarvas read the note from Kelban to Hunter detailing Kelban's fears about his involvement with the Russian mafia and the existence of a "drive" that could bring them down. They surmised that Hunter probably had hidden a mini hard drive and the note the morning that Kelban was killed. Stanton said, "This note could explain why Kelban was killed and why the Russians tried to frame Hunter—so that they'd have more time to get to him before he could turn the drive over to us."

"Yeah. But assuming that Hunter got the drive back, I don't like the looks of those gunshots in the wall outside. Do you think he'll actually be able to stay alive long enough to get the drive to us?"

"I don't know, but from what we know about how the Russian mafia operates, I don't like his chances out there on his own."

As soon as she read the note, Stanton's concern was renewed about what information might be on the drive that Kelban had sent to Hunter just before he was killed. Her source had given her Kelban's name, which meant that they might have known about each other. It was possible that Kelban's drive contained the identities of members of the Russian mafia, such as Stanton's informant. Stanton couldn't risk that information falling into the wrong hands. If Hunter was still alive somewhere, she had to get the drive from him before the Russians did.

"Hey, Jimmy, can you wrap things up in here with the evidence guys? I've got to make a couple of calls—report in to the office and see what our next move should be. I'll meet you downstairs."

"Yeah. No problem."

Stanton knew that the note provided strong evidence of the likely motive behind Kelban's murder. She did not know whether this detail would prove helpful or not, but after exiting Hunter's apartment building, she practically ran across the street to a pay phone and anxiously dialed the familiar number from the back of the plain business card that had been given to her in the Russian Vodka Room.

When the familiar raspy voice answered, Stanton felt her heart flutter with relief as she said into the phone, "I've got news for you."

CHAPTER 33

Sergei Ilanov, Sunday, 9:52p.m.

Sergei did not like the unknown. He paid vast sums of money to informants because, often, the intelligence that he obtained allowed him to make even more money. But the most valuable aspect of information to Sergei was that it enabled him to prevent the occurrence of unforeseen circumstances that could lead to his downfall. Right now, some punk kid possessed a computer drive that could destroy Sergei's empire, and that kid's whereabouts were unknown. Sergei certainly did not like that.

Sergei's initial plan of having Hunter apprehended by the authorities, and then paying off one of his people on the inside to hand over the flash drive, was being stymied by the fact that no one was able to locate Hunter. Sergei was particularly enraged upon hearing that Ivan had found Hunter back at his apartment, but allowed Hunter to escape, swearing that he'd been waylaid by some mysterious accomplice who had attacked him from behind. Seeing that his original plan, which called for patience and stealth, had failed, Sergei realized that he hadn't risen to his position of wealth and power by waiting around for other people to make things happen. Rather, his methods involved striking aggressively and decisively, showing no mercy, and leaving little to chance. And so Sergei called once again for Boris and Ivan.

Like most native Russians living in New York, Sergei occasionally frequented the upscale Russian Vodka Room. But he refused to meet with his own people there, making certain that no one could ever publicly link him to his underlings. Instead, Sergei always went to small, out-of-the-way bars or restaurants to meet with his associates, and threatened them with death if they were ever followed to a meeting with him. On this particular night, Sergei met with his two top lieutenants in a dark, dingy bar on West Seventy-fifth Street, between Broadway and Amsterdam Avenue, appropriately named *Dive 75*. Sergei was sitting at a booth in the back of the bar, sipping a glass of vodka, when Boris and Ivan arrived and sat down across from him. Ivan spoke first, in a rushed, worried tone.

"Sergei, I am sorry that I could not grab Hunter at his apartment. He must have had someone there helping him. Whoever it was almost smashed my skull in and knocked me down the stairs. I should have seen it coming, but I was focused on chasing Hunter. Again, I am very sorry."

Sergei thought to himself that in the old days Ivan would already have been punished severely for failing to capture Hunter. But there were more important matters to deal with at the moment, and Sergei could always mete out Ivan's punishment once he had Hunter and the flash drive in his possession.

"That's all right, Ivan, you could not have known that Hunter would have an accomplice there to ambush you. But we must move forward and protect ourselves by finding the young attorney quickly before he goes to the authorities."

"How do we find him again?" Boris asked. "He certainly won't go back to his apartment after Ivan nearly blew his head off."

"We don't find him. We make him come to us."

Sergei pulled several pieces of paper from beneath his coat, consisting of blueprints, sketches, and other instructions, and proceeded to describe to his trusted lieutenants how they would get Hunter to come out of hiding.

Several hours later, a team of highly skilled men silently approached a house on a quiet suburban street. The home was a two family model, and was identical to the houses on either side of it, as all three had been built at the same time. In front was a driveway, leading up to a garage on the left, with a set of concrete stairs on the right going up to the front door. Once inside, two sets of stairs led either up to the main floor, or down to the lower floor. From the lower floor landing, there was a third staircase leading to the furnished basement. All three sets of homeowners had put up fencing around their backyards, and each home had a private side door entrance to the lower floor of the house.

The middle house, where Jake Hunter had spent most of his childhood and teenage years, was still occupied by his mother and brother. Up until recently, his grandmother had lived in the lower floor of the house, but she'd retired and moved to San Diego, and the lower floor was currently empty.

FBI Agent Lynch sat on the hard stoop in front of the side entrance to the Hunter house. Behind him was a set of steps going down to a basement entrance and a wooden gate leading to the back yard. Agent Lynch listened to the traffic rolling along behind him on the Seaford-Oyster Bay Expressway, but never heard the back gate open, or the man sneaking up behind him with the garroting wire, until it was too late.

The lock on the side door was expertly picked, and several men, including Boris and Ivan, made their way to the upstairs floor of the Hunter home. The other two FBI agents assigned to watch over the Hunter family were playing five hundred rummy at the kitchen table, and neither had time to react to the trained killers who fired well-aimed bullets through silenced pistols and into the agents' foreheads. The killers, not new to their trade, moved deftly to catch the slouching agents' bodies before they fell from their chairs and could wake anyone else in the house.

Moving stealthily down the hall toward the bedrooms, two men entered Mrs. Hunter's room. Jake's mother had finally been able to fall asleep after being awake since first seeing Jake on the news on Friday morning. One of the men poured some liquid out of a bottle onto a plain white rag and held it firmly over Mrs. Hunter's nose and mouth. After a moment, her eyes opened wide with fear, but her frightened state only caused her to inhale the chloroform more deeply, and she was soon unconscious.

Boris and Ivan watched from the doorway of Bret Hunter's bedroom as two more henchmen approached the sleeping figure under the blankets. With the chloroform-doused rag in his hand, one of the men pulled back the blankets and was surprised to find several pillows where he'd expected to find Bret. The closet door rifled open, and an aluminum bat, which Bret had used earlier that year to help lead Wantagh High School to a New York State Baseball Championship, slammed forward as Bret drilled the rag-toting henchman right between the eyes.

Bret stepped out of the closet and, as the second henchman approached, he took a fierce swing and made direct contact with the man's right knee, shattering the kneecap. With the first two assailants already writhing in pain on his bedroom floor, Bret turned toward the doorway ready to keep swinging, but Boris and Ivan were both holding guns and pointing them directly at Bret. Boris spoke calmly, knowing that his superior weapon placed him firmly in control of the situation.

"You'd better hand that over, before someone really gets hurt. You wouldn't want Ivan here to decide to take your mom with us too, now would you?"

"You're not taking her?" Bret was breathing heavily and clearly was scared, despite still holding his bat in a cocked position.

"The boss said to just take you," Boris answered. "Now, drop that bat and kick it over here."

Bret remained uncertain, but didn't think he had much of a choice. It was obvious that these men would not hesitate to kill him, and he was hopeful that they weren't lying about not taking his mother with them. Bret slowly placed the bat on his carpeted bedroom floor and, with the front of his foot, pushed it forward, watching as it rolled over to Boris. Bret's arms were quickly pinned from behind by Ivan, and he felt the wet rag cover his face. He tried not to breathe in, but he couldn't hold his breath for very long. Soon, Bret began to feel woozy, and then everything faded to blackness.

CHAPTER 34

Jake Hunter, Sunday, 9:58p.m.

One of the first things Jake had done after moving to New York City and starting law school two years earlier was look for a place to work out. He'd checked out one popular chain of gyms, with a location near his apartment, but found it too expensive for someone who was taking out loans to pay for school and building up some pretty hefty credit card debt as well. Once school started, Jake asked one of the guys he met in class if he knew of an inexpensive place to work out in the area. Jake's friend told him about a Holiday Inn Hotel on Fifty-seventh Street between Ninth and Tenth Avenues, which had a small gym in the basement for hotel guests. A one-year membership cost only two hundred and fifty dollars—a huge bargain compared to most New York gyms. The price was right, the location was nearby, and the gym had all the essential equipment Jake was looking for, so he had joined.

The Holiday Inn was familiar and close, and Jake and Anna checked into the hotel under the names Jack and Diane Mellencamp. On the walk over, they'd discovered that they shared a similar taste in music, and Jake suggested that they use the fake names, which Anna thought was a great idea. They ended up borrowing the last name from one of their mutual favorite singers, and took their first names from one of his most popular songs. At the front desk, Jake paid for the room in cash and they headed upstairs. As they walked down the dimly lit hallway toward their room, Anna, seemingly in a much better mood, asked playfully, "Do you think they gave us the honeymoon suite, Mr. Mellencamp?"

"I just hope they gave us a key to the mini-bar. I could use a drink."

"Are you trying to get me drunk so you can have your way with me?"

As Anna spoke, she stopped in the middle of the hallway and turned to look at Jake. Jake stopped as well, and they were staring into each other's eyes as Anna continued in her sultry, southern voice, "Because you don't need to get me drunk, you know."

Anna pulled Jake toward her and they kissed deeply and aggressively. Jake began running his hands along Anna's back, reaching underneath her shirt and gently massaging her tanned skin. His fingers pressed into her shoulders as they continued to kiss, and Jake's hands were soon running down her back and tracing the skin directly above her jeans. Anna's hands began exploring Jake's body as well. Her left arm was wrapped tightly around his midsection, and her right hand was caressing Jake's left thigh and steadily rising. Their breathing was heavy, and as Anna began to kiss Jake's neck, he opened his eyes and realized that they were still in the middle of the hallway. Jake's hands rose to Anna's face and he again gazed into her eyes for a moment before saying, "Maybe we should continue this inside the room."

"Good idea."

Jake opened the door to their hotel room, and Anna ran inside and jumped onto the bed with two feet. Part of Jake wanted to forget everything else and jump into bed with her, but he knew that there was something more important he had to do first.

"You know what—I'm gonna go get us some ice and sodas from the machines now, because I have a feeling once we're comfortable in this room, I'm never gonna want to leave."

"Okay. But hurry back."

Jake left the room and raced down the hall, leaving the ice bucket next to the machine. He pressed the down button next to the elevator at the end of the hall, jumped inside when the doors opened, pressed the button marked "B," and rode down to the basement. Jake exited the elevator, walked down a short hallway, and through a door marked *Men's Locker Room*. The basement gym was just around the corner, but Jake was only interested in using his gym locker at the moment. He spun the dial of his combination lock, pulled it open, and placed the flash drive that Kelban had sent him into the locker, covering it with an old gray t-shirt. Jake thought that he had Kelban's note in his pocket as well, but he couldn't find it and figured that it was probably still behind the secret brick from his fire escape.

Jake took the elevator back up to the fifth floor, grabbed some ice and two bottles of Coke from the vending machine, and paused outside the door to his room for just a second to catch his breath. He entered the room and saw Anna standing in front of him topless, and wearing nothing else except for the sexiest pair of black lace panties Jake had ever seen. His mouth dropped open at the sight of Anna's slim, tan-line-free figure, and certain other parts of his body began to react as well. Anna smiled coyly and said, "What took you so long? I almost had to start without you."

"If I knew you'd be waiting here like that, I'd have been back much sooner."

"Well, now that you're back, get over here."

Jake dropped the sodas and ice bucket to the floor, pulled his shirt over his head as he strode toward Anna, picked her up, and flopped down onto the bed on top of her. As he began kissing her neck and running his hands all over her luxurious body, Jake's mind raced with thoughts—from the attempt on their lives earlier that night, to his plans for the following morning, to what he would do when he saw his family again. Despite everything else Jake was thinking, one thing kept repeating over and over in his head as he moved lower, kissing Anna's breasts and stomach. That thought, which reverberated through Jake's brain for the rest of the evening, was: *I could be going to jail tomorrow, so I might as well enjoy tonight.*

CHAPTER 35

Jake Hunter, Monday, 8:35a.m.

When Jake woke up the next morning, his first thought was that he never wanted to leave the hotel room. He was still holding Anna in his arms and, for the briefest of moments, he almost thought that everything else that had happened must have been a dream. But then the memories of the past three days came rushing back, and Jake frowned at the thought of just how real the situation was. It was time to turn himself in, straighten everything out, and let the FBI figure out how to protect him and Anna from the killers that were surely still searching for them.

Jake got out of bed and started getting dressed, which woke Anna from her slumber. She looked up at him and, with her voice still heavy from sleep, said, "I guess you're going to call the FBI soon, aren't you?"

"Yeah. I have to. Apparently they have an International Organized Crime Unit that is familiar with the kind of people we're dealing with. I'm going to call them and see if I can talk to an agent that's working on Kelban's murder case."

"Well, before you call them, how about grabbing us some breakfast while I jump in the shower? That way we can at least have a little bit more time together before they come get us and split us up."

Jake didn't want to stall too much longer, but Anna looked so convincing that he figured it would be okay to wait one more hour.

"All right. I'll go grab some breakfast sandwiches and juice from the deli downstairs. I'll be right back."

"Good. And, Jake, please be careful."

As Jake left the room, Anna got out of bed to take a shower. When he returned ten minutes later, the water was still running, so he put the bag with their breakfast down on a table and turned on the television to wait for her to get out. Jake sat down on the bed and received a stunning shock at the news playing out in front of him.

The house on the TV screen was his mother's house. The camera panned out, revealing a pretty, red-haired reporter, speaking into a microphone.

"Here in the normally peaceful town of Wantagh, Long Island, a grisly triple homicide and kidnapping took place last night."

Jake's mouth opened as if to scream, but all that came out was a low-pitched wailing sound. As Jake inched toward the television, reaching his hand up toward the screen, the reporter continued with the story.

"Many details are still unknown at the moment, but we do know that this was the childhood home of Jake Hunter, the New York City law student suspected of killing his boss, humanitarian attorney Michael Kelban, just a few days ago. Channel twelve has also been able to confirm that three FBI agents who had been guarding the Hunter home were brutally murdered sometime overnight. And it appears that Hunter's younger brother, eighteen-year-old Bret Hunter, was kidnapped. Mrs. Hunter was found unconscious and was taken to a nearby hospital, but appeared otherwise unharmed. It is unclear whether or not the events that took place here last night are connected to the murder of Michael Kelban, but law enforcement officials have stated that they are not ruling anything out at the present time."

The reporter glanced to her right and behind her, as a woman wearing a dark blue FBI windbreaker came walking down the driveway toward the street. With her cameraman following close behind, the reporter approached the FBI agent that she had learned earlier was Agent Charlene Stanton, who was working the Kelban murder.

"Agent Stanton, can you confirm whether or not what took place here last night is connected in any way to the murder of Michael Kelban?"

Speaking into the reporter's microphone and looking directly into the camera, Stanton responded, "At the present time, I can neither confirm nor deny any connection between the two events. However, if anyone has any knowledge as to the current whereabouts of Jake or Bret Hunter, I encourage you to please contact your local authorities or the FBI with any information. Thank you."

The reporter tried asking a follow-up question, but Stanton brushed her off and walked away. After a quick sign-off, the reporter's image disappeared from Jake's screen and was replaced by the in-studio anchors, promising an update on the weather and sports in their next segment.

Jake was sure that the Russian mafia had kidnapped his brother, and that they'd taken him because they knew that Jake had the flash drive. At first, Jake couldn't figure out how the Russians were planning on contacting him about exchanging the drive for his brother. But then he remembered that he'd taken his cell phone out of the secret hiding place in his apartment the night before.

Jake realized that he needed to check his voicemail messages right away, but couldn't risk doing so from the hotel room in case incoming calls to his cell phone were being traced. He scribbled a quick note of apology to Anna, who was still showering, saying that there was something he had to take care of alone. Jake then left the room, speed-walking out the front of the hotel to a set of pay phones standing in front of the underground parking garage located next door. Jake picked up one of the two available pay phones, inserted a quarter, and dialed his own cell phone number. Because his phone was turned off, the call went straight through to Jake's voicemail, and he quickly punched in the necessary code to retrieve his messages.

The first message was from Jake's mom. She was obviously crying and told Jake that she knew he didn't kill anyone and just wanted him to come home so that she would know he was safe. Her message had been left on Friday afternoon, and Jake was immediately overcome with guilt. He was so wrapped up in himself last night that he hadn't even tried to contact his family. And now Bret had been kidnapped, which might never have happened if Jake had called and told them to leave the house because it wasn't safe. Jake felt so strongly about wanting to contact his mother that he almost hung up the phone in order to call her. But he realized that the one thing working in his favor at the moment was that no one knew where he was. Plus, calling his mother might put her in danger. Jake was frustrated, but decided there was nothing he could do about contacting his family.

The second message began so abruptly that it took Jake a moment before he understood its importance. A bland, male voice spoke slowly, giving Jake instructions.

"Jake Hunter. I have your brother. You have something I want. Call me back at the following number: 917-555-1207. But only call from a pay phone. I will know if you try to trace the call or the number. If you ever want to see your brother alive again, do exactly as you've been instructed and don't even think about going to the authorities. After you've memorized the phone number to call, erase this message and get rid of your cell phone. Don't forget—do exactly as I say or your brother dies."

While the first voicemail had upset him, this message left Jake seething mad. He did not like hearing the threats against his brother, and felt as if the voice on the phone was mocking him, even though the caller sounded very calm and straightforward. Jake immediately deleted the message and hung up the phone. The phone number was seared into his memory as soon as he heard it. Jake had a photographic memory and once he pictured the number in his mind, there was no way he would forget it. Jake inserted a second quarter into the pay phone, dialed the number left by his brother's kidnapper, and waited anxiously for someone to pick up on the other end.

***

Sergei sat at his desk, reviewing video footage on his computer screen. Unlike the surveillance video from Kelban's office that he'd been watching several nights ago, these videos were of women. One of Sergei's highly profitable businesses involved the sale of women from his native country and its Eastern European neighbors. There were men in countries all over the world who were willing to pay top dollar for Sergei's "mail-order brides." Attractive, young, and poor, these girls were recruited with promises of a new life in America or elsewhere, and were instead sold and kept in line by threats to them and their families. Sergei was reviewing the videos to decide which women would bring the highest price, when a nearby phone began to ring. There was only one person who had been given the number to that line, so Sergei knew who the caller was.

"Hello, Jake."

"Where's my brother!" Jake was hardly able to contain his emotions as he spoke.

"He's fine. Although he did give one of my men a broken leg and another quite a headache before coming along quietly."

Jake's spirits lifted briefly at the thought of Bret hurting two members of the Russian mafia, but he remained focused on the task at hand.

"Yeah, well, I've got what you want. So, you let him go and I'll give it to you."

"As much as I'd like to trust you, Jake," Sergei responded, "that's just not possible. So here's how this is going to work—are you still in New York City?"

Jake hesitated, but somehow knew that the man on the other end of the phone would be able to tell if he was lying. So he told the truth.

"Yes."

"Good. On the northeast corner of Sixty-sixth Street and Central Park West there is a bench. At ten o'clock this morning, you will meet one of my men there and give him the flash drive in exchange for your brother."

"I'll be there."

"I know you will."

Then Jake heard a click, and the man on the other end of the phone was gone.

CHAPTER 36

Peter and Nicholas, Monday, 8:51a.m.

As Peter and Nicholas were keenly aware, patience is one of the most critical characteristics that a person must possess to be successful in the intelligence business. Fortunately, they were both extremely patient men. However, the people they worked for were not always willing to wait for results. The two men knew that time was a factor on their current assignment, but Hunter had vanished again, and they had no new leads to follow in their efforts to track him down. Still, Peter and Nicholas remained prepared for any scenario whereby they obtained information on Hunter's location. They were sitting in a plain white van, which contained various stick-on placards that could readily be applied to the sides of the vehicle to disguise its appearance. They also had several changes of clothing, and corresponding props, in the van that would allow them to access different buildings or locations, including police uniforms, exterminator outfits, and even prison jumpsuits.

When Peter's cell phone rang, he hoped that it would be one of their many underground contacts, calling with information that could help them find Hunter. But when he answered, Peter was mildly surprised to hear the voice of their current client—a voice he knew well from their time growing up together in Russia.

"Hello, Peter."

"I have to apologize," Peter replied. "We have nothing to report at the moment."

"Well, I have some news for you, and it includes Hunter's location."

"How did you find out where he is?"

"Just because you two are the best, doesn't mean you're the only ones I've got working for me."

"You have never been afraid to use multiple resources to achieve your objectives. I've always admired that about you. So, if you've found Hunter, how can we help with the rest of the mission?"

"For now, just get into position at the address I'll give you. And be ready to move on a moment's notice. I have a feeling things are about to start unfolding very quickly."

"We'll be there," Peter said, nodding at Nicholas to drive as he spoke. "And we'll be ready."

CHAPTER 37

Boris, Monday, 9:55a.m.

Whenever Boris visited New York City's Central Park, he was amazed at the level of restraint it must have taken to allow the prime stretch of midtown real estate to remain undeveloped in the modern age of constant expansion and growth at the expense of nature. Despite Manhattan's eight million residents and skyrocketing rents and real estate prices, the powers-that-be in the city realized that the Park provides a critical outlet for its inhabitants, whether they used it for exercising, attending concerts, or just lounging around on the Great Lawn.

On this particular summer morning, there were hundreds of runners and cyclists traversing the many paths inside Central Park. But Boris sat just outside the Park on a wrought-iron bench, facing the morning traffic on Central Park West and waiting for Hunter to arrive. Boris was not happy to be exposed in such an open, public location, but Sergei felt that Hunter would be more likely to show up if he believed that he was safe because the meeting was set in a public place in broad daylight. And Boris knew better than to question Sergei.

Sergei's plan was simple enough. Boris was wearing a tiny earpiece and wireless communicator through which he could speak to Ivan, who was parked around the corner on Sixty-fifth Street. When Hunter showed up, Boris would alert Ivan to come pick them up, subdue Hunter by whatever means necessary, get the flash drive, and leave with Hunter along for the ride. At that point, Boris would insert the drive into a laptop to confirm its authenticity, and the Russians would head to a more private location where they would torture Hunter to ensure that there were no copies and that he hadn't told anyone else about the flash drive or the information it contained. Once Sergei was sure that they had the only copy, poor Mrs. Hunter would never see either of her sons again.

It was just about ten o'clock, when a disheveled homeless man staggered up to Boris and asked, "Can you spare some change, man?"

Boris, clearly annoyed at the distraction, responded gruffly, "That's the third time you've asked me for change in the last ten minutes."

"I know. That's because you haven't given me any yet."

"Get out of here, you lousy bum."

"Man, no one appreciates a good sense of humor anymore. C'mon, can't you help out a brother who's down on his luck?"

"I said, get out of here before I call the cops."

Boris checked his watch as he spoke. It was now five minutes after ten and he began to wonder whether Hunter was going to show up.

"Oh yeah right," the intrusive homeless man continued, "you're gonna call the cops on me. Are you gonna tell them 'bout how you kidnapped that kid and killed that lawyer when they get here?"

Boris cocked his head sharply toward the man in front of him and, for the first time, truly examined his face.

"Where is Jake Hunter?" Boris asked quietly, his voice barely containing his seething rage.

"You need to forget about where is Jake Hunter, and tell me where is Jake Hunter's little brother. You give me the little brother, we walk out of here, and I'll tell you where you can find your computer drive thingamajig."

"Jake Hunter's little brother is not here, and if you don't tell me where Jake Hunter is, I will kill you right here in the street."

"Well, seems to me you've made two mistakes. First, why isn't Jake's brother here like he's supposed to be?"

As he said this, Ollie flailed his arms up in the air, as if exaggerating the question. Oddly, he kept raising his arms up and down in this manner while he continued speaking.

"That was the deal, right—bring Jake's brother in exchange for the drive? Well, you can't make an exchange if you don't bring what you were supposed to trade. So not bringing Jake's brother, that's your first mistake.

"And your second mistake," Ollie turned away from Boris as he spoke, but continued waving his arms, "is thinking that you can kill a man in the middle of a busy New York City street and get away with it."

Boris was about to ask this clearly insane friend of Hunter's why he felt the need to keep flapping his arms up and down like some kind of deranged bird, when he realized that the man wasn't crazy at all. He was signaling to someone, and Boris knew who the signal was meant for—Hunter was nearby. As Boris reached beneath his coat with his right hand, he began speaking to Ivan, who was listening over the communicator.

"Ivan, Hunter is not coming to meet me, but he is close. Keep your eyes open for him."

Turning his attention back to Ollie, Boris spoke in a softer, more congenial tone.

"Excuse me, my friend, there's something I have to tell you."

"What do you want?" Ollie said as he turned and looked scornfully over his shoulder at the still-seated Russian. "Now you got something to say to me?"

"Yes, I do," Boris answered with a sneer. "You told me that I made two mistakes. Well, you have made a mistake too. A very big mistake."

As he spoke, Boris pulled a gun out from beneath his coat, and his lips curled into a cruel smile.

CHAPTER 38

Jake Hunter, Monday, 10:12a.m.

On the northwest corner of Sixty-fifth Street and Central Park West, Jake stood across the street and one block down from the bench where Boris sat. Jake watched Ollie approach Boris several times and speak to him briefly, with the big Russian repeatedly brushing him off while glancing from side to side expectantly. On Ollie's third approach, Boris's head snapped up, and he stared hard at Ollie as they engaged in a lengthier discourse. Suddenly, Ollie threw his arms up into the air and began waving them in an almost frantic display.

Jake's heart sank as he saw the signal that he and Ollie had agreed that Ollie would use to alert Jake that his brother was not present. Jake hadn't had much time that morning to come up with a plan to ensure both his own and his brother's safety, but he'd remembered Ollie's offer to help him, and they had figured out a scheme that would enable Ollie to warn Jake if the Russians reneged on their promise to bring Bret with them to trade for the flash drive.

As Jake watched Ollie begin to flail his arms, he understood the signal immediately, but Ollie, in an effort to make sure that Jake could see him, continued flapping his arms as he talked to Boris. After a few seconds, Jake began to worry that Boris would realize that Ollie was signaling and figure out that Jake was watching their interaction from somewhere nearby.

Jake's concern for himself quickly dissipated as he observed Boris's actions. Jake saw Boris reach beneath his coat and surreptitiously pull out a gun, with what looked like a long, thin extension added on to the end of the barrel. With the noise from the early morning traffic and the silencer on the gun, Jake could not hear the shots as they were fired into Ollie's midsection. But he did see the two flashes of light emitted from the end of the gun and Ollie's body lurching backwards twice before crumpling to the ground. Jake's eyes widened and he reflexively took a step toward the street in Ollie's direction, but then he saw Boris rise and begin to move toward him, scanning the surrounding area as he hastily distanced himself from Ollie's twitching body.

Jake turned around and forced himself to walk away from the horrifying scene on the other side of Central Park West. He was traveling west on Sixty-fifth Street, in the opposite direction of the vehicular traffic crawling down the one-way street. A car that was parked on the same side of the road that Jake was walking on started its engine, catching Jake's attention and causing him to look over at the driver. At the same moment, the driver happened to be closely examining the people walking by, and the two men locked eyes.

Jake and Ivan immediately recognized each other, having crossed paths before as Ivan had chased Jake and Anna through the apartment building on Sixty-third Street less than twenty-four hours earlier.

"Hunter!" Ivan yelled, pushing open the car door while turning off the ignition.

Jake took off, sprinting west on Sixty-fifth Street as Ivan yelled to Boris through the wireless communicator.

"Hunter's here! He's heading west on Sixty-fifth."

Boris was still on the far side of Central Park West, too far away to catch Jake, and unwilling to start running down the street less than a block away from a man he'd just killed. But Ivan was only about ten yards behind Jake, although he was losing ground to his quicker, younger prey.

Jake's legs were pumping hard as he reached Columbus Avenue, where he began to dart across the wide city street, attempting to reach the entrance to the uptown subway line. As he ran from the sidewalk into the road, the traffic heading downtown had a green light, and Jake found himself directly in the path of a white van, which was screeching toward him as the driver slammed on his brakes. Jake extended his arms in front of him and his hands hit the hood of the van just as it was coming to a stop. The impact knocked Jake slightly to the side, but he quickly regained his balance. A brief look over his shoulder told Jake that Ivan had reached the corner and was about to enter the street just a few paces behind him. The driver of the van was screaming obscenities, but Jake did not hear them as he ducked his head around the passenger side of the van, saw a break in the traffic pattern, and ran across the remaining two lanes and onto the sidewalk.

Jake took the steps two at a time down the entrance to the subway. His escape plan if he was spotted while watching Ollie was to enter this subway station because Jake felt that there was no better place to get lost in a crowd in New York City. He also knew that the subway station at Sixty-sixth Street had several tunnels leading to exits on Sixty-fifth, Sixty-third, and Sixty-second Streets, including one right in front of Jake's law school at Fordham.

As he ran down the stairs, Jake decided that if a train was arriving or already stopped at the station, he would board it only if he was certain that Ivan would not have time to get on as well. If there was no train, Jake figured he would have to lose Ivan somewhere in the underground tunnels. As he hit the bottom step, Jake could see that a train was pulling to a stop in the station. He yanked his Metrocard from his back pocket as the train doors opened, knowing that he would have just enough time to board the train before the doors closed, and that Ivan would not make it in time to catch him. Jake swiped his Metrocard, pushed through the turnstile, and boarded the train as the doors began to slide shut. He saw Ivan at the foot of the stairs several feet away and breathed a sigh of relief.

Just as the subway doors were on the verge of closing, they snapped back open, and the train conductor's voice rang out over the public announcement system.

"Please do not hold the doors in the back of the train."

Jake could not believe his bad luck. Some passengers were holding the doors open to allow their friends or family to catch the train. Unknown to them, these passengers were also putting Jake's life in danger. Ivan saw Jake enter the train and the Russian ran at top speed straight into the turnstile, which stopped him, but only for a second. The subway doors finally began closing again just as Ivan jumped over the turnstile and jammed his right arm between the nearly-closed doors, stretching out his fingers mere inches from Jake's face.

Jake knew that when passengers prevented the subway doors from closing, the conductors always reopened them—but usually only for a moment. Still, if a passenger wanted on badly enough, getting an arm in the door would give him enough time to push the doors open and get on once the conductor opened them, no matter how quickly they were closed again. And Jake had a strong feeling that Ivan wanted to get on his train badly enough.

When the bell rang, signaling that the doors would briefly reopen a moment later, Jake reached out and grabbed Ivan's hand by the fingers and the wrist. Just as the doors were about to open, Jake lunged his face forward and sunk his teeth deep into the meaty part of the hand directly beneath Ivan's thumb. The subway doors opened and Ivan reflexively yanked his arm backwards, howling in pain. As the doors closed, Jake spat out the small piece of Ivan's hand that he'd bitten off onto the platform floor, next to a wailing Ivan. The train began to move, and Ivan composed himself and reached out toward the doors, but he was too late. Jake had gotten away from him again.

The next stop on Jake's train was at Seventy-second Street. The other passengers in the subway car were shooting him strange and dirty looks following his assault on Ivan but, in typical New York fashion, no one actually said anything to him. Jake thought it was best to get out at the Seventy-second Street stop, where he transferred onto a downtown express train. After exiting at Forty-second Street, he walked uptown for fifteen blocks on Eighth Avenue, passing a wide variety of strip clubs and peep-show rooms. Jake initially found it strange that this stretch of seedy clubs was located just a block away from the tourist central of Times Square. But he soon figured out that setting up these shops so close to the city's biggest tourist attraction made perfect sense after all.

Jake realized that he was only thinking about strip clubs and tourists because he couldn't bring himself to think about what he'd just seen happen to Ollie. Or about the fact that the men who had kidnapped his brother hadn't kept their promise to return him and, even worse, there was no doubt that these men were cold-blooded killers. Jake shuddered involuntarily as he approached the entrance to the Holiday Inn. The hotel reminded him of Anna.

At first, Jake hoped that Anna had already left the hotel. When he'd departed early in the morning to find Ollie and set up his plan for the meeting with the Russians, Jake hadn't known what to say to her. Returning to the hotel, Jake again struggled with how much to tell Anna about what had just happened if she was still there. But Jake wanted nothing more than to unburden himself of everything that had been happening to him, and he thought that if he could tell Anna about his brother, and Ollie, and the stupid flash drive, she could hold him and whisper that everything would be all right, like it had seemed with her the night before. Yet as Jake entered the elevator to head up to the fifth floor, he decided that he would not say anything to Anna about the day's terrible events. The more she knew, the more danger she would be in. Enough people had been hurt already, and Jake didn't want to risk losing her too. If she was still at the hotel, he would make up some excuse about running into a friend when he went down to get breakfast.

Jake slid his key card into the door and the lock clicked open. He pushed the door inward and entered the room. The curtains were closed, the lights were turned off, and it took a few seconds before his eyes acclimated to the darkness. When they did adjust, Jake couldn't believe what he saw. Anna was sitting in front of him in a chair, her ankles bound, her mouth covered with tape, and her arms pulled behind the back of the chair, tied at the wrist. Jake could barely make out the traces of tears running down Anna's cheeks. As he took a couple of quick steps forward to untie her and find out who had done this, he noticed the man to his right, sitting on the edge of the bed and holding a gun, which was aimed directly at Jake's heart.

CHAPTER 39

Jake Hunter, Monday, 10:32a.m.

"Who are you?" Jake angrily asked the sloppy looking stranger, who was wearing the same Hawaiian print, short-sleeve, button-down shirt he'd been wearing when Jake had seen him at the Port Authority the day before. The top two buttons of the shirt were undone, revealing a large tuft of curly, black chest hair, and the man was nearly bald, yet had still vainly attempted to comb his few remaining strands of hair across his shiny pate. Jake could barely control his emotions after the disastrous and harrowing morning he'd just experienced, and if not for the gun pointing at him, surely would have attacked the thug who had tied up Anna.

"I'll ask the questions here, kid. Now where's the mini hard drive?"

Jake wasn't surprised by the request, but could not determine who his latest pursuer was possibly working for. The man spoke with a thick New Jersey accent, and did not have the look or the clothes of a member of the Russian mafia. Jake wondered who else besides the Russians could possibly be searching for the flash drive.

"It's not here," Jake lied, stalling for time and hoping to get a clue from the stranger with the gun as to who had hired him.

"Wrong answer, Jake. I'm only gonna ask you one more time and then your girlfriend over here is gonna have a new hole in her body for you to explore. Now, where is the drive?"

Jake shot a quick glance at Anna and could see how frightened she was, but the flash drive was his only hope of getting his brother back, and he couldn't risk giving it to this man and sealing his brother's fate. Jake decided to tell the gunman the truth in the hope that he might understand Jake's dilemma and not hurt Anna.

"I can't give the drive to you. My brother's been kidnapped and I need to trade it to get him back."

The man cocked his head slightly to the side, considering Jake's story, and Jake grew hopeful that he would let them go. But instead, the gunman pursed his lips, shrugged his shoulders, and responded, "Fine, have it your way."

The stranger turned his gun away from Jake and pointed it at Anna. The tape over her mouth prevented her from talking, but Anna's eyes spoke to Jake, pleading with him to do something. Tears streaked down her face and she strained against her bindings as the man cocked his gun. Jake saw Anna push her toes into the floor, trying to lean back in the chair and propel herself away from the gunman. But she was too late.

As Jake stared helplessly at Anna, he heard the near-deafening explosion of the gunshot, in stark contrast to the silent bullets that had been fired into Ollie's body an hour earlier. But the effect was the same. Anna's chair toppled over backwards from the impact and she let out a scream, muffled by the tape covering her mouth.

The sound of the gunshot and the sight of Anna tumbling over in the chair snapped something inside of Jake. Although he was unarmed, he began charging toward the stranger, who still held his gun and clearly was not afraid to use it. The man did not expect Jake's aggressive and immediate reaction, and his half-second hesitation before swinging the gun back toward Jake gave

Jake enough time to rear back and throw a vicious punch into the gunman's jaw, knocking him sideways off the bed, stunned.

Jake lunged forward and grabbed the man's right arm near the wrist, as he was still holding the gun in his right hand. Jake began ferociously slamming the stranger's arm against the thick, wooden leg of the chair, to which Anna was still tied, her feet hanging limply between the chair's legs. Jake heard a cracking sound and, though he was unsure whether it was the chair leg or the man's arm, the gun dropped to the floor. Jake quickly picked it up and tossed it across the room.

The gunman was sprawled out on the floor, holding his broken wrist, which was swelling almost as rapidly as the left side of his face. Jake turned around and grabbed a metal lamp off the dresser behind him, yanking the plug from the outlet, and held it over the stranger, ready to swing. As much as Jake wanted to hurt the man, he needed information more.

"Who sent you? Who are you working for?"

"I don't know," the man mumbled painfully as he lifted his good arm to try and block Jake from hitting him with the lamp.

"Wrong answer," Jake mimicked the gunman, his rage clearly visible in both his tone and his posture. "I'm only gonna ask you one more time, who are you working for?"

"I swear, I don't know. If I knew, I'd tell you."

"Fine, have it your way."

Jake swung the lamp, delivering a knockout blow to the side of the stranger's head. But as soon as he had done so, Jake's arms fell limp in front of him, and the lamp slipped through his fingers and dropped softly to the floor. No matter how much anger Jake had toward this man, he didn't want to kill him, because killing an unarmed and wounded man would mean that Jake was no better than the man he was attacking. When Jake leaned closer and saw that despite the man's sagging posture, he was still breathing, Jake found himself feeling slightly relieved.

Jake moved toward Anna's prone body and noticed that she too was still breathing. As he began to pull the tape from her mouth, there was a loud banging on the door of the hotel room. Realizing that someone must have heard the gunshot and called the hotel manager, Jake was about to yell, *Just a minute,* when he heard a voice from outside the room shout, "FBI, open the door!"

CHAPTER 40

Agent Stanton, Monday, 10:33a.m.

Stanton's source hadn't been surprised to hear that Hunter was still alive. In fact, after delivering what she'd assumed was relatively secret information the night before, Stanton was the one who received a shocking phone call the next morning, during which she was provided with information about Hunter's location. After hanging up the phone, Stanton called Zarvas, told him to pick her up in fifteen minutes, then quickly dressed and went down to the street to wait for his arrival. A few minutes later, Zarvas pulled up to the curb, Stanton got into his car, and they went to verify the tip.

The two agents were standing in the lobby of the Holiday Inn on West Fifty-seventh Street talking to the hotel manager and reviewing a list of guests, when a porter came running up to them, clearly agitated.

"Mr. Windwer, sir," began the nearly breathless young employee, wearing a nametag identifying him as *Adam,* "I just heard something that sounded like a gunshot on the fifth floor!"

"What room number did you hear the shot coming from?" Zarvas demanded.

"I think it came from room five fourteen."

Zarvas waved for the manager to come with them as he nodded at Stanton and said, "Let's go."

Outside of room five fourteen less than a minute later, Zarvas banged on the door and announced their presence. When there was no response after a few seconds, Stanton instructed the manager to insert his key card, unlocking the door. She then motioned to him to step aside, pressed down on the door's handle, and swung it open, while standing with her back against the wall directly next to the door. Stanton spun into the doorway with her gun drawn and entered the room, with Zarvas following close behind. Stanton covered her partner as he pushed open the bathroom door, quickly scanned the room, and announced that it was, "Clear."

Stanton entered the main section of the hotel room and couldn't help but be confused by what she saw there. Expecting to find Hunter, Stanton instead found herself staring at an unconscious man with a bloody wound on his head and a swollen right wrist. On the ground a few steps away from the man, bound to a toppled-over chair, was a young, thin, attractive blond girl, who had been crying and also appeared to be either unconscious or in shock. Stanton's first thought was that the information she'd been given was wrong and that Hunter had never been here at all. But then she noticed the curtains flapping in the breeze coming through an open window.

Stanton ran to the window, pulled the curtain aside, and peered out. The fire escape extended down to the second floor, but she noted that the ladder from the second floor landing had been lowered to street level. Stanton scanned the street below but did not see anyone matching Hunter's description. She was confident that they would find Hunter's fingerprints in the hotel room and on the fire escape, but proof that he'd been in the room was of little use, and she grimaced at the thought that they had narrowly missed catching Hunter yet again.

While Stanton arranged to have additional agents and NYPD search the area surrounding the hotel for Hunter, Zarvas called for an ambulance. He then knelt down to untie the young woman, who seemed to be in shock. Unsure of what else he could do to help her, Zarvas turned to Stanton and asked, "What do you make of this situation?"

"I don't know. The longer this case goes on, the stranger it gets. At this point, it's hard to say exactly what Hunter is involved in. Hopefully, after we get them to the hospital, these two can give us some answers."

"One good question to start off with is—whose gun is that on the floor over there?"

Before Stanton could hazard a guess, two emergency medical technicians rushed into the room, rolling a portable hospital gurney. One immediately knelt down next to the injured man, checked his pulse, and pulled open his eyelids, shining a flashlight into each eye. The second EMT set up the gurney on the floor next to the young woman, and then turned back to the first and asked, "How is he?"

"He's unconscious, but stable. We're gonna take the girl down first. Excuse me, agent, could you help us lift her onto the gurney?"

Zarvas broke away from Stanton, who continued bagging the gun and searching the remainder of the room. He helped the technicians gently lift the woman onto the gurney, which the first EMT then adjusted to waist height and began wheeling toward the door. The second turned to Zarvas and said, "We've got to get her out of here. Another team will be right up for the other guy. Thanks for your help."

After the EMTs left the room, Zarvas said to Stanton, "Those guys got here really fast, didn't they?"

"Yeah," Stanton responded. "There's a hospital a couple of blocks from here. I guess they were right in the neighborhood."

About ten minutes later, a second set of EMTs arrived and began tending to the man with the head and wrist injuries, who started coming to as he was loaded on and strapped to the gurney. The FBI's forensics team also showed up, and Stanton and Zarvas decided to leave the techs to process the scene while they went to the hospital to question the two strangers they'd found in what they believed to be Jake Hunter's hotel room.

On the drive to the hospital, Stanton flipped through the injured man's wallet. She was surprised at what she found and filled in Zarvas on the interesting new twist.

"The guy is a private investigator from Paramus, New Jersey. His name is Santo Alampi. Would someone have hired a PI to find Hunter?"

"It's possible. But who? And where does the girl fit in?"

"Not sure. She didn't have any ID on her, and I couldn't find anything in the room with her name on it. That's the problem with this case—we've got too many questions and not enough answers."

When they arrived at the hospital's emergency room, the agents located the attending physician, who briefed them on one of their interview subjects.

"Mr. Alampi is awake. He's got a fractured wrist and quite a headache, but you can see him now."

"What about the young woman who came in around the same time as Mr. Alampi? Is she okay?" asked Stanton.

"I haven't treated any young woman. Perhaps one of the other doctors saw her."

Zarvas went off to find the girl, while Stanton went into Alampi's room and began interviewing him.

"Mr. Alampi, what were you doing in that hotel room?"

Grimacing, and looking utterly miserable, Alampi answered, "It was supposed to be some kind of half recovery of stolen property, half scare tactic job. I was hired to go to the hotel room, tie up the girl, wait for the kid, and ask him for some kind of mini computer drive. If he didn't give it to me, I'm supposed to act like I'm gonna shoot the girl. I was a little suspicious, but it was ten grand for a couple of hours work. That's not an offer I could afford to turn down. Some scare it turned out to be—the kid ends up going nuts and attacking me."

"So who hired you?"

"I honestly don't know. I got a phone call in my office early this morning. I had slept there last night—things ain't so good with the missus these days—and somebody disguising their voice asks me if I want to make a quick ten grand. Says all I gotta do is take a ride over the GWB and scare a couple of kids in some hotel and get the drive back. I figured it was one of the kids' parents, and the kids stole the thing and ran away or something. The caller told me to drive to the Holiday Inn, and that there would be a package waiting for me at the front desk with my money in it, but there were strict instructions that the hotel would not let me have the package until I showed them the drive I was supposed to get back. I figured, how hard could it be."

"What about the girl?"

"I don't know anything about her either. When I got to the hotel room, she was already tied up with her mouth taped. She looked like she'd been crying, so I told her not to worry, that I was just waiting for her boyfriend so I could get back something he'd stolen, and that once he gave it back, everything would be fine. I thought that made her feel better, but she got real upset again when the kid got back."

"So what exactly happened when the kid came back to the room."

"I did just like I was supposed to—I asked him for the hard drive, threatened the girl, and when he said he wouldn't give it to me, I pretended to shoot her. That's when the kid went nuts."

"Wait a second, what do you mean you *pretended* to shoot the girl? We found her at the scene and she was hurt."

"Maybe she hurt herself when her chair tipped over. All I know is, there's no way I could have hurt anything other than her eardrums."

"How do you know that?"

"Because my gun was loaded with blanks. I was only hired to scare the kids, remember? I'm sure your forensics people are checking my gun out right now. Why don't you give them a call."

Stanton didn't believe all the details of Alampi's story, like the part about being hired by a mystery caller. But even if he did know who had paid him to get the flash drive, he wasn't going to give up his client's name, and Stanton knew that pressing him for it would be a waste of time. One thing she was sure of was that the Russians would never use a second-rate private investigator to muscle Hunter if they knew his location. But whoever had hired Alampi clearly knew where Hunter could be found. Stanton hoped that her partner's interview with the girl had provided more answers than her session with Alampi.

She found Zarvas on the phone by the hospital's admitting desk. He appeared frustrated, and as he hung up the phone, Stanton asked him, "How'd it go with the girl? Did you find out anything useful?"

"Stanton," Zarvas answered in a strained and serious tone, "that girl never arrived at this hospital. I've checked every other hospital in the area and she's not at any of them. I just hung up with the ambulance response unit. Only one set of EMTs was dispatched to our scene. The guys who took the girl were not real technicians. She's gone."

CHAPTER 41

Sergei Ilanov, Monday, 12:45p.m.

It had not been a good morning for Sergei. He'd expected Boris and Ivan to confirm that they had captured Hunter pursuant to his plan. Instead, they reported that Hunter had managed to escape yet again. Although their story of the morning's events with the homeless man and the chase into the subway station was disappointing to Sergei, he did find some perverse pleasure in hearing that Hunter had bitten off part of Ivan's hand.

Sergei also was informed by his sources within the FBI of some interesting details about the search for Hunter at the Holiday Inn. He was intrigued by this situation, especially the disappearance of the young woman. Sergei was far more concerned, however, by the fact that there was someone else, other than himself and the authorities, who was trying to locate Hunter. Sergei was convinced that anyone chasing Hunter was doing so to get at the information that could incriminate him.

Despite the likelihood that an unknown party was somehow involved in the search for Hunter, Sergei remained optimistic. After all, he still had Hunter's brother, and Hunter had no choice but to contact Sergei if he ever wanted to see his sibling alive again.

A couple of hours after the feds missed catching Hunter at the Holiday Inn, the phone line that Sergei had set up solely for him began ringing. Sergei purposely let the phone ring several times in order to demonstrate that he was not anxiously awaiting Hunter's call. When he finally picked up the receiver, Sergei could not stop himself from mocking Hunter's pain.

"Mr. Hunter, so good of you to call. I hear it's been a bad day for some friends of yours. I can't say that I'm sorry about that, since you are the one who got them involved in the first place."

If Hunter was angered by Sergei's taunting, his voice didn't show it. Instead, his tone was calm and clear as he responded, "I have what you want. It's in an envelope addressed to the FBI. If anything happens to me, or my brother, that's where it's going to be sent. Based on this morning, I obviously can't trust you to set up a meeting. So here's how it's going to work. I will give you the flash drive in exchange for my brother tonight at ten p.m. I will be in Atlantic City at the Hilton Hotel and Casino playing blackjack. Have one of your goons bring my brother to the blackjack table that I'm playing at. My brother sits down at the table with me, and I give your guy the drive. After that, I turn myself in to the cops, telling them nothing except that I didn't kill anyone, but got scared so I ran and hid out for a few days. You'll have what you want, and you can stay away from me and my family. This plan is not negotiable. I'll see your man with my brother tonight at ten o'clock."

This time, Sergei was left holding the phone after listening to the click of Hunter hanging up on him. Although he was surprised at Hunter's confident tone, Sergei was quite pleased by Hunter's plan because he loved Atlantic City. He had an ownership interest in two casinos and frequented them several times a year, but it had been a few months since his last visit. On this trip, Sergei would recover the flash drive and his empire would be secure. Sometime shortly thereafter, he would have Hunter brought to him, and would make Hunter suffer for the irritation he'd caused over the last four days.

Sergei picked up a different telephone and pressed a single digit. After one ring, Boris answered.

"Yes, boss?"

"Book us a suite at the Hilton Hotel in Atlantic City for tonight. Get Ivan and Hunter's brother and arrange a car service to drive you to the hotel. Once you arrive, have the driver park in front and await further instructions. I will meet you there later tonight around eight o'clock. Understood?"

"Yes, boss. We will be there."

While Boris was calling the Atlantic City Hilton to reserve a suite under the name of one of the many shell corporations that Sergei and Kelban had set up for business purposes, Sergei dialed the Hilton's reservation line as well. Using a false name, he booked himself an ordinary room at the hotel, which no one else would know about—not even Boris. Depending on how things played out with Hunter, Sergei wanted to be prepared to depart Atlantic City on a moment's notice, and would leave his trusted comrades behind if necessary. Though he may not have been particularly loyal, Sergei was always cautious. And he was not about to have his carefully crafted empire brought down by some would-be lawyer whose good fortune up to this point was bound to come to an end. If Sergei was right about how the evening was about to unfold, Hunter's luck would indeed be running out very soon.

CHAPTER 42

Jesse Halpern, Monday, 12:58p.m.

Jesse was nervous. Actually, nervous was an understatement—Jesse was scared. Since the first day he started working with Alampi, the private investigator had been in control of every situation. He always seemed to know the right things to do and say to avoid trouble. One time, Jesse saw Alampi get attacked by a much larger man after taking some compromising photos that ultimately led to the man's divorce. Alampi had easily subdued the man before the guy even landed a punch. But Alampi just called Jesse from the hospital with a broken wrist and stitches in his head, even though he'd said earlier that it would be no trouble getting the flash drive from Hunter.

Despite Alampi's injuries, he sounded okay on the phone, and his boss being hurt was not the cause of Jesse's fear. Alampi told him that the client on the Hunter case would be calling the office, and that Jesse would have to take the call and explain that Alampi hadn't been able to get what the client wanted. Jesse was not a big fan of interacting with people in general—he much preferred interfacing through his computer—but he was especially not looking forward to dealing with a possibly angry client. After staring at the office phone for nearly an hour, when it finally rang, Jesse jumped backwards, startled by the sound. But he knew that he had to help his boss and so, hand trembling, Jesse answered the phone.

"Hello."

"Where's Alampi?" the client's harsh voice came across the line.

"He's, uh, he's in the hospital," Jesse stammered. "He, um, he wanted me to tell you that he tried to scare Hunter, but when he pretended to shoot the girl, Hunter attacked him and hit him over the head with a lamp, and now he has a broken wrist and stitches in his head. And he's really sorry, and we'll keep trying to find Hunter for you, and I'm supposed to ask if there's anything I can do until he gets out of the hospital."

Jesse found it easier to get out all the information he was supposed to relay in one long, rambling speech, rather than trying to explain it in pieces. Now that he'd said everything, he exhaled, feeling only slightly better, and anticipating the client's angry response. Jesse was pleasantly surprised when the client spoke in a calm, measured tone.

"Well, that's rather unfortunate news. I'm afraid my time to find Hunter is running short. But, actually, there are two things you can do for me while Mr. Alampi is recuperating. You're the computer genius, right?"

"Um, yeah, I guess so."

"Do you have access to an aging program, one that can show various samples of what a person might look like after a certain number of years have gone by?"

"Yes. But, um, hasn't Hunter only been gone for a few days?"

"I don't need you to run the aging program for Hunter," the client snapped. "I'll e-mail you a photo of someone else that I want you to run through the program."

"Okay," Jesse said sheepishly. "What's the second thing you want me to do?"

"I need you to run another detailed search on Hunter's potential locations, places he's visited frequently, phone calls he's made and received—anything that might indicate where he is or where he could be heading. I'll call you back in half an hour for an update."

"Do you want me to run any aliases for Hunter this time?"

A few moments passed in silence, and Jesse was about to check that the client had heard him, when he got his response.

"Just one."

CHAPTER 43

Jake Hunter, Monday, 1:01p.m.

Jake hung up the pay phone he was using in a secluded corner of the Port Authority, put his right hand to his forehead, covering his eyes, and exhaled deeply. He knew that he'd been on the line with a very dangerous individual, and Jake hoped that his plan would work. More importantly, he prayed that his brother was unharmed and would be completely safe by later that evening. After fighting his nerves in order to remain composed throughout the call, Jake collected himself and walked over to the platform where his bus to Atlantic City was waiting. Of the fifteen passengers already on the bus at one o'clock on a Monday afternoon, fourteen were women over the age of sixty, and the other was a man in his seventies surveying the rest of the passengers like a lion stalking his prey in the jungle. When Jake boarded the bus, the older man scowled, considering him competition for the ladies' attention. But the elderly gentleman was pleased when Jake took a seat in the last row of the bus, far away from most of the other travelers.

After scurrying down a fire escape to narrowly elude the authorities for the second time in the past four days, Jake had ridden a downtown subway train into the East Village. From the moment he'd called the number left on his voicemail and listened to the man who answered the phone order the exchange outside Central Park, Jake had been working on his own backup plan. He expected to be double-crossed by a group of people who had already killed his mentor, set him up for the murder, and then kidnapped his younger brother. Even now that he was going to meet the Russians on his terms, Jake knew that he would have just one chance to succeed—and would be lucky to survive the encounter. When he was deciding where to set up the meeting in a public, well-populated location, Jake figured that since a good deal of luck was necessary, there was no better place to go than Atlantic City.

As Jake sat in his seat in the back of the bus, out of the view of the other passengers, he went through his bag, taking out and examining some of the items he'd purchased while he was down in the Village. First, he pulled out a set of handcuffs and the small metal key that unlocked them. Jake practiced deceptively pulling the cuffs out of his pants pocket with his right hand and then quickly slapping them down over his left wrist. After several tries, he was able to operate the handcuffs rather smoothly, and he placed the cuffs and the key back into his right front pocket.

Next, Jake pulled a fake driver's license out of his bag. The phony ID probably wouldn't fool the cops, or even a bouncer at a high end New York City nightclub, but Jake was sure that it would be good enough for a hotel desk clerk, especially when the room and deposit were being paid for up front in cash. If necessary, he would throw in a couple of extra twenties to ensure that the clerk would look the other way regarding Jake's failure to provide a credit card upon check-in.

Jake had been distracted—going over his plan in his mind—while the fake ID-maker, an overweight man in his late twenties with multiple piercings and bad skin, was taking his picture. Speaking with a slight lisp, probably due to a recent tongue-piercing, the man asked Jake, "Hey, man, what do you want your name to be?"

Jake answered with the first phony name that popped into his head, "Jack Mellencamp."

Looking at the name on his fake license reminded Jake of Anna. Specifically, he thought about her eyes, filled with fear and begging him to help her. Jake was forced to leave the hotel room when the FBI had shown up, knocking on the door. He hadn't had much of a chance to check on her, and had no idea if she was okay, or even alive. Wondering about Anna led Jake to think about his brother, Bret, and all the other people who had been hurt because of whatever incriminating information was on the flash drive. One question kept repeating itself in Jake's mind—why was the damn thing worth so much?

Jake knew that whatever was on the drive, he needed to move it to a secure location—somewhere safer than his locker outside the Holiday Inn's basement gym. When he was trying to figure out who he could trust to hold on to it for him, Jake first thought about his close friends like Jason, who had helped him get out of the city and had lied to protect him, and Ollie, who had risked—and lost—his life helping Jake. But Jake didn't want to involve his friends any further and, truth be told, there was only one person he felt he could turn to that would make sure the information got to the right people if anything happened to him or Bret, and Jake hadn't seen that person in almost fifteen years.

Three years earlier, at Jake's college graduation, someone took a picture of Jake and his best friends during the commencement speech. Because it was their last weekend in college, they'd been awake for the seventy-two hours prior to the graduation ceremony, partying and celebrating the fact that they'd all managed to pass the classes they needed to graduate. During the droning oration, one by one, Jake and all of his friends passed out in various positions in the uncomfortable folding chairs, with their heads occasionally bobbing and waking them, only to fall back asleep moments later. The picture of the dozing group provided a humorous memory, but another event that occurred at graduation left Jake with a far more serious recollection.

When the keynote speaker finally finished talking, everyone woke up long enough to toss their caps into the air and take some pictures with their families. As Jake and his friends posed for photos in the middle of the main campus, he noticed a man standing by himself beside a nearby tree. Jake wasn't sure at first but, after a while, he became certain that the man was watching him. Jake's mom decided to walk his grandmother back to the car, and they made a plan to meet up with Jake back at his house off campus. The rest of Jake's friends soon scattered with their families, and Jake approached the man.

"Do I know you?"

"You're Jake Hunter, right?"

"Yes. How do you know who I am?"

"It's kind of a long story, Jake. So I'll give you the abridged version. I'm from the Midwest. Where exactly isn't important. A long time ago, I was married to a beautiful woman, had two amazing daughters, and worked hard to provide for my family. One day, my wife left me for another man—a wealthy man—and she made up certain lies about how I treated her to keep me from seeing my kids. Needless to say, I was devastated, and I soon developed a drinking problem.

"A while back," the man continued, "another single guy moved in next door. We became friends, but neither one of us spoke very much about our past. One night last year, on my older daughter's birthday, my wife wouldn't let me speak to her on the phone. I went on a drinking binge and started throwing things around my house in anger. That's when my neighbor came over to try to calm me down. I told him I didn't want to hear it because he didn't know what it was like to not be able to talk to his kids. You know what he said to me then?"

"What?" Jake asked, growing more and more curious at the man's strange story.

"He said that he hadn't spoken to his kids for fifteen years. And they didn't even know that he was alive. You see, he'd been forced to go into the witness protection program because he testified against these two Italian brothers, who were big-time mafia bosses back in the 1980s. My neighbor was a large man, and he'd been a star athlete in his younger days. But his dream was to open a successful restaurant, and he borrowed some money from the brothers to buy a place. When the restaurant failed and my neighbor couldn't pay back the money he'd borrowed, they decided to put him to work until he paid off his debt. The guy had a wife and two young kids, and was willing to do whatever he had to so that he could provide for them and keep them safe. At first, the job wasn't really that hard. He worked as a bodyguard, and didn't have to do much other than look mean and drive the brothers around. But one night, during a simple dinner meeting at a restaurant in Manhattan, one of the brothers shot and killed a famous judge.

"My neighbor knew," the man went on with his story, "that he couldn't continue to work for these men after witnessing them commit murder in cold blood. In fact, in the months leading up to their trial, all of the other witnesses in the restaurant were killed. My neighbor was sitting in a back room at the courthouse, preparing to testify, when his lawyer approached him with a note that he'd been told to pass along. The note was from the brother that had shot the judge, a man named Carmine Valenti. It said that if my neighbor told the truth and fingered Carmine as the shooter, both he and his family would be killed, regardless of any promises of witness protection by the authorities. But, the note said that if my neighbor would lie and say that Anthony Valenti was the shooter, Carmine would tell his brother that he'd killed my neighbor, and his family's safety would be ensured while my neighbor was put into witness protection. The only other catch, besides risking perjury, was that my neighbor would never be allowed to contact his family again, because if Carmine Valenti found out, he would have them all killed."

Even though he already knew what the response would be, Jake had to hear the man answer his next question.

"So, what does this neighbor of yours have to do with me?"

"He's your father, Jake."

His emotions swirling, Jake was unable to speak. The man rested a hand on Jake's shoulder and spoke again.

"No one else knows about this, Jake. Not even your mother. Your father was only able to deliver a cryptic message to her through the authorities that his old life was over and she'd have to take care of you and your brother alone."

Tears began rolling down Jake's cheeks and he was finally able to ask, "Why are you telling me this now?"

"Because your father wanted to be here, Jake. He wanted you to know that he's kept tabs on you and your brother from afar, and he wanted to tell you how proud he is of you. But he couldn't risk coming here today. If Carmine Valenti were to ever get word that your father came out of hiding to see his family, he could still order you all killed tomorrow. It's a chance your dad just couldn't take. So, I offered to come and see you and tell you his story, so you would know how much he loves you and how sad he is that he's missed out on being a part of your life."

The man reached into his pocket and pulled out a small plastic bag containing a thin stack of folded bills and a yellow piece of paper. He took Jake's hand and placed the bag into it as he spoke for the last time.

"Jake, this is a graduation gift from your dad. The money is a thousand dollars. He's not trying to buy you off with the gift, he just sincerely wanted you to have some emergency spending money to use whenever you might need it. The piece of paper has a phone number on it. Unfortunately, you can't use the number unless you find yourself in a life-or-death situation. And as much as your father would love to hear from you, he knows that it's for the best if you never have to use that number. Congratulations on your graduation, Jake, and I'm sorry to be the one to have to tell you all this. But I think you'll realize it's better that you know the truth. When you feel like the time is right, you should tell Bret about his dad too. I gotta go now, Jake. You take care though, okay?"

As the man turned to walk away, Jake asked him a final question.

"Hey, mister. Will you do one thing for me?"

"Sure, Jake, what is it?"

"Tell my dad that I love him too."

Before he'd called Sergei and boarded the bus to Atlantic City, Jake had dialed the phone number on the crumpled piece of yellow paper, which had been given to him three years earlier. Now, Jake hoped that he could count on his father—a man that he hardly knew.

PART THREE

THE GAMBLE

CHAPTER 44

Jake Hunter, Monday, 4:38p.m.

As he had hoped, Jake had no trouble checking in at the front desk of the Hilton. He took the elevator up to his room, number eight twenty-five. Jake opened the door, stepped inside, and closed it behind him. Directly in front of him was a short, narrow hallway, and the bathroom was immediately to Jake's left. The hallway opened into the main room, which had a king-sized bed in the center of the room to Jake's left, with an end table on either side. Past the bed, in the corner of the room farthest away from the door, was a small table and two chairs. The television was in the middle of a large wall unit, which was positioned directly across from the bed, and contained several drawers and two closets for clothes.

Jake walked straight ahead into the room until he reached the far wall, which was actually a large glass window covered by two sets of drapes. He pulled the curtains open and observed the scene outside his window, staring down at the boardwalk, which was cluttered with people taking a late afternoon stroll, or perhaps just heading from one casino to the next. Jake looked out at the Atlantic Ocean, with its waves crashing gently onto the sand, as hundreds of swimmers and sunbathers enjoyed the beach. On the near side of the boardwalk, directly adjacent to Jake's hotel, was a small concrete parking lot. He looked at the cars parked below his window eight floors down, and couldn't help but think that there wasn't going to be a fire escape to climb down if he found himself trapped in this room.

Turning away from the window, Jake thought about one more lesson that Kelban had taught him, just as they were about to head into an extremely delicate meeting involving the construction of a sports stadium in New York City. Kelban's corporate client owned certain land surrounding the proposed stadium site, and the value of the property had been estimated by several expert appraisers at anywhere between twenty and two hundred million dollars. Throughout earlier negotiations, it became clear that several other parties with competing interests against Kelban's client wanted to minimize the purchasing costs of this land. Jake and Kelban spent countless hours preparing their presentation and the offer they would make on behalf of the client.

As they were about to enter the meeting room, Kelban explained to Jake that there was no doubt in his mind that they'd settled on the right asking price for the property.

"All those hours we put in, Jake, researching the land values, understanding the politics, unearthing the full economic potential of the site, and formulating our presentation and offer—they all pay off when we walk into this room. When you've done everything you can do, learned everything you can learn, prepared for every last detail, then you can't go wrong in the end. Whether the people in this room accept our offer or not, it won't be because we didn't do our homework and come up with the exact value of this property. And when I'm done laying out the facts and the projections, I'm telling you, Jake, they will pay our asking price. In fact, they'll jump at it."

Walking into that meeting, Jake hadn't felt nearly as confident as his boss. But as he watched Kelban lay out their research and listened to him speak—particularly the confident way he handled any question thrown at him—Jake began to realize that Kelban was right. All of their preparation had led them to the right result, and Kelban's crisp, informed presentation left no doubt that their figure was correct. When Kelban announced at the end of his speech that his client was making a one-time offer to sell the entirety of the property as a whole, instead of breaking it down and selling it off as individual lots, the purchasers took less than twenty minutes to accept his offer of two hundred and twenty-five million dollars. Needless to say, the client had been pleased.

Jake hadn't had anywhere near the same amount of time or resources to plan for what was about to happen over the course of the evening, but he was confident that he'd done everything in his power to prepare the best strategy possible. With this confidence, Jake began to feel a calm come over him. He did not know whether he would survive the night, but if he didn't, it would not be because he hadn't done all he could to prepare for every last detail.

Although Jake didn't think he'd be able to sleep, he laid down on the bed and set the alarm clock for eight p.m., just in case. Apparently, Jake didn't realize how tired and drained his body was, because he drifted off to sleep almost immediately.

***

Shortly after Jake fell asleep, Boris checked into one of the suites at the Hilton, then joined Ivan in half-dragging a sedated Bret Hunter to the room. Sergei, who came to Atlantic City in a separate car to avoid being seen arriving with his men, went up to the suite shortly after them and outlined his plan.

"I will be gambling downstairs in the casino, where I will be able to keep an eye on everything. Boris, at ten o'clock, you take the brother and go find Hunter at the blackjack tables. For now, the most important thing is getting that drive back."

"Once I have it, do you want me to kill them?" Boris asked.

"Not on the casino floor. That would be too risky. I expect that we will have our chance to make Hunter pay before he ever leaves Atlantic City, but we have to be patient. Ivan, I want you to wait here. Shortly after Boris returns, I will call you in the suite and tell you where to meet me. Understood?"

"Yes, boss."

After instructing his men, Sergei headed downstairs to the casino and played some baccarat in the high stakes VIP section. While he gambled, he thought about Boris's offer to kill the Hunters, and his decision to put it off for the time being. Sergei wondered if he was getting soft as he grew older, but quickly dismissed the notion. If anything, he was just being cautious, and, after all, patience was a virtue. Sergei was confident that Jake Hunter would eventually get what he deserved.

Less than an hour later, Sergei had won almost forty-thousand dollars. Although he'd only played for a short while, he followed his usual gambling strategy of quitting while he was ahead. Sergei cashed in his chips, left the table, and walked back to the hotel lobby. Using the alias he'd previously booked the room under, and a heavy Boston accent, he checked in at the front desk. Instead of a suite, Sergei's second room was a standard model with two double beds, located on the seventh floor.

Sergei went upstairs, perused the room service menu, and decided to have a steak for dinner. After ordering his food, Sergei made another call to the pilot of his private jet, which was being fueled and serviced in a hangar at the nearby Atlantic City Airport.

"Is the plane ready to leave tonight if necessary?"

"Absolutely," the pilot answered. "If you let me know about twenty minutes before you arrive, we can be ready for take off when you get here."

"Good. I'm looking forward to getting out of the country for a while."

CHAPTER 45

Agent Stanton, Monday, 4:55p.m.

For the second time in less than a week, Stanton and Zarvas spent the better part of a day searching for a missing person who seemingly had disappeared into thin air. Zarvas's initial inquiries proved to be correct—the injured young woman they'd discovered in Hunter's Holiday Inn hotel room hadn't been admitted to any hospital in New York. The agents even checked all of the hospitals within a fifty-mile radius, with the same result. In addition, they hadn't been able to find anyone who could identify the two men posing as EMTs, or who had seen them leaving the hotel with a girl on a gurney.

After their frustrating day, Zarvas dropped off Stanton at her apartment a little before five o'clock. Leaning out the driver's side window as Stanton walked toward her building, Zarvas shouted to his partner, "Hey, Stanton. Eventually, this case will start making sense. We've just got to keep working it, make sure we're seeing all the angles."

"I know, Jimmy," Stanton responded. "You're right. Hey, I'm gonna order some dinner and then go through the file on Hunter again, see if I can figure out where he might have run to. You wanna come upstairs, get some Chinese or something?"

"No, thanks. I'm gonna check back in at the office and keep working the leads on the Russian mafia connection to the dead lawyer. Thanks for the invite though. Call me if you find anything on where Hunter might have gone."

Zarvas waved as he pulled away from the curb and out into the street. Stanton watched him drive off down the block and then entered her apartment building.

Half an hour later, Stanton was sitting on her living room floor eating General Tso's Chicken with papers from Hunter's file spread out all around her and Bruce Springsteen playing on her stereo. Her phone rang, and Stanton jumped to her feet to grab it, pausing to lower the volume on the Boss singing *Rosalita*. The familiar voice of her source once again delivered information on Hunter's whereabouts that Stanton never would have guessed no matter how many times she reviewed his file.

"Hunter is in Atlantic City. I think he may have arranged a meeting to exchange the flash drive for his brother. How soon can you meet me there?"

Stanton checked her watch and saw that it was almost five thirty. Depending on the traffic getting out of the city, she knew it would take her about three hours to get there.

"I think I can get there by eight, eight thirty," Stanton answered hopefully, not wanting her source to risk an interaction with the Russians alone, especially if Hunter was going to give them the drive.

Fortunately, the time frame seemed acceptable to Stanton's source.

"I'll be in the lobby of the Hilton hotel reading the newspaper and wearing a Boston Red Sox hat. When you arrive, ask me what time it is. Whatever answer I give you will be the number of the room I want you to meet me at. Take the elevator upstairs, and I'll meet you there a few minutes later. Understood?"

"Yes. I'm leaving right now."

"And, Charlene, make sure you come alone."

"I will."

Stanton was excited at the prospect of making another big bust and bringing in Hunter. But she was more eager to see her lover, recover the flash drive, and prevent any potentially harmful information about her source from getting to the Russians.

Stanton went down to her building's underground parking garage and got into her car, a ratty, steel gray, nineteen ninety-one Toyota Camry. She started the engine, backed out of her assigned space, and drove forward onto the street in front of her building. Stanton was so focused on getting to Atlantic City as fast as possible that she did not notice the vehicle that pulled away from the curb behind her as she exited the parking structure. In fact, Stanton was so intent on getting to her destination, she never noticed that the same car continued to follow her for the entire length of her trip.

CHAPTER 46

Amy DiPippo, Monday, 9:04p.m.

Amy DiPippo had been dealing blackjack in Atlantic City for almost a decade. For the last four years, she'd worked at the Hilton—five days a week, eight hours a day, from eight p.m. until four a.m. Amy grew up in Red Bank, New Jersey, which was not far from Atlantic City, and she was glad that she could still go home and visit her parents whenever she felt like it.

Amy married her high school sweetheart, Josh, a charming, handsome, athletic boy, one grade ahead of her. They moved together to Atlantic City when his post-high school construction job brought them there during a busy period of hotel expansion. Their first few years together, things worked out well for the young couple. Amy developed a taste for playing blackjack and, at first, her winning sessions at the tables were more frequent than her losing ones. One afternoon, she came home early after making more than three thousand dollars during her usual morning session, and found Josh in their bed with two cocktail waitresses from Caesar's Palace.

Following their divorce, Amy moved into her own apartment in Atlantic City and figured that she would support herself with her gambling winnings. Six months later, with her credit cards maxed-out and two months behind on her rent, Amy took a job dealing blackjack at the Tropicana. It was supposed to be short-term work to help pay the bills until she got back on her feet.

Ten years had somehow passed. Amy had managed to save a small bankroll, and poker had replaced blackjack as her game of choice. She was planning to head to Las Vegas for the World Series of Poker the following spring. But at the moment, an hour into her usual shift, it was just another dreary Monday night in late August, with seven more hours of dealing to go.

At least tonight there was a young, cute guy sitting at Amy's table. He seemed preoccupied and looked slightly familiar, but he was tipping well and that was all that Amy really cared about. The guy was betting twenty dollars per hand, and he was playing three hands at the same time—the one directly in front of him, and the hands on either side of him as well. Every time he got dealt a blackjack, which pays out at odds of three to two, he'd win thirty dollars, which Amy paid to him with a green twenty-five dollar chip and a red five dollar chip. And each time, the guy would give Amy the five dollar chip as a tip for dealing the blackjack. Players who tipped in this fashion made the hands more interesting, because every time the cute guy started one of his three hands with an ace, a ten, or a picture card, Amy was rooting for him to hit the blackjack. Although she was more interested in his cards and his money, Amy had no idea how interesting Jake Hunter's presence at her table was about to become.

***

In the past, time always seemed to fly by while Jake was gambling, but the last hour he'd spent playing blackjack felt like an eternity. A short distance away from his table, there was a large group of *Wheel of Fortune*-themed slot machines. Every five minutes, the machines would erupt in noise, starting with a loud siren going off and then a harmonized crowd of mechanical voices chanting the words "Wheel—of—Fortune!" Ignoring the nearby clatter for the time being, Jake went over his plan in his head while the dealer, a nice woman in her early thirties wearing a nametag identifying her as *Amy*, shuffled the eight decks of cards. The first part of Jake's plan—the most critical part in his mind—was to make sure that his brother was safe, and to get him out of harm's way. The second part of the plan would be much trickier.

When Jake was still in college at Brown University, the largest casino complex in the country, Foxwoods, had been a mere forty-five minute drive from campus. Although Jake and his roommate, David Lairson, were both underage, they loved to gamble and frequently made late night excursions to "the Woods," as they called it. They were able to get into the casino using fake IDs that they borrowed from their older friends. On one such occasion during their sophomore year, Dave got carded while he was playing blackjack, and the pit boss realized that his license was phony. Jake, sitting at a nearby table, had grown extremely nervous as a couple of beefy guards led his roommate through a door marked *Security*. But after about twenty minutes, Dave came back out the door and was escorted to the exit. Jake had followed at a distance and met up with Dave outside.

"What happened, man?"

"I got busted," Dave answered, in his typical accent-free California drawl.

"The pit boss just randomly checked your ID?"

"No, it wasn't random at all." Dave hung his head sheepishly as he continued, "The guy probably wouldn't even have noticed me if I hadn't been harassing the waitress to bring me my rum-and-cokes two at a time."

"So what happened in the security office?"

"They took my picture with a Polaroid camera and took away my fake ID. Oh, and get this, the head security guy actually says to me, '*We know who you are now kid, so consider yourself banned from the casino for life, until you turn twenty-one.*' How funny is that?"

"Banned for life, until you're twenty-one. That's pretty good. Not sure the security guy comprehends the meaning of the phrase *for life* though. So, basically, once you're of age, they'll be happy to lift your lifetime ban and start taking your money again?"

"I guess so."

"Well, let's get back to campus. I've got an early class tomorrow morning that I was planning on sleeping through."

Sitting at the Hilton blackjack table, Jake smiled briefly at the thought of Dave, now living in Pasadena with his wife and new baby boy. If he was ever able to get himself out of the mess he was in, Jake decided that he'd have to go visit them sometime soon. He checked his watch and saw that it was ten-oh-one. But before he had a chance to get worried that the Russians weren't going to show up, he felt a presence behind him. Sure enough, when Jake turned his head, he saw Boris and Bret standing there, although Bret looked a bit groggy.

"Are you okay?" Jake asked his younger brother.

Bret nodded in response, and his eyes locked on Jake's in a way that told Jake his brother was all right—for now.

Jake then turned his attention to Boris and immediately felt a wave of anger come over him, as he recognized Boris as Ollie's killer. Jake knew he had no choice at the moment but to contain his emotions, so he took one deep breath and, nodding toward Bret, said, "Let him sit here," motioning to the open seat directly to his right.

"And you sit here." Jake indicated to Boris that he wanted him seated on his immediate left.

As the dealer finished shuffling the cards, Jake pushed a few of the green twenty-five dollar chips in front of Bret.

"Here. Play a couple of hands."

As the cards were dealt, Boris began to grow impatient and quietly asked Jake, "Where's the flash drive?"

"It's here," Jake answered, but seemed more focused on the cards being dealt as he said, "Hey, look at that—you got a twenty. I mean, I got a twenty."

The dealer turned over her one face-down card, revealing that she had a total of nineteen. She paid the hand in front of Boris and took away the money in front of Bret and Jake. After she had either paid or taken money from everyone at the table, Jake addressed the dealer.

"Hey, Amy, would you mind calling the pit boss over here?"

"Sure. No problem."

Boris was now getting extremely concerned, and he asked Jake through gritted teeth, "What are you doing?"

"Just hang on a second," Jake answered calmly. "I think I should have gotten paid on that last hand."

The pit boss approached the table and said affably to Jake, "Is there a problem sir?"

"Well, I hate to do this but," Jake pointed to his right at his younger brother, "this kid just sat down to play, and I don't think he's twenty-one."

Boris could barely contain his anger, but he managed to keep his cool by telling himself that getting the drive was his top priority and that he would get it from Hunter, with or without the brother, and in spite of whatever trick Hunter was trying to pull.

The pit boss asked Bret if he could see his ID, and Bret mumbled something about not having it on him. The pit boss immediately radioed his security personnel to come to table twenty-four to remove an underage gambler. Jake turned to Bret and winked at him out of sight of both Boris and the pit boss.

"Sorry, kid. Don't worry about it though. Just stay with casino security until someone comes to get you. Call your mom if you have to. Okay?"

"Okay," Bret answered, and his eyes began to moisten with tears, understanding that Jake had just orchestrated his rescue, but that Jake himself was still in danger.

Within moments, three guards, wearing windbreakers that read *Hilton Security*, escorted Bret away from the table and were headed toward the casino offices. As they led his brother away, Jake felt an urge to simply get up from the table and run away from Boris alongside Bret and the security guards. But knowing that Boris had killed Ollie in the middle of a crowded city street, Jake had little doubt that Boris would shoot him and Bret right on the casino floor if he tried to leave the table. When the small commotion died down, Boris leaned toward Jake and menacingly stated, "You got what you wanted, now give me the drive."

Jake began reaching into the right-hand pocket of his pants as he answered, "Okay. Let me get it—hey, what's that? Did someone just hit a jackpot?"

Jake was pointing with his left hand out toward the casino floor where the slot machines were located. The *Wheel of Fortune* machine had just started its recurring racket, which Jake hoped to use as a distraction once his brother was out of harm's way. Boris turned his head in the direction Jake was pointing, and Jake quickly pulled the handcuffs from his pocket, slapping one side of the cuffs over Boris's right wrist. Jake lunged forward intending to lock the other cuff through one of the holes in a shelf protruding from the table beneath the playing surface, which the players could use to hold their beverages. But Boris reacted with unexpected speed and yanked his arm away, pulling the cuff from Jake's hands. Boris then grabbed Jake's left wrist with his large, meaty fist and snapped the other handcuff around it. This action took place so fast that no one other than the dealer at their table had noticed.

Staring at Jake with desperate rage, Boris seethed as he spoke, reaching beneath his coat toward his gun and making it clear that there would be no more opportunities for games or stalling.

"Where...is...the...drive?"

Jake knew there was only one acceptable answer to the question. So as he pocketed the remainder of his chips from the table with his right hand, he responded, "It's in my room."

"Well then," Boris stood as he spoke and pulled Jake from his seat by tugging on the handcuffs binding them to each other, "I guess we're going to go and get it together."

***

Amy watched the unusual scene unfold, and as the two handcuffed men walked away from the table, the younger one tossed her a green chip as a final tip. She thought about reporting this strange activity, but there were already three new players sliding into the recently vacated seats. Besides, to a lifelong gambler and dealer, the odd scene was nothing more than another wild night in Atlantic City.

CHAPTER 47

Agent Zarvas, Monday, 9:25p.m.

Agent Zarvas had been suspicious of his partner ever since Stanton led him to Hunter at the Holiday Inn in Manhattan. It was one thing to have reliable sources. It was something else all together when you could track a person down at the most random of places without a hint as to where the information was coming from. It almost seemed like someone had placed a homing device on Hunter, and that person was communicating only with Agent Stanton about his location.

After Zarvas dropped Stanton off in front of her building, he circled the block and pulled over to the side of the road not far from the exit of her underground garage. He was only mildly surprised when, about forty minutes later, Stanton's car came careening out of the driveway and went speeding down the street. Over the next two hours, Zarvas became much more intrigued while he continued following her as she headed south into New Jersey on the Garden State Parkway.

Stanton finally left the Parkway at Exit 38—the Atlantic City Expressway. Zarvas kept her car within view as she pulled into the parking structure of the Atlantic City Hilton Hotel and Casino, but he was afraid to get too close to Stanton, fearing that she would notice him. By the time Zarvas entered the enormous parking garage a couple of minutes later, slowly circled the first few levels, and found Stanton's car, his partner was long gone from the vehicle. He would have to track her down inside the building.

Zarvas wondered what Stanton could possibly be doing in Atlantic City. She'd driven over eighty miles per hour for most of the trip, and he knew that she hadn't merely gotten the urge to go on a late night gambling excursion. But if she'd received more news about Hunter, why hadn't she called him? Zarvas began to wonder what *he* was doing there. Would he be backing up his partner on a successful bust? Or would he find her involved in some sort of illegal conspiracy? Either way, Zarvas knew he had to be careful because he didn't have any backup of his own.

Zarvas tried to keep a low profile as he approached the hotel's registration desk and asked to speak to the manager. Soon, a tall, well-tanned man with a large nose and graying hair walked up to Zarvas from behind the front desk.

"How can I help you, sir?"

Zarvas discreetly flashed his badge and credentials and asked, "Is there someplace we can talk in private?"

"Of course. Follow me."

The manager reached beneath the counter in front of him and pressed a button that unlocked a small, latched opening, which allowed Zarvas to approach the manager, who then led Zarvas through another door behind the registration desk and into a back office. Once they were alone in the office, the manager, in a more serious tone, asked, "What can I do for you, Agent Zarvas?"

"I need a list of names—all the reservations for tonight that were made within the past twenty-four hours, starting with the suites."

"No problem. That will just take me a few minutes to pull up on the computer."

Twenty minutes later, Zarvas was still sitting in the manager's office. He'd gotten about halfway through the list of names of people that had booked rooms in the past day, when the manager came rushing back inside.

"Agent Zarvas, I have some news. You asked about suites, right?"

"Yes," Zarvas responded eagerly.

"Well, no suites were booked in the past twenty-four hours and entered into our computer system. But, you see, I realized that some of our more publicity-shy customers don't always book their rooms through our traditional reservation system."

"Get to the point," Zarvas snapped at the manager, feeling like he had no time for detailed explanations of the hotel's booking procedures.

"Okay. Sorry," continued the now-flustered manager. "Well, I just checked with the assistant manager and she told me that she took a booking for a suite around one o'clock this afternoon. The person she spoke to asked her to hold the suite, but not book it through the computer system, and that there would be a nice tip in it for her when they arrived. The gentleman showed up a few hours later, and my second-in-command was apparently quite pleased with the tip she received."

"Did she tell you what the man looked like?"

"I thought you'd want to know, so I asked her that already," said the manager, now pleased with himself at having had such foresight. "She said he was a large white man, and she also said that he was very Eastern European looking, whatever that means."

Growing tired of the manager's attempts at detective work, and anxious to see if the suite had been booked by someone in the Russian mafia, Zarvas sought one last piece of descriptive information.

"What name is the suite booked under?"

"Actually, it's not booked under an individual's name. It looks like a corporate entity—DVI Industries, Inc."

As soon as he heard the name, Zarvas knew that it was indeed the Russians. DVI Industries was one of the corporate fronts that the FBI had been watching after receiving credible intelligence that the shell company was engaging in money laundering for the Russian mob.

Zarvas obtained a key to the suite from the manager and told him that he would be contacting additional officers who would be arriving soon at the hotel. He looked at his watch and saw that it was almost ten o'clock, about an hour since he'd last seen Stanton. Zarvas pulled his cell phone off his belt and punched speed dial number one—his supervisor at the New York office.

"Boss, it's Zarvas. I've been chasing a hot lead on the Hunter case and ended up in Atlantic City, at the Hilton Hotel. There's a suite booked here under the company name DVI Industries, the front set up by the Russians that we've been watching. I think they may be here looking for Hunter. I want to go check it out, but I need a backup team out here just in case."

"It'll take at least half an hour to mobilize a team and get them there," Zarvas's supervisor responded. "Is Stanton there with you?"

Zarvas paused for a second before answering, knowing that no matter how he responded, his answer would not be entirely truthful. Finally, he simply said, "Yeah, she's here."

"All right then, you two check out the suite. But be careful, and don't take any unnecessary risks. The backup team will be out there ASAP."

Zarvas appreciated the concern and hoped that his backup would arrive soon, but without knowing anything about where Stanton or Hunter were located, he had no choice but to take a risk. And he'd be taking it alone.

CHAPTER 48

Ivan, Monday, 10:07p.m.

Ivan sat on the bed in the suite with his back propped up against the wall, watching the ten o'clock news. He was pleased that Sergei had ordered him to wait in the suite, as he was still in pain from the injury that Hunter had inflicted on him. Ivan examined his bandaged hand, which still stung whenever he moved his fingers. Sergei had promised him that he could get even with Hunter as soon as Sergei had the flash drive. Hopefully, Ivan thought, Boris was getting the drive right now.

Sure enough, at ten fifteen, there was a knock on the door of the suite. Ivan assumed that Boris's hands were full, perhaps with the Hunter brothers, or that he simply didn't feel like reaching for his key. Still, as Ivan was about to pull the handle and open the door, he thought that it couldn't hurt to check who was knocking. He leaned toward the peephole and shouted through the door, "Boris, is that you?"

Just as his eye was focusing through the peephole, Ivan heard the familiar electronic clicking sound, indicating that the door had been unlocked with a key card from the outside. In the very next instant, the door exploded inward, cracking Ivan in the head and knocking him backwards onto the floor. Agent Zarvas busted through the doorway with his gun drawn and shouted, "FBI, don't move!"

Ivan's head was pounding and a trickle of blood ran down his forehead, but he knew that he hadn't done anything wrong at the hotel. He was confused by the fact that only one agent had come through the door, as opposed to the team of multiple agents that usually would be present for a sting operation. Despite these strange circumstances, Ivan recalled Sergei's instructions, as he often counseled his men to let the authorities arrest them, and then simply ask to call their lawyer without saying another word.

Zarvas immediately began asking questions as he removed Ivan's gun from his shoulder holster, stood him up, and handcuffed his hands behind his back.

"Where are Jake and Bret Hunter? Who else is here at the hotel with you? Where's the rest of your people?"

Ivan simply responded, over and over, "I want my lawyer. I want my lawyer."

Zarvas was getting frustrated with Ivan's stonewalling, when the phone in the suite suddenly began to ring. He looked at Ivan and asked, "You expecting a call?"

"I want my lawyer."

Zarvas quickly grabbed a small hand towel from the bathroom and forced it into Ivan's mouth to prevent him from making any noise. Then, in the friendliest voice he could muster, Zarvas picked up the ringing telephone and said, "Hilton Hotel, suite twenty-five seventeen. May I help you?"

There was only silence on the other end of the phone, and Zarvas tried not to reveal the strain in his voice as he spoke again.

"Hello?"

"Yes. I'm sorry," the man on the other line finally responded, in an accent that sounded like it came from somewhere in the mid-western United States. "I thought a friend of mine was staying in that suite."

"Yes, sir, I believe he just stepped down the hall to the ice machine. I'm setting up room service at the moment. Can I take your name and number and have the gentleman call you back?"

The line was quiet again, but Zarvas hoped that maybe he would get a name or some clue as to who was on the phone. Instead, the voice that responded merely sounded disappointed and resolute as it stated, "No, no you can not."

And then the line went dead.

Zarvas believed that he'd been talking to Boris and Ivan's boss, and he knew that wherever the man was, he was likely going to disappear for a while after figuring out that at least one of his men had been discovered in Atlantic City. Even if he'd missed his chance at apprehending the Russian mafia kingpin, Zarvas hoped that he'd be able to track down Hunter somewhere at the hotel. He also thought that if he could find Hunter, he'd find Stanton as well.

Suspecting that he'd get neither help nor trouble from Ivan, Zarvas pulled the towel out of Ivan's mouth, but re-handcuffed his wrists around the headboard of the bed. He called in to the New York office again to alert the backup team to pick up Ivan in the suite whenever they arrived. With little else to do, Zarvas closed the slightly damaged door to the suite and positioned himself in a chair facing the entry, hoping that maybe one of Ivan's pals would return. He then pulled the list of names that the manager had printed out for him from his pocket and continued reviewing it from where he'd left off.

All of a sudden, much to Ivan's surprise, Zarvas jumped up from the chair he was sitting in and muttered to himself while shaking his head back and forth.

"Unbelievable. The kid checked in under the same name."

Close to the bottom of the list he was looking at, Zarvas came across the name that he knew to be Hunter's favorite pseudonym, Jack Mellencamp. Mr. Mellencamp had checked into room eight twenty-five, and that was where Zarvas hoped to find him still in one piece. As he headed out of the room and into the hallway, he turned to Ivan and said, "Now you be a good boy until the cavalry gets here."

Zarvas was closing the door behind him as he heard Ivan's familiar response.

"I want my lawyer."

CHAPTER 49

Jake Hunter, Monday, 10:23p.m.

Boris and Jake exited the elevator on the eighth floor still handcuffed to each other. Boris turned toward Jake and asked, "Which room?"

"Eight twenty-five," Jake answered lethargically, though his mind was working feverishly to come up with some way to get free from Boris.

Boris half-dragged Jake toward the door to room eight twenty-five. When they arrived, Jake slid the key card into its narrow opening and heard the door unlock. As he pushed the handle down and prepared to walk inside, Jake asked Boris, "You want to go first?"

"No. You go."

Jake stepped through the doorway into the short hallway that led into his room and immediately noticed that something wasn't right. When he went down to the casino, he'd left the bathroom door completely open and the lights on, but now the room was dark and the bathroom door was barely cracked.

As Jake hesitated inside the doorway, Boris closed the door, drew his gun with his un-handcuffed hand, and stepped forward into the room. Just as Boris was about to turn to his left to make sure that no one was hiding behind the wall separating the bathroom from the bedroom, Jake saw a flash of light and heard a click and a whooshing sound. The light came from the barrel of a gun, which sent a bullet directly into Boris's temple, practically destroying the entire left side of his face.

Boris's body was blasted sideways, and as he fell to the ground, he pulled Jake down with him. Jake landed on his side, and when he was finally able to tear his eyes away from the hideous sight of Boris's lifeless form, he looked up and saw two women standing in front of him. They walked out from behind the wall to the foot of the bed and stood side by side facing the door and looking down at Jake.

As he looked up at them, Jake recognized one of the women as the FBI agent he'd seen on television in front of his mother's house the morning after his brother was kidnapped. At first, he felt a wave of relief and believed that he was finally safe. He could surrender to the authorities, explain everything he'd been through, and clear his name. But Jake then noticed that the other woman, dressed in all black and wearing a Boston Red Sox hat, was pointing her gun directly at him and asking, "Where's the flash drive, Jake?"

"What?" was all Jake could manage to say in response. He was extremely confused and felt like he might vomit from the pungent smell of blood and charred skin coming from Boris.

"I need that drive, Jake," the woman in black stated. "The one that Kelban sent to you."

"Why do you need it? And who are you? Agent Stanton, what's going on here?"

Jake turned to look at Stanton, but she simply stood there and did not respond. It seemed that she'd relinquished all control of the situation to the other woman, who now decided to answer Jake's questions.

"My name is Svetlana Ilanov. I need that drive so that I can finally track down my bastard father, and avenge my mother's death. You see, Jake, your boss, Michael Kelban, and many men like him, they all work for my father, who was born with the name Sergei Ilanov. He uses these other men to do his dirty work so that he can stay in hiding, using fake names and identities, pretending to be things he is not.

"After my father beat my mother to death and left the Soviet Union, my little sister and I were taken to an orphanage—a cruel, horrible place where we were also beaten. But there is a saying that I learned at that orphanage. The American translation I believe is—*That which does not kill you, only makes you stronger.* Well, though I sometimes felt as if I wanted to die in that place, I grew very strong there in both my body and my mind. My father used fear, threats, and violence to take power and control of people, but I found other ways to get what I wanted from people that were just as successful and ensured even greater loyalty."

As Svetlana rambled on with the tale of her difficult childhood, Jake desperately tried to figure out what to do about a situation that he feared would soon escalate out of control. It seemed to Jake that Svetlana's story had been bottled up inside her for a long time, and she must have felt the need to tell it, as she continued her explanation while Jake continued racking his brain for ideas.

"My father had a fifteen-year head start on me in America, and, at first, I wasn't even sure that he was still alive. He'd done an excellent job of erasing any traces of his past, his former name, his former life. Thankfully, his old protégé, Yevgeny Pulachin, did not. He was simple to seduce, and the pig could not help himself from bragging about his illegal activities while we were together in the bedroom. Perhaps he needed to feel like he was a big man in certain ways, because he certainly was not in others.

"Unfortunately, Yevgeny was smart enough to protect whatever secrets he knew about other powerful men—like my father. Finally, after one night of heavy drinking, including a little something I added to his drinks to help loosen his tongue, I was able to get Yevgeny talking about the good old days in Russia, and he mentioned that there was a man who he both respected and feared more than any other man.

'Who is this man?' I'd asked innocently.

'He was the leader of my old gang in Mother Russia. Now, he has many names and is involved in many affairs—more businesses and schemes than even myself, but he is like a ghost.'

"I knew that he was talking about my father, but he would not reveal his location or aliases, so I made one last attempt at getting some useful information by asking, *'Does anyone help this great man keep track of all of his affairs and businesses?'*

'Some hot-shot lawyer named Kelban. Thinks he's a real big man.'

"And then fat Yevgeny passed out in his bed." Svetlana practically spat as she said the name, clearly still disgusted at the thought of the acts she'd performed in order to gain his trust and get information out of him. Yet she went on with her story, focusing on a new man in her life.

"That same night, I started keeping tabs on Kelban. I had built up a few of my own resources and had a small staff of trusted people working for me, doing surveillance, computer-hacking, whatever was necessary. While watching Kelban, it wasn't long before I started seeing quite a bit of you, Jake. Three weeks later, I set up Yevgeny to get arrested at his weapons warehouse.

"I then began trying to discreetly contact Kelban to feel him out about getting information on my father and his whereabouts. But my efforts seemed to make Kelban nervous, and I think his altered behavior must have alerted my father, who probably sent this goon," Svetlana motioned her gun toward Boris, "to kill him. But before Kelban died, he sent you the flash drive, which I suspect has all the information I'll need to find my father and kill him. So, Jake, I'll ask you one more time, where is the drive?"

"It's not here right now, but it's being brought here. I swear!" Jake was telling the truth, and he hoped that would be enough to save his life.

"Not here, but on the way." Svetlana seemed to be considering Jake's story, as Stanton stood nervously beside her absent-mindedly chewing on a fingernail. "Well, that sounds like bad news for you, Jake."

As Svetlana aimed her gun at Jake's chest, he heard a faint noise that sounded like the door to the room being unlocked. Agent Zarvas burst through the door and into the room with his gun raised and pointed directly at Svetlana.

"FBI!" Zarvas shouted. "And I've got bad news for you lady. The cops have this floor completely surrounded, so drop your gun."

Svetlana's expression immediately changed from a cruel, wicked sneer to a look of exasperated sorrow. The shift was so drastic, Jake almost found himself feeling sorry for all of the psychological trauma she'd experienced—being abandoned and orphaned as a child, and then searching for her father in an effort to kill him, only to have the search end in failure and arrest.

"Are you all right, Jake?" Agent Zarvas asked.

As Jake turned to respond, he noticed something black and metallic sticking out from the crack in the bathroom door. Before he could open his mouth to warn Zarvas, a shot fired through the silencer on the end of the gun and flew into the back of Zarvas's arm. The agent's gun fell from his hand, as the force of the gunshot knocked him into the wall and he crumpled to the floor in a seated position. The bathroom door opened and another woman walked out and reached down to pick up Zarvas's gun, while keeping her own gun pointed at him.

Jake looked up and could muster only one word.

"Anna?"

"Oh, that's right," Svetlana chimed in, her false expression of sadness after Zarvas's entry replaced with a dark, mocking visage. "You two already know each other. Jake, surely you remember my baby sister, Anastasia."

Jake could do nothing but stare, mouth open, at Anna. He couldn't bring himself to speak to the woman he had feared might be dead, but his eyes asked the question that his voice could not—*Why*? Anna refused to look at Jake or to speak, but her sister was happy to continue talking for the both of them.

"Since you barged in here without any backup, Agent Zarvas, I know you were lying about having this floor surrounded, although I'm sure this place will be crawling with agents soon. So, because you're a late arrival and I'm short on time, I'll give you the quick version. My sister and I need the information on Mr. Hunter's hard drive so we can find our father—the same man you've been searching for for the past few years—and kill him. And your partner here has been helping us try to obtain that information."

Zarvas, holding his wounded arm with his other hand, asked the one question that Svetlana hadn't already answered.

"Stanton, why?"

Although Stanton finally opened her mouth to speak, Svetlana, clearly the room's dominant personality, cut her off and answered instead.

"I'll tell you why. Because tough Agent Stanton here has her own secrets and insecurities that no one had ever paid any attention to. I made her as an agent the minute she started working at the Russian Vodka Room, but, as it turned out, we shared a bond of having been made to feel like unwanted, damaged goods. Once she was convinced I was connected to the Russian mob, we agreed to work together. I helped her succeed in her career, and I made her feel things and brought her pleasure that no man ever could. In return, I used her to get information on your investigation of my father and, eventually, on your investigation of Hunter. Working with me as partners, and lovers, created a feeling of trust and loyalty that Charlene would never break."

Nodding her head as she listened to Svetlana's explanation, Stanton finally spoke.

"I'm sorry, Jimmy. But I'm in love with her. I never wanted to involve you in this. How did you find me here?"

"I followed you from your apartment. I'd been suspicious ever since your source," Zarvas looked distastefully at Svetlana as he said this, "gave you the tip about finding Hunter at the Holiday Inn."

"Wait a second," Jake cut in on the conversation. "That still doesn't explain how you knew that I would be here."

"Oh, poor, naive Jake," Svetlana cooed obnoxiously. "Don't you remember that sad little story you told my sister about how you loved coming to Atlantic City with your parents when you were a boy? I'll admit, I didn't think it was anything important at the time, but when we lost track of you after the fiasco at the Holiday Inn in Manhattan, I had a hacker friend of mine monitor the reservation information for all the hotels in Atlantic City. Imagine my surprise when Jack Mellencamp checked into the Hilton. You almost made it too easy for us."

Jake realized that the encounter with the stranger at the Holiday Inn had been a setup. He grew angry at Anna and was practically yelling as he addressed her.

"So you moved in to my apartment building to spy on me because I worked so closely with Kelban? And then you made up all those stories about your family and your feelings just so you could try to get the drive from me?"

"I'm sorry, Jake." Anna finally turned to look at him as she spoke, with sincerity in her eyes but without a trace of her former southern accent. "I was just supposed to get close to you as a connection to Kelban. And when he was killed, I wanted to get the drive from you for my sister. But I couldn't find it, and then, you were so nice to me that I wasn't sure what to do. My sister planned that whole scene back at the hotel."

"Anna, shut up!" Svetlana glared at her sister as she spoke. Then, turning to Stanton, she said, "And you, you couldn't even make sure that you weren't followed here. It seems that perhaps you have outlasted your usefulness to me."

Stanton was taken aback by Svetlana's harsh words. She was sincerely hurt and stunned as she tried to respond.

"What are you talking about, Svetlana, we're in—"

Svetlana raised her gun toward Stanton and everyone in the room burst into activity of some sort. Jake reached into his pants pocket with his right hand, grabbed the key to the handcuffs, and began unlocking himself from Boris. Anna's eyes were drawn toward her sister, and Zarvas took the opportunity to drive his foot hard into her shin. Anna yelped as her leg gave out and she collapsed onto the floor.

Svetlana pulled the trigger of her gun twice, and two silenced bullets ripped through Stanton's torso. Her body was propelled backwards onto the bed, with her arms extended above her head. Blood began pooling beneath her body onto the comforter and through to the sheets below.

Zarvas reached forward and pulled a small-caliber gun from his ankle holster. He turned toward Svetlana and fired two shots, which were much louder than those that Svetlana had just fired. But Zarvas's aim was poor due to his wounded arm. The first shot nicked Svetlana's arm, spinning her slightly sideways. The second shot missed Svetlana completely and went through the window a few feet behind her, sending a spiraling series of cracks through the glass, but not shattering it.

Anna recovered from her fall and swung her arm downward, with the butt of her gun making solid contact with Zarvas's wrist. There was an audible crack, and Zarvas yelled out in pain as he again dropped his gun to the floor. Anna quickly tossed it across the room and kept her vision and gun trained on Zarvas.

Jake, no longer handcuffed to Boris's corpse, looked up and saw Svetlana turning back around, regaining her balance after the impact from Zarvas's bullet. Knowing that she would steady herself and shoot him in mere seconds, Jake leapt to his feet and began running toward her, keeping his body low like a sprinter bursting out of the starting blocks. Svetlana had just raised the gun to firing level when Jake's right shoulder drove hard into her midsection. His speed and the force of the impact lifted her off the ground. Jake, unable to control his forward momentum, took two more strides and crashed hard into the glass wall. When their bodies made contact with the already-splintered window, the glass gave out, and they hurtled through it.

As Jake started to fall, he swung his left arm out wildly, grabbing on to the fabric of the curtain that was barely within his reach. While he held on, his muscles strained under the weight of both his own body and Svetlana's, as she'd managed to wrap one arm around his waist and was hanging on to him with all of her strength. Jake reached up with his right arm to grab the curtain with both hands and better support the weight, but knew that he would not be able to hold them both up for much longer. He shook his legs and twisted from side to side as much as he dared, and as he looked down, he saw the fear in

Svetlana's eyes as her grip began to loosen. Jake was still staring into those frantic eyes when he suddenly felt the weight that he was supporting decrease. Svetlana lost her grip, and he was unable to turn away as he watched her fall eight stories to the concrete below.

Jake gripped the curtain tightly, but was unable to pull himself up. The muscles in his arms began to seize, and he was sure that he was going to follow Svetlana to the ground if someone didn't come to his aid soon. From inside the hotel room, Jake heard an unfamiliar voice yelling, "Federal Marshal, put the gun down!"

Next, Jake heard what sounded like someone being handcuffed and footsteps racing around the room. He was about to shout for help when a voice directly above him said, "Jake, give me your hand."

Jake looked up at the speaker and then reached out with his left arm. Two strong hands grabbed him around his wrist and helped pull him up and into the hotel room. When he was on his feet, Jake saw Anna being led out of the room by a man wearing a *U.S. Marshal* jacket. Another man with the same jacket stood near the doorway, watching as several medics helped Zarvas up from the floor and strapped Stanton onto a stretcher.

Jake then turned to look at the man who had helped lift him back into the room and said, "Is it really you, dad?"

"It's me, son."

Jake took a quick step forward and wrapped his arms around his father, hugging him tightly as several tears fell silently down his face.

CHAPTER 50

Peter and Nicholas, Monday, 10:25p.m.

Unlike Svetlana Ilanov, Peter and Nicholas had never known either of their parents. In fact, even though the two boys had been left at the orphanage at the same time, no one had ever bothered to confirm whether they were actually related to one another. But whether they were brothers by blood or not, Peter and Nicholas were brothers through life, as their experiences growing up together had bonded them as close as any family ties ever could. In that same Russian orphanage, Peter and Nicholas had befriended Svetlana and Anastasia, who had been sent there when their father left and their mother died. Years later, the four of them accumulated enough money to travel together to the United States—Peter and Nicholas in search of a vast clientele that would pay top dollar for their already well-developed espionage skills, and Svetlana and Anna in search of revenge.

When Svetlana had approached Peter and Nicholas in the Russian Vodka Room several days earlier, she'd hired them to help her kill her father, as she felt that she was finally close to tracking him down. Jake Hunter, and the information he'd been given by Michael Kelban, were merely a means to achieving that goal. Once Hunter took Anna into his confidence and on the run with him, Svetlana altered her original plan of finding her father through Kelban. Instead, she hoped to use Hunter's feelings for Anna to get the flash drive, which the security guard had described to Peter and Nicholas, by having Santo Alampi threaten her life during the hotel room setup. But the ruse backfired when Svetlana's father had Hunter's brother kidnapped. Once again, he'd been one step ahead of her.

At that point, Svetlana used her resources to track down Jake, who made the mistake of checking into the Atlantic City Hilton under the same alias he'd used previously to check into the Holiday Inn with Anna. When the private investigator's computer-hacking sidekick found the name she suggested he search for, Svetlana set in motion her plan to find Jake and her father, and to tie up the one remaining loose end that could connect her to their deaths—by getting Agent Stanton to meet her in Atlantic City.

Well before Svetlana called Stanton, she'd sent Peter and Nicholas to the Hilton in case she needed their help, and to have two extra sets of eyes there to search for her father. The two men had stationed themselves near the front entrance to the hotel and, at approximately six o'clock that evening, they'd watched as a black town car with tinted windows dropped off a strange group of three passengers—two large men and a teenage boy. Peter recognized one of them as the same man who had taken a couple of shots at Hunter in his apartment building before Nicholas had slowed the man's pursuit. Peter and Nicholas carefully noted that, after dropping off his passengers, the driver pulled the car around to the front of the hotel's circular driveway, positioning himself to be able to leave quickly if necessary. Upon witnessing this, Peter went to their van in order to change his attire. Nicholas remained at his post in front of the hotel, occasionally glancing at the printouts that Jesse Halpern had created using his aging program and a fifteen-year-old picture that Svetlana had provided of her father.

Just before ten thirty p.m., the two men watched as the driver of the town car received a call on his cell phone and started the engine. Peter and Nicholas moved quickly to set up what they hoped would be the final stage of their present job.

CHAPTER 51

Sergei Ilanov, Monday, 10:31p.m.

Less than twenty minutes had passed since Sergei dejectedly hung up the phone in his hotel room. When Ivan hadn't answered his call, Sergei immediately knew that something was wrong. Ivan would never have disobeyed his order to remain in the room and wait to hear from him. And if Boris had escaped with either Hunter or the flash drive, he would have called Sergei on his cell phone by now. Aware that he might be discovered if he stayed where he was, Sergei called the driver waiting downstairs and gave instructions to meet him at the front of the hotel with the car. He then called his pilot at the airport and ordered him to have the plane ready to fly within the hour.

The car pulled up just as Sergei exited the hotel, and Sergei waved off the driver, who was in the process of exiting the car in order to open the rear door.

"I've got it," Sergei said gruffly. "Just drive."

"Yes, sir."

When they were both situated, the driver asked, "Where to, sir?"

"Atlantic City Airport."

"Yes, sir."

As they drove away, Sergei opened his briefcase and began working on his laptop. He confirmed a reservation at the island villa he would be staying at, and checked on several money transfers and bank transactions he'd set in motion earlier that day in the event that he needed to leave the country for a while. Satisfied that everything was in order, he shut down his computer, locked his briefcase, leaned back in his seat, and closed his eyes. For the remainder of the trip to the airport, Sergei went over in his mind the mistakes that had caused his present situation. He felt that it was important to review such errors immediately in order to make sure that they never occurred again. Hunter may have gotten away from him once, but Sergei would make certain, when he was able to safely return to New York, that Hunter would not escape his wrath again.

Sergei opened his eyes as the vehicle slowed down to pull into the airport's main gate. He directed the driver, "Take me to hangar seventeen, straight ahead and to the right."

"Right away, sir."

The car crept forward along the row of private hangars before finally creeping to a stop in front of hangar sixteen. Sergei, annoyed at his driver's mistake, shouted, "No. I said hangar seventeen. It's the next one up."

The black partition between the front and rear of the car slid down and the driver turned to face Sergei as he spoke.

"I'm sorry about that, sir. But I don't think you're going to make it to hangar seventeen."

Before Sergei had a chance to react, Peter, dressed in an outfit very similar to the one that the driver had been wearing, raised his gun and extended his arm through the open partition. Before he pulled the trigger, he said to Sergei, "Your daughters wanted you to have this."

The two shots went directly into Sergei's forehead and immediately produced small crater-like cavities, each leaking a thin trail of blood. Peter quickly and quietly exited the car, threw the gun onto the driver's seat, and jogged back in the direction he'd just driven, where Nicholas had stealthily followed in their van.

Minutes later, the two men were driving away from the airport, pleased that they'd completed another job so successfully. The only thing they couldn't understand was why Svetlana was not picking up her cell phone to revel in the good news. Oh well, Peter thought to himself, she'll find out eventually.

EPILOGUE

Tuesday, 2:17a.m.

In the back of a United States Marshals Service van heading toward New York City, Jake sat between his brother and his father, feeling completely safe for the first time in what felt like a lifetime. He was thrilled that his dad had made it to Atlantic City in time to pull him back up into the hotel room, but he was curious how his father was able to get there so fast when Jake had only contacted him earlier that day. Rather than try to make sense of it, Jake simply asked, "So, dad, how did you get to the Hilton so fast? I mean, I checked the area code of the phone number your neighbor gave me, and it's located in Omaha, Nebraska. I thought it would be days before you'd get to New York and pick up the flash drive from my gym locker."

"Jake, my sons were in danger. I'd already come to New York and had been waiting for that call from you ever since I first saw you on the news the day that Kelban was killed. I'd already contacted the Federal Marshals—they're the ones that run the witness protection program—and they were with me when you finally called. You're right about it being an Omaha area code, except it wasn't my home number. It's my cell phone number, and I always keep that cell phone with me. I just wish we could have gotten down to Atlantic City sooner, but the Marshals insisted on stopping to get the drive first. Once they had it in hand, we got down here as fast as we could."

"But what about the Russian mafia guy, Sergei Ilanov, that the daughters were trying to find from the information on the drive? I heard Agent Zarvas telling the Marshals that he was afraid he'd tipped him off on the phone earlier and let him get away."

"Well, when the feds checked the flash drive right after we picked it up, one thing they found out was that Ilanov owned his own jet and kept it in a private hangar at the Atlantic City Airport. If Ilanov had boarded his plane, the FBI would have been there waiting for him."

"You said *if* he'd boarded the plane. Does that mean he never went to the airport?"

"Actually, from what the Marshals told me, Ilanov went to the airport, but before he could get to his plane, someone shot and killed him. They found his body in the back seat of a rental car."

"Are they sure it was him?" Jake asked. "I mean, he seemed like the kind of guy who might try to fake his own death or something just to throw the feds off his trail."

"No. It was definitely him. Sergei Ilanov won't be causing our family, or anyone else, any more pain and suffering."

His father's comment about the pain and suffering Ilanov had caused made Jake think about all the people that had been hurt or killed, just in the past several days—Stanton and the other FBI agents, Ollie, Ilanov's own daughter Svetlana, and Michael Kelban. Thinking of Kelban reminded Jake of their last real conversation at the end-of-the-summer party for the new associates, when he'd finally asked, "What's the story with the wax figures in the back of your office—judge, jury, and executioner?"

"It's simple really," Kelban explained in his usual charming, yet slightly didactic manner. "Whenever people talk about decisions of fate—at least in the justice system—going back to the Middle Ages, the arbiters of fate were always considered to be those three categories of people. But I think people have been getting it wrong all these years. See, the judge, jury, and executioner get credit for rendering the decisions or committing the acts that seal someone's fate, but the person who draws those three actors to their conclusions is, and always has been, the lawyer."

"So, your wax renditions serve as a metaphor then." Jake's response was more statement than question. "All three characters are posed so that they're facing your desk. They are looking to you—the lawyer—to lead them to their ultimate decisions."

"Absolutely," stated Kelban, patting Hunter on the back as he continued. "Right on, as usual, Hunter. I think they also do a pretty good job of intimidating some of the summer associates."

"Emphasis on *some*," Jake responded.

Looking back, Jake realized that he'd sounded cocky and had been echoing Kelban's persona. After everything he'd just been through, Jake wasn't sure that he could ever go back to being that kind of person. Regardless of how certain he'd been about his career path a week ago, Jake began to think that maybe being a lawyer was not the way he wanted to spend his life after all.

As Jake thought about both his past and his future, his father interrupted his thoughts by saying, "I want to tell you boys how proud I am of both of you. I've had to keep tabs on you from afar, but I've been so pleased by everything I've heard. Bret, you've grown into such a strong young man, leading your team to that baseball championship and about to go off to play college ball at Florida State. And, Jake, soon to be a high-powered New York City lawyer. I'm so proud of you guys."

Bret, who had been quiet and somewhat overwhelmed since meeting his father back at the hotel, finally spoke.

"Thanks…dad. Are we going to get to see you again after tonight?"

"Well, I don't know how much of the story you've heard, but the people who I was hiding out from—the Valenti brothers—are both dead now, and neither of them had any kids, so their family isn't really around anymore. The Marshals told me that we've still got to be real careful for a while, but they'll help us set up some meetings at secret locations, and I'll be able to see you guys. You know, sometimes I feel so guilty about my stupid past and not being around for you kids while you were growing up."

Their father started to get a bit choked up, and Jake was about to say something reassuring, but Bret beat him to it.

"Don't feel bad, dad. You didn't have a choice."

"Yeah," Jake chimed in. "You were only doing what you had to do to protect your family. Can you promise us one thing though?"

"Anything for you guys. You just name it."

Cracking a half-smile and with a mischievous glint in his eye, Jake said, "Just promise that the next time we go gambling together as a family, we can do it in Vegas instead."

ABOUT THE AUTHOR

Cort Malone graduated from Brown University and moved to New York City, where he attended Fordham Law School and studied international criminal law. Currently, he is a litigator at a law firm in midtown Manhattan, and has published several articles on various legal topics. He lives with his girlfriend in New York.

Made in the USA
Charleston, SC
08 December 2010